FOR THE WIN

WYNN HOCKEY

KELLY JAMIESON

CONTENT NOTES

Content notes for this book and all my books are available
on my website at
https://www.kellyjamieson.com/content-notes

THE WYNN DYNASTY

Bob Wynn, owner of the California Condors. Originally married to Grace Rogers (deceased), parents to Mark and Matthew with Grace. Parents to Everly, Asher, Harrison, and Noah with Chelsea Wynn. Grandfather to Jean Paul (JP), Théo, Jackson, and Riley.

Chelsea Wynn (formerly Clark), married to Bob Wynn, mother of Everly, Asher, Harrison, and Noah.

Matthew Wynn, owner of the Long Beach Golden Eagles. Son of Bob Wynn. Married to Aline Gagnon. Father of Théo and Jean Paul (JP).

Mark Wynn, coach of the Long Beach Golden Eagles. Son of Bob Wynn. Divorced from Victoria (Tori) Kendall. Father of Jackson and Riley.

Théo Wynn, general manager of the California Condors. Son of Matthew Wynn and Aline Gagnon. Grandson of Bob Wynn (with Grace).

Jean Paul (JP) Wynn, son of Matthew Wynn and Aline Gagnon. Grandson of Bob Wynn (with Grace). Plays for the Long Beach Golden Eagles.

Jackson Wynn, son of Mark Wynn and Victoria (Tori)

Kendall. Grandson of Bob Wynn (with Grace). Plays for the Chicago Aces.

Riley Wynn, daughter of Mark Wynn and Victoria (Tori) Kendall. Granddaughter of Bob Wynn (with Grace). Goalie coach for the San Diego Hawks, affiliate team of the Long Beach Golden Eagles.

Everly Wynn, daughter of Bob and Chelsea Wynn. Executive director of the Condors Foundation.

Asher Wynn, son of Bob and Chelsea Wynn. Sports reporter for *Playmaker* (hockey blog).

Harrison Wynn, son of Bob and Chelsea Wynn. Plays for the Pasadena Condors, affiliate team of the California Condors.

Noah Wynn, son of Bob and Chelsea Wynn. Plays for the San Diego Hawks.

HARRISON

"Smith is out. Lower body."

I nod slowly, sitting in coach Dave Martin's office in the Santa Monica Coliseum.

"He's out for the season," Coach adds glumly.

"Damn."

"Yeah. On top of Yatsyshyn already being out, we're pretty light on the left wing."

"Yeah."

I've been called up from the farm team, which is nothing new for me. This season I've been up and down more than an Amazon drone.

I *do* have a contract with the California Condors, but it's a two-way contract, meaning I can get sent down to the AHL any time. People say "sent down," but technically I'm being loaned to the Pasadena team. I get paid more when I play NHL games, based on my contract, but still a helluva lot less than most NHL players. But don't get me wrong— it's not just about the money.

"We're gonna need you, Milo, and Jack to fill some big holes. I haven't decided yet what lines we're gonna run." He rubs his silver beard. "We may have to toss things in the blender and see what we come up with."

"That's fine." I'm nothing if not adaptable. I think I've filled in on left wing and played with nearly every line on this team at one point or another.

This shit is getting old.

I mean, I'm grateful I have a chance to play hockey for a living. But everyone wants to play in the NHL. I've had so many chances, but it never sticks. I end up being sent back down to the minors. They give me the "you're a valuable veteran resource for that team" speech. I know it's true. I'm not bragging; it's a fact that at twenty-six years old, I'm the second-oldest player on the Pasadena Condors. Our team feeds players to the Santa Monica Condors and there are new guys coming in every season, teenagers who've just been drafted, guys being traded, and I've watched too many of them make the move.

We've been lucky with our draft picks the last few seasons. That's the upside of being a team that sucks and never makes the playoffs—higher draft picks. A bunch of eager, talented, young guys have come into the team, and then moved onto our NHL affiliate. This year the Condors have done a lot better, thanks to new management and coaching. It looks like they (we?) might make the playoffs. But injuries are killing them right now and it's late in the season.

"I'll do whatever I can," I tell Coach.

"Will you?" He sits back in his chair and crosses his

arms, looking at me over the rims of his black reading glasses.

I gaze back at him. "Uh . . . of course."

He gives me another long look that has my nuts shriveling. "What?"

"You have a lot of natural talent for this game."

I guess that's true.

"You also have a lot of experience. Been playing pro hockey for ten years now, right?"

"Yeah." He knows exactly how long I've played, how many NHL games I've played, and all my numbers.

"When I say we need you to step up, I mean *we really need you to step up.*" He straightens and sits forward, his intense gaze fixed on me. "Let me be very frank here."

"Of course." I keep my face expressionless, not sure where this is going, but fairly sure it's not going to be good.

"You've coasted for a lot of years."

My jaw drops. "What? That's not true!"

"You make it look easy," he continues. "You have amazing hands and a fantastic ability to read the play. You make good choices with the puck at both blue lines. But there's a sense you're only putting in as much effort as you need to."

"No. Absolutely not." *I think . . .*

"I've always wondered what it would look like if you really put some effort into it. I bet you didn't have to try hard in junior hockey. I bet you knew you were going to be drafted."

Ugh. Here we go. Just because my dad is a hockey legend, everyone expects me to be just like him. "If you're referring to my family, no—"

"No, that's not what I'm saying. Even Wynns don't get drafted if they can't play. No GM is stupid enough to waste a draft pick. But you knew you were good, you knew you'd get drafted, and you figured you'd play in the NHL. Am I right?"

"Yeah," I mutter.

"I get that it hasn't worked out for you, but maybe you need to take a long look at why that is and what you could do differently." He gives me a wry smile. "You're a popular guy with both teams. Easygoing personality, fun in the dressing room."

I stare at him, not sure where he's going with this.

"Those are good qualities, and important. Never underestimate the power of changing the mood in the room." He eyes me shrewdly. "But if you demonstrated hard work, you'd be even more of a leader."

Heat is pressing up inside me, squeezing my windpipe. I curl my hands over the arms of the chair. "I can't be my dad," I say tersely.

Bob Wynn, King of Hockey. Four Stanley Cup rings, long and legendary hockey career. But I've never measured up.

Coach's eyes soften minutely. "That's not what I'm saying."

"Sure it is. Everyone expects that. And I do work hard." I'm annoyed but I keep my tone polite. This is bullshit, but he's the coach.

"I'm not saying you don't. But I think you have another level inside you. We want to see that next level from you."

To be honest, I don't know what that means. And I

don't know how to do that. But I nod my agreement as if I do as Coach stands to end the meeting.

"Thanks for the chance," I tell him.

"Life is ten percent what happens to you and ninety percent what you do with it."

Great. Now he's spouting cute motivational sayings.

"You don't always get what you wish for," he adds. "You get what you work for."

I nod. "Yes, sir."

I head to the dressing room to change for the game-day skate. I got here early because Coach wanted to talk to me, but other guys are arriving now too.

"Called up again, eh?" Jimmy says with a slap on my shoulder. "We're falling like dead trees here."

I grin. "So I hear."

Out on the ice with assistant coach Stanislav Petrov blowing the whistle and putting us through a few easy drills, I let Coach's words run through my mind. I'm a little pissed, to be honest. I shove that aside to focus on what I'm doing.

Maybe it's anger that gives me an adrenaline boost. I'm laser focused on the puck and the net. I'm shooting harder. I'm skating faster.

When we're done, I stay on the ice, working on a few things I wasn't happy with.

"Good skate, Harry," Scotty says, tapping my leg with his stick as he skates off.

"You're on fire," Jimmy, the team captain, says. "Hold onto that for tonight."

I'm gonna fucking try.

"You need to up your transition game," Stan says to me when we're the only two left on the ice.

I stare at him.

"You wanna work on that?"

The only answer is, "Yeah."

He nods, skating backward. "We can work on some drills. Get you breaking for openings. Working on your passing angle. Moving into open space when the D-men move to cover a high breaking forward."

"Okay."

We stay on the ice awhile longer, and I agree to come back again tomorrow to work on more.

After I'm showered and dressed, I head to the players' lounge for lunch, loading up on chicken, pasta, and a big salad with sweet potato and avocado. I've been here enough that I'm comfortable with all these guys. And now, Wyatt Bell is dating my sister.

Don't ask me how the hell that happened. He is *so* not Everly's type. But she seems really happy, and hell, so does he. He's kind of a player, though, so he better not screw her over. I'd have "the talk" with him, but Everly was ranting the other day about how Dad embarrassed her with that kind of conversation, so I'm keeping my mouth shut.

After I eat my bowl of ice cream, definitely my favorite part of the meal, I head home for a nap. As I drive, I reflect more on what Coach said.

I do want to play in the NHL. I've always wanted it. And it's pissing me off that it hasn't happened.

Is he right? Do I think that because I'm a Wynn, I should get a free ride?

My dad is Bob Wynn, a hockey legend, known as the King of Hockey. I have a big family and a lot of them were, or are, hockey players, including two half brothers who now own and coach our local rival, the Long Beach Golden Eagles. My nephew JP plays for that team, and my brother Noah plays for their farm team. He's younger than me, so that doesn't make me feel any better that I'm not the only Wynn playing in the AHL. My aunt is the goalie coach for their farm team. My other nephew, Théo, is the GM of the Condors.

I'm pretty sure none of us got where we are because of our name, nor did we expect to.

I gnaw on my bottom lip as I change lanes on Pico Boulevard.

Home. I don't even have my own home, at twenty-six years old. I share the rent of a house here in Santa Monica with my brother Asher. But I also share the rent of an apartment in Pasadena, because that's where I've spent most of my time. Driving over an hour each way sucks on game days, so when I'm playing in Pasadena I stay there, and when I get called up, I stay here with Ash.

I park in front of the house, a two-story Spanish style with white stucco and red tile roof. It's old, but some of it has been updated. The front yard is full of drought-tolerant plants instead of a lawn, a few flowers but lots of tall reed grasses, shorter fescue, lavender, sage, and spiky agave. I thought maybe we could make tequila from the agave, but apparently it's not that easy. I haven't given up the idea, though.

The only reason I know what these plants are is because

my dad has taken an interest in gardening the last few years, and I've kind of gotten into it too.

Now I'm thinking about Dad, and my mood dips even lower. I'm not a worrier, I like to take things as they come, but even I'm concerned about what's happening with him.

I pull the mail from the mailbox and walk inside. Asher's sitting in his office, the third bedroom of the small house, typing away on his computer.

Ash never even tried to make it into the NHL. Maybe he was the smart one out of the two of us. Maybe neither of us inherited the right talent genes from our dad. Ash played hockey in college, but he was more focused on getting his journalism degree and now works as a sports reporter for *Playmaker*, an online hockey blog that's getting huge.

"Hey," I call to him. "I'm home. Mail for you." I walk in and toss envelopes on his desk.

He glances at them. "Bills and junk mail. Why do I get the bills? Both our names are on the lease."

I grin. "Because you're more stable and responsible than I am, and we don't want our electricity cut off."

He smiles and shakes his head.

"I pay my share," I add, before heading to my bedroom.

I still believe in a good, long nap on game day. Part of it is probably just the routine, but whatever, if it helps I'm not stopping. It's only about one-thirty, but my room is dark with the blinds drawn. I strip off my clothes and climb into bed naked, setting my phone on the nightstand with the alarm set.

As I lay in bed, I can't stop thinking about my meeting with Coach. How many times have I heard from coaches that I'm not living up to my potential? It makes me nuts. I may be Bob Wynn's son, I may have some of his talent, but that doesn't mean I can be a god like him.

The challenge of being in the AHL is that it's so close to that ultimate goal—and yet making it that next step is sometimes the biggest hurdle. All of us are good players. We've all probably been top performers at some point in our hockey lives. And then here we are, one step down from the major leagues. From being the best.

Have I let it wear me down? Have I given up the goal, subconsciously?

I won't have too many more chances. After this season, I'll be twenty-seven, which is the average age of an NHL player. I still feel like I'm in good shape. I take my health and fitness seriously. I'm not injury prone, like some guys. I probably have a lot of years left in me to play. But . . . realistically, not many guys make the permanent move from the AHL to the NHL at this age.

The one person I need to talk to right now is Dad. He's always been my best coach, my biggest supporter. He'd be honest with me about whether I've been coasting, about whether I really need to work harder. He'd understand.

But right now, he's the last person I can talk to.

My dad may have Alzheimer's.

We've all been worried lately about his memory and confusion. When my brother and I tried to talk to him about it, he denied it. I haven't seen a lot of evidence of it myself, but everyone else apparently has. And now we know Mom is worried too, it scares the shit out of me.

I may not have that much longer to prove to *him* I can do it. My gut becomes a rock, and I try to relax.

I'm not ashamed to admit that I want my dad to be proud of me. Especially when it comes to hockey. He's the King.

Fuck. I have to figure things out on my own. I have to prove myself. This time I *have* to do it.

2

ARYA

It's a gorgeous morning in Marina del Rey. The sun is warmer now spring is here, and we've even had a little rain, so things are fresh and green. I'm inside Makara Yoga, which is part of Stand-Up Guy Paddleboards, owned by my friend and roommate Taj, getting ready for my Saturday morning stand-up paddleboard yoga class. I didn't invent this kind of yoga class, but there aren't many places that offer it, and it's getting more and more popular.

I have a small studio space here where I do a couple of other Saturday classes, and I also work at Prana in Venice a few times a week. I'm enjoying this new career as a yoga instructor. I'm not making a ton of money, but it's a start, and my classes at Prana have become really popular.

"Hey," I greet Taj, who's also preparing for a SUP lesson.

He shakes back the long, dark hair falling over his face and gives me that sexy smile he's known for. "Morning."

He's so freakin' gorgeous it's hard to look away from him. He'd probably be modeling if he was taller than five foot nine. We've been friends since college. I had a big crush on him then, and I was pretty bummed when I discovered he had a boyfriend. I've gotten over it, though, and I'm so glad he's my friend, because I've needed him—and *any* friends I can get—the last while.

I go onto my laptop to check how many people have registered for this morning's class. I use an app that makes it easy for people to register for blocks of classes or just drop-ins, and to pay online. I've learned a lot about running a business from working at Prana, and now having my own small place.

I limit the class to twenty and it looks like we're full up today. Yay.

I love these classes on the water. There's something extra calming and strengthening about being on the ocean, absorbing the boundless energy of the water, wind, and sun.

Standing behind the counter Taj and I share in the space, I lift my head when a male voice says, "Hi, Arya."

I see a familiar face. My pulse leaps in response. This guy came to one of my classes a few months ago. With Everly and Taylor, a couple of my regulars. I thought he was so cute and fun, and he was definitely flirting with me, making dumb jokes about yoga that had me laughing and nearly losing my focus. But then he turned the class into a gong show, knocking a friend of his—no wait, apparently that was his nephew—off his paddleboard into the water as class was finishing.

He's good-looking, but not in the stunning way Taj is.

His chiseled jaw gives him an air of strength, his ocean blue eyes gleam with charm and humor, and his nose has a bump on it that suggests it's been broken at least once. A scar bisects one eyebrow. His dark hair isn't the near-black of Taj's, more of a walnut brown, and it's shorter. The curve of his mouth in a perpetual smile gives him a boyish, roguish look. And yes, he's a big fat flirt.

Wait, not fat. His body is amazing—lean and muscled, probably six foot two, with hard-packed abs and an ass that is truly biteable. I may not be into dating or relationships anymore, but I can appreciate a nice smile and a ripped body.

"Hi." I give him a polite smile so as not to reveal my heart is beating fast. "You're back."

"Yeah. I really got a lot out of that class. I think it elevated my brain to a higher state."

Oh my God. I bite my lower lip on a smile. "Well, good."

"I've truly come to believe in a higher sense of self, a divine energy in the world."

"Trying a little too hard, dude," I tell him, then turn away. "Okay, everyone," I call. "Grab your board and let's head out onto the water."

We all pick up boards and paddles and the anchors we use to keep us from floating out to sea, and head outside.

"I've been practicing," I hear him tell his friends behind me as we all enter the water.

Once we're all in position on our boards with our anchors dropped to keep us in place, I begin the class. "Let's start with Mountain Pose, feet hip-width apart, your knees in a micro-bend." I position myself to demonstrate, ignoring the fact that my flirty customer is right near me, his eyes focused on me. "Bring your palms in to your heart." I press my hands together in front of my chest. "Inhale the arms up." I lift my arms as I pull air into my lungs, all the way into my belly. "Inhale, reach the arms to the sky, lifting the heart."

"I love it when my heart lifts," Flirty Dude says.

I can't stop the little snort that escapes me. "Exhale and fold forward . . ." I bend over.

"Fold over and let your brains spill out of your head," Flirty Dude says.

With everyone bent over, one of his friends says, "Also known as 'preparing your anus.'"

My eyes pop open wide and I freeze. I nearly burst out laughing, which would be totally inappropriate. These guys are throwing me off my game! Again!

Flirty Dude chokes and starts laughing. Next thing I know, there's a huge splash as he tumbles into the water, splattering my feet and legs.

Now everyone is distracted as he flails around, still chortling.

Everly, who I know a little, yells at him. "Harrison! You're embarrassing me!"

Harrison. Okay, that's his name. I'm about to tell him to get a grip and get back on his board, which he's already trying to do, but as he attempts to climb on, he knocks his board into mine.

My arms flap as I try to regain my balance—and I have excellent balance—but the water's choppy from his thrashing around and there's no way I can do it. I fly into the air and land in the water.

I sink beneath the surface, cold water closing around me. I push up, spluttering and shaking water out of my eyes. I cannot believe this is happening!

3

ARYA

"Oh my God!" Everly cries.

I grab my board and rest my forearms on it, staring at Harrison. I'm befuddled. And cold.

"Are you okay?" he asks. "I am so sorry."

The class is totally disrupted now. Everyone is murmuring and making shocked noises. I don't even know what to say. This has never happened to me. "I'm fine," I say through clenched teeth. "Wet, obviously."

"I'm really sorry," he says again, and he does look contrite. "You can blame him." He jerks his head at the guy who made the anal joke.

That guy gives me a guilty grimace. "Sorry."

I blow out a breath and turn my glare back on Harrison. I'd like to tear a strip off him, but that's not what yoga is supposed to be about. Peace. Oneness. Harmony. *I am capable of anything.* Also, he does look really sorry. I take another breath and relax my body, including my face. "Are you able to continue with the class?" I ask him.

"Yeah, yeah," he says quickly. "For sure. Uh, are you?"

I roll onto my paddleboard and strip off the thin zip-front hoodie I'm wearing. I drop it to the board behind me. "Yes." I find my center and stand, now in my wet sports bra and yoga shorts. My hair's in a ponytail, which is good, although it's dripping water down my back. Shivering, I gaze around at the group. "Sometimes you need yoga. Sometimes you need a beer." I pause. "Sometimes you need both."

Laughter ripples through the morning air.

"Let's resume." I keep my voice calm, a half-smile on my face. "One more time . . . exhale, fold forward . . . inhale, reach up." I hold that pose for a few seconds. *I am capable of anything.* "Exhale, fold forward, and bring your hands to the board as we squat down and bring the right foot back."

This time there are no smart-ass comments from the peanut gallery. I survey the group to see how everyone's doing, including Harrison. His face more serious, he seems focused on the pose.

"You want two ninety-degree angles with your legs," I continue, moving my knee and foot into the correct position and watching the others. "Good. Coming up into Half Warrior . . ." I lift my arms and stretch them out in front of me. "Shoulders back . . . inhale . . . and lift the arms up."

I sense Harrison's gaze on me. Which is weird, because almost everyone in the class watches me to see how I do it, but I *feel* his eyes on me. I say the next words, just waiting for his reaction. "Lift your heart to the sun."

He stretches his arms up and lengthens his torso, not making any jokes. How about that.

Sweet smiling Jesus, he has an amazing body. Although a bit tight. If we were in the studio, I'd be setting a hand in the small of his back, making adjustments to his pose.

We go through the rest of the class without incident. "Let's finish up with a nice Child's Pose." I stretch my arms out in front of me on the board. "Let your body melt into the board."

I follow my own advice, shutting out the rest of the class, particularly that one guy with the naughty-boy smile and hot body, letting my muscles relax, tension seep out of me. I focus on the gentle movement of the water beneath me, my breathing, the warmth of the sun on my back.

Class is over and we all paddle back to shore. This basin is quiet and calm, perfect for my classes. I'm so lucky that Taj has his paddleboard business here and I get to piggyback onto that.

I have another class in my studio at noon, so I head toward the change room so I can put on dry clothes and dry my hair. As I approach the change room, Harrison steps in front of me.

"I want to apologize again," he says earnestly.

He has amazing blue eyes.

"I didn't intend for that to happen, it was an accident, and I'm really sorry that we disrupted your class."

"It's fine. Forgiveness and letting go are an important part of yoga."

He studies my face. "That's very . . . generous of you. We were assholes." He scrunches up his face. "Sorry."

I have to smile now. "It's okay, I may have thought that myself. But exhalation is the act of letting go."

"Could I take you out for a drink . . . or dinner? To make it up to you?"

I blink. "That's not necessary."

"I know it's not, but I'd like to." His smile is genuine and open.

Getting hit on by customers is not usual, since my classes are made up of mostly women, although it has happened. I don't date *anyone*, never mind customers, and especially not men I don't know. For a moment, I'm tempted . . . that unpretentious smile, those warm eyes focused solely on me . . . he's making it hard, but I just can't. "I'm sorry, but no."

"Oh." His face clouds. "Everly said she thinks you have a boyfriend."

What? "No," I say before I can stop myself.

His eyes brighten. "Okay, then!"

"But I can't go out with you."

Disappointment tugs at his lips again. He opens his mouth to say something more, and I sense he's going to try to persuade me. My fingers and toes tingle as adrenaline surges through my body, my stomach clenching. "I have to go."

I bolt into the ladies' changing room and shut the door behind me. My heart knocks in my chest, and for a moment I wish I could lock the door behind me. There are other women in the room, though.

I am brave.

I lift my chin and smile, making my way to the locker in the back where I keep my things. My insides knotted, my skin clammy, I fake a calm that I don't feel as I change into a pair of cropped yoga pants and a top. Then I head to the counter and mirrors along one wall to dry my hair.

I convinced Taj to let me make some improvements to this changing room, so it didn't look like the marina bathroom it once was. I added a couple of hair dryers and a few feminine accessories. It's not the ideal setup, but it works for the classes I do here.

Breathe in courage . . . breathe out doubt.

Harrison Whoever is probably harmless, and I probably could have gone out for one drink, and it probably would have been fun . . . but I'm still uneasy about doing that.

WHEN I EXIT THE CHANGING ROOM, I FIND EVERLY still hanging around. The man with her is the one who made the joke that caused Harrison to fall into the ocean. She approaches me, and he's a couple steps behind her. Big guy, very handsome.

"Arya," she says. "I'm so sorry about the class."

I smile at her. I like Everly. She's been coming to my class for a while, along with her friend Taylor, and she's always been into it and respectful of the practice. "No need for you to apologize."

"He's my brother," she says. "Harrison." She rolls her eyes. "I convinced him to come that first time, so I feel responsible for his antics."

"You're not responsible for anyone but yourself."

"You're so sweet. You handled that amazingly well."

"*I* apologize," the guy with her speaks up. "I'm Wyatt." He extends a hand and I shake it. "We shouldn't have been joking around like that."

"I told your . . . Harrison that it's fine. I've let it go." I smile. "Shit happens."

They both let out surprised laughs. "It does," Everly agrees.

"It's healthy to find the humor in things," I add, smiling. "I need to get to my next class."

"Do you have a business card?" Everly asks.

I blink. "Yes." I move over to the counter and pluck one from the holder. "Here you go."

No idea why she wants it, but whatever.

"Thanks. See you next week."

Is she going to bring her brother again? Crap.

It doesn't matter. *I am capable of anything.*

TAJ AND I ARE SITTING ON THE PATIO AT THE GOLDEN FISH on the Venice Boardwalk later that day. The tables are wooden, the sun is low over the ocean, and we're with some of Taj's friends, Arlo, Indigo and Janey, who are now my friends too. Taj's boyfriend Ziggy owns this place, so we hang out here a lot. It's got that casual beach vibe, cool and laid-back, with the scent of ocean and sun-warmed sand mingling with coconut sunscreen and marijuana. Lots of marijuana.

I sip my beer, one of the many interesting choices Ziggy has on tap here. Taj is drinking kombucha with Longboard lager. I've finished off my tuna poke bowl, which was delicious.

I look around as Taj and Arlo talk about the beach

cleanup they're organizing for next weekend.

I can't believe I'm living here.

This is so far from home. Back in Fargo, North Dakota, the snow might be melting . . . or they might be having a late season blizzard. I'm letting the sun warm my face, sitting near the Pacific Ocean, listening to Hozier, drinking a delicious beer. I let out a long, slow breath of peace.

It might sound weird, but sometimes I get homesick, no matter how wonderful it is here. We all complained about the snow and cold, but weirdly, there are moments I miss it. And I miss my family. But life is good here. Uncomplicated. Relaxed. Chill.

Maybe a wee bit boring, but that's my own fault. I'm learning to take bigger steps, bigger risks. Not like skydiving or anything, just . . . small risks.

"Tell these guys about your class today," Taj says to me with a grin.

I shake my head, smiling ruefully. "I got dumped in the water."

Arlo, Indigo, and Janey laugh, Janey's eyes going wide. "No!"

"Some guys were joking around, and one of them laughed so hard he fell in." I pause. "Actually, I was having a hard time not laughing myself."

"What did they say?"

I repeat Harrison and Wyatt's comments and everyone cracks up.

"So, he's flailing around in the water, knocks into my board, and I go in too." I roll my eyes, still smiling. "Oh my God, I was in shock! I couldn't believe that just happened."

"Why are they coming to your class if they're just going

to fuck around?" Indigo frowns and flicks her black hair off her face.

"Yeah, I don't know. This guy's been before. His sister is one of my regulars, I guess she convinced him to come, but clearly he's not really into yoga." I pause. "He wanted to take me out to dinner to make up for it."

"Ah!" They all react with the same knowing nod.

I frown. "What?"

"He's just trying to get your attention," Janey says. "That's why he's acting out."

"That's probably why he came to your class," Indigo adds.

He *was* flirting with me and trying to impress me, but I doubt that was the reason he was there. "We're not in grade school," I mutter. "He doesn't need to pull my hair or snap my bra strap to get my attention."

They all laugh.

"You obviously turned him down." Taj nudges me with his elbow.

"Of course I turned him down." Taj knows better than anyone why that is.

"Seriously, though . . ." He regards me with a notch of worry between his eyebrows and touches my shoulder. "You were okay after falling in?"

"Oh yeah. Fine. Good thing I can swim!" I appreciate his concern. He's a good friend.

"That would be important if you're doing classes on the water," Arlo says with a grin.

"Let me know if you need me to hang around or get rid of him if he shows up again," Taj adds.

I want to deal with life on my own. But it's definitely

comforting to know there's someone close by who's got my back if I need it.

We have one more beer. The Edison lights strung around the patio glow as the sun lowers below the horizon and the music gets a little louder. It's Saturday night in Venice and crowds of people are still walking along the boardwalk, taking in the little shops and bars. Arlo and Indigo head out first. I watch them walk out, heads close together, Arlo's arm around her shoulders. They're such a sweet couple. Then Janey leaves too. I hug her goodbye.

"Bike ride tomorrow?" she says.

Sundays I have no classes. "Sounds good."

"I'll text you."

Ziggy saunters over and takes a seat at our table across from Taj and me. "Hey," he says, with a special smile for Taj.

Another sweet couple. I'm happy for my friend that he's found someone so great here in California. He went through some shitty relationships in college. It gives me a flicker of hope that there's someone for everyone, but after what I went through, I don't know how I'll ever have the guts to take a chance again.

MONDAY AFTERNOON I'M RIDING MY BIKE TO PRANA WHEN my phone rings in my backpack. I don't stop to answer it. It's most likely a call about SUP yoga class hours or fees, even though all the information is on my website.

At Prana, I lock up my bike outside on one of the racks.

A lot of customers use bikes as transportation, so we accommodate that. I carry my backpack inside.

The studio is housed in an old building with exposed brick walls, high ceilings, and dark hardwood floors, but it's been modernized with fresh coats of paint inside, new lighting, private showers, and cellphone lockers. The main floor has a small retail area with big windows looking onto the street, one studio, and the showers and lockers. A new open staircase leads to the second floor, where two more studios are located, as well as the teachers' lounge, where I now head.

I drop my backpack onto a couch and sit beside it to pull my phone out. There's a voice mail, so I tap the button to take me there and listen while I toe off my running shoes.

It's from someone I don't know and it confuses me a bit. The guy's name is Gary Jones, and he works for the Condors. I don't know what the Condors is. Are. They want someone to give private yoga classes for the team.

Is this a new kind of corporate team building? Surely they only want one class. I don't really know how I'd make yoga a team-building exercise; that's not my thing.

I listen to the message again, trying to make sense of it.

Oh, wait—the *Condors*. The hockey team. I do know what that is. Hockey's a popular sport in North Dakota. I went to a lot of games at UND. I wasn't so much into NHL games, but once some friends and I went up across the Canadian border to watch a Jets game in Winnipeg.

Okay, the Condors want their own yoga instructor.

Yoga for hockey players? I grin. That's . . . crazy.

I don't have time to deal with this right now since I'm teaching classes right away.

Later, when I'm home and Taj is there helping me make Mediterranean quinoa bowls, I tell him about the voice mail.

"Holy shit." He pops a slice of cucumber into his mouth and chews. "That's so amazing, Ari!"

"Is it? I guess it is. How on earth did they get my name?"

He shrugs. "Google?"

That seems doubtful to me. "I can't do it. I don't know anything about yoga for hockey players! And honestly, teaching a class in front of thirty big goons kind of scares the crap out of me. I don't think I can do that."

He nods slowly, eyes thoughtful. "I get it. But it sounds like a great opportunity. You want more work."

I scrunch my face up. "I do."

"Let me hear the message."

I replay it on speakerphone so he can hear.

"I don't know much about hockey, but sounds legit." He rubs his stubbled chin. "It would be at least worthwhile talking to him about it."

"It would be a waste of his time. I should just tell him no."

"I know you're scared." He grabs my hand.

I meet his eyes.

"But you keep saying you need to take bigger steps. Take some risks. Why not try this? It's a professional sports team."

"Oh yeah, like professional athletes don't have any issues of domestic abuse."

He winces. "Okay, maybe there have been a few

instances. But not every player is an asshole. And this is a class. A whole bunch of people."

"I know." I sigh. "This just seems way out of my comfort zone."

"I get that. But you know how you grow and heal and get stronger, right?"

"Yes," I mutter, then recite, "I love taking risks."

He laughs. "That doesn't sound convincing."

It's one of my fearless affirmations, and he's right. "I am capable of anything," I say aloud, sounding surer of myself.

"Yes, you are." He pulls me in for a hug. "Do it."

"I'll think about it."

We finish making dinner and eat in front of the TV, watching a local news show. After we've eaten, I get out my laptop and start googling. I'm curious about how yoga would help hockey players. I mean, I think yoga helps everyone, but how would it benefit specifically these athletes?

Stress reduction. Reducing inflammation. Breathing. Sleep. Okay, yeah. I can cover all that.

Flexibility. Mobility. Balance. I nod as I read.

I find a blog by a woman who teaches yoga to the Pittsburgh Penguins. Okay, this is a real thing. I read about hockey injuries and strength training. While yoga can build strength, I don't see it as valuable for professional athletes for that; I'm sure they're already strong. But I can certainly see that there would be great benefits from adding it to a strength-and-conditioning plan.

Groin and hip flexors . . . oh yeah. There are a number of poses that will help with that, opening up the hips and strengthening groins and adductors. Warrior 2 for balance.

Absolutely. Balance must be incredibly important for hockey players. And strengthening shoulders for protecting them when they get checked into the boards.

I read about structural imbalances, stability and range of motion.

I look away from my monitor and stare at the wall, imagining a class full of hockey players. It makes me nervous . . . but it also intrigues me. Being able to help athletes who are in top physical condition be even better . . . of course that appeals to me.

Wasn't I just thinking the other day that life is good . . . but a little boring? I enjoy what I'm doing right now, but it's not enough for forever. I've thought about expanding Makara into a full-time business, maybe hiring other instructors, offering different types of classes. And my goal in moving here to California and starting a new career was to expand my limits. To be brave and confident and in control of my life.

Can I do this?

I nibble my bottom lip.

"What are you thinking about?" Taj is kicked back on the couch, bare feet on the coffee table, still watching TV.

I wrinkle my nose. "Yoga for hockey players."

He smiles. "Good."

I pull air in through my nose and let it slowly out. *I breathe in courage and breathe out doubt. If it doesn't kill me, it makes me stronger.*

I'll call back Gary Jones in the morning. *Aaaaah!*

4

HARRISON

I'VE BEEN PLAYING IN SANTA MONICA FOR TWO WEEKS NOW. Six games. I'm feeling pretty good. Working hard.

We've won five of those six games. I have four goals, four assists. Not too shabby.

And yet, I have a feeling I'm still not doing my best.

The first game I played after getting called up was against the Long Beach Golden Eagles, which is our big local rival. The fans get super worked up for every "Beach Barn Battle" against the Eagles. A lot of Eagles fans come too, so the atmosphere in the Coliseum is pretty crazy.

It was a big game for me. The two teams are adversaries because of more than just a local rivalry. My half brother Matthew owns the Eagles, and my other half brother Mark is the coach. This is a confusing, long story, but Matthew apparently bought the team after Dad fired Mark as coach of the Condors. He fired him because he was pissed that Mark and Matthew were suing him, accusing him of stealing money from them. It's nuts, but we're trying to sort out this crazy conflict.

So, a bunch of my family was at that game. My dad comes to every game, obviously, as the team owner, but my mom, Everly, and Ash were there too. And because it was the Eagles, Mark and Matthew were there, and I was playing against my nephew Jean Paul, known as JP.

We lost that game, which was disappointing. Personally, I felt good about how I played. I was still irritated about the little talk I'd had with Coach where he basically told me I was lazy and I needed to get off my ass. Maybe that lit a fire under said lazy butt, because I was determined to show him he was wrong.

You don't get what you wish for, you get what you work for.

The loss just made me even more determined to do better. Hockey's a team sport and it's not about me showing off for my family, though I'll admit I want to impress them; it's about winning. We need to *win*.

I've been working with Stan on transitions. He got Bellsy to come and practice with us and he's a damn good D-man, so it's been great. He gets us doing one-on-one drills, making me backcheck then transition to offense, and a bunch of other drills.

There are only three weeks left in the regular season. We have a playoff spot locked up, but we still don't know if we'll have home-ice advantage, since we've been neck and neck with Vancouver in the points race. Every time we get ahead of them, they win and jump over us.

It's Saturday. We practiced this morning, but we don't have a game tonight. We just got back from a short road trip where we had back-to-back games in Denver and Phoenix.

It's great having a Saturday night off, but I'm spending it with a bunch of family.

Not that I don't love my family. I do. But we have a lot of, er, issues.

For this family meeting, I don't have to come all the way from Pasadena. Asher and I drive together from our place on Pine Street to our nephew's place in Marina del Rey.

Our dad had two kids with his first wife, our half brothers Matthew and Mark. Théo is Matthew's son, so yeah, he's our nephew, but he's only two years older than us.

"Hopefully this shit is getting fixed," Asher mutters as he drives along Lincoln Boulevard.

"Yep."

There's been a black cloud over the family for years. Maybe I should say "clouds." When my dad remarried, the family was pretty upset. His first wife had died only a couple of years before that, and our mom is twenty years younger than him. You can see why the family thought she was marrying him for his money and that Dad was blinded by her youth and good looks. Dad's sons from his first marriage had a hard time dealing with Mom and Dad having kids while they were also having kids. So there were already some bad feelings when Mark and Matthew started pestering Dad about some money issues a few years ago, and now they're freakin' suing him. Not only that, Matthew bought the rival team and stole Mark away from Dad's team.

A while back I suggested to Everly that we, meaning the

younger Wynn family members, should try to figure out what's going on with this lawsuit to see if we could end this family feud. We've had a couple of meetings and each of us has spoken to various older Wynn family members and reported back.

Then Everly lost her shit at a hockey game, that same first game I played at, which meant my great play didn't even get noticed. Whatever.

This was not like Everly, and kind of shocking. She does not lose her shit. Ever. That was why I suggested she be the one to lead this plan. She likes to be in charge of everything. And I'm speaking as her little brother who she put makeup on, whose hair she curled, and who she dressed in a flowered dress to have a tea party with her dolls.

Anyway, with Mom and Dad, Asher, and Matthew all in one room, Everly told Matthew our suspicions about Dad. Now it's all out in the open.

We park and walk a block or so to Théo's house, right on the beach. He and his wife, Lacey, have rented this place since Dad hired him as general manager last summer. He hasn't even managed the team for a full season, but I think he's doing amazing. It has to be challenging, though, working for Dad. Especially now.

It's late afternoon, a sunny day with the ocean sparkling blue and gold in the distance, people walking and biking on the path and playing volleyball on the beach. I ring the doorbell and then open the door to step inside.

Lacey appears. "Hey, Harry! Hey, Ash."

I roll my eyes at the nickname. It's what my teammates have always called me, so I'm used to it, but it's not my name. "Hey, Lace. How's it going?"

"Good. Come on in. You guys want a beer?"

"Oh, hell yeah," I answer.

"Yep," Ash replies.

She laughs and heads to the fridge while we turn in to the living room. Everly's already here, along with JP, his girlfriend Taylor, and Théo, of course. My other brother Noah and our niece Riley drove up from San Diego. Only Jackson isn't here. He lives in Chicago and lucky him, he's missing out on all this shit.

We exchange greetings and take seats. Lacey hands Ash and me beers.

"Okay, we're all here now," Everly says. "So." She looks around at us. "I guess you all know that I confronted Matthew and Dad at the game a couple of weeks ago."

We all nod. "What's up with that, Ev?" I ask, loosely holding my beer. "We had a plan."

"I know." She gives me a toothy grin. "Sorry about wrecking the plan. I . . . well, the truth is . . ." She pauses and I can see she's getting emotional. Shit. "Well, I'll just be blunt. If Dad is dying, this all seems so ridiculous."

"He's not dying," I immediately object.

Everyone exchanges uncomfortable glances.

My gut cramps. "I mean, not right away."

I don't know much about different kinds of dementia, but I talked to one of my Pasadena Condors teammates about it once. His grandma has Alzheimer's, and he makes it sound pretty goddamn terrifying.

"Maybe not," Everly concedes. "But we don't know for sure what's going on with him. Mom's taking him to the doctor next week. She's going with him."

"Maybe you should go too," Ash suggests to Everly.

She shakes her head. "Mom can handle it."

"Are you sure?" I ask. "I know she's strong, but this is tough stuff."

"I'd totally go if she wanted me to. But I think she's got this. We're all just happy he finally agreed to go."

"It hasn't happened yet," Noah mutters.

"True." Everly sighs.

We've had a hard time convincing Dad he needs to see a doctor. It would be easy to just take his word for it that he's fine, but we all know he has to do it.

"I've discovered a few bad business decisions he made the last couple of years," Théo says quietly. "This has been going on for longer than we realized, I think."

"He's damn good at covering it up," JP puts in. His girlfriend reaches for his hand and squeezes it.

"He is," Everly agrees. "Anyway, we'll see what comes of that. But I kind of had a moment . . . fighting over money is stupid. I basically told Matthew that family is more important than money." She tips her head. "And I know it's privileged to say that, because we all have more than enough money. But seriously, we don't know how long Dad has left, or how long we'll have *him* . . ." She makes air quotes with her fingers. "Because this disease is stealing him from us. I'm sure Mark and Matthew don't want that to be how things end with their father."

"I think you're right," JP says. "Dad wants to go to the doctor appointment next week too." His dad, meaning, Matthew, Dad's oldest son.

My eyes pop open wide. "Wow. Really?"

"Yeah." JP winces. "But Chelsea won't let him."

"Well, that sucks," Riley says. She's Mark's daughter. "He should be able to."

"Do you blame her?" Everly challenges Riley. There's always been tension between these two, since Riley's dad has never liked our mom, and we've always tried to defend her. "Nobody trusted her for years. Why would she trust them?"

Riley purses her lips. "Fair, I guess."

"Mark and Dad are going to sit down with Dad and Chelsea," JP adds. "They're waiting until after the appointment."

"Okay." Everly nods. "That's good."

"You were great that night," Ash tells Everly, smiling. "I damn near died when you went off like that."

Ash was at the game in the press box and had stopped by Dad's box between periods when this all went down.

"Thanks." Everly beams.

"And you're right, Everly," JP says. "About family and money." He looks around. "Hopefully they can settle things. It really seems that Grandpa owes Dad and Uncle Mark money."

We've learned that Dad didn't steal money; he actually borrowed it from a trust fund that belonged to Mark and Matthew, which was their inheritance from their mom, with legal documents all drawn up. But he was supposed to pay it back, and he hasn't, which is why they ended up suing him.

The media had a field day with that, holy shit. It's died down from when the suit was first filed, but everyone knew it was going on and that there was bad blood between the King of Hockey and his sons.

I don't know why he's not paying them back, but that

worries me too. Is it the Alzheimer's? Is it because he has no money? Christ, I hope he hasn't bankrupted the team. Or himself.

"Théo," I say. "Can Dad afford to pay back the money? We all know that the Condors aren't a big money-making team."

Théo blows out a breath. "I don't know. I know the finances of the team, but not his personal situation."

"What if . . ." I hesitate. "What if he can't pay it back? What then?"

Everyone trades uneasy glances again. Silence as heavy as a Zamboni falls over the room.

Everly speaks first. "We'll deal with that when we come to it."

We all nod.

"What else do we need to do?" Everly gazes around at us.

"Make sure Dad goes to the doctor," I say.

"And make sure Uncle Mark and Dad sit down with Grandpa and Chelsea," JP adds.

"If they don't . . . we'll need to get involved. Are you all ready for that?" Everly asks.

We all speak up in the affirmative.

"Okay. We'll check in with each other in a couple of weeks. No need to meet unless things don't go right."

"Sounds good to me." I lift my beer bottle to my lips.

Everly pulls her phone out and starts tapping the screen with her thumbs. "Texting Wyatt," she says. "Telling him he can come over now."

Her boyfriend Wyatt Bell, known to players as Bellsy, lives in the same building, a three-unit condo.

"He could've been here," I say.

"He wouldn't." She sets down her phone and lifts her wineglass. "He says it's family stuff, and it's awkward that he plays for the team."

I respect that.

Lacey heads to the kitchen and Théo heads outside to get the barbecue going. They offered to make dinner for us. Bellsy arrives and heads straight to Everly, sliding a hand around the back of her neck and kissing her forehead.

She closes her eyes briefly, smiling.

I've never seen my sister like this. It's weird, but nice. I'm happy for her.

When we're not talking about our family issues, we all get along pretty well. Riley offers to help in the kitchen, JP and I head out to the patio to stand with Théo around the barbecue in manly fashion while drinking beer, and Taylor and Everly come sit outside and start talking about their yoga classes.

Yoga. Damn.

"Don't remind me about yoga class," I tell them. I was crushing on the sexy yoga instructor until I accidentally knocked her into the water. Way to make a good impression. The humiliation still burns every time I think of it.

They grin. "I'm sure you want to forget that," Taylor says.

"I'll never make you come to class again," Everly adds.

"You seriously went to another of her classes after that?" I ask.

"Yeah." Everly shrugs. "I considered changing to a

different class, but she's a great instructor. I really like her classes."

"Same," Taylor says. "She's really down-to-earth."

"Or down-to-water," Everly says.

They both laugh.

"So funny," I mutter.

Riley, Noah, and Ash haven't heard the story, so Everly entertains them with an exaggerated version of it. A little exaggerated.

Hey, I'm a good sport. I can laugh at myself.

Théo starts flipping burgers on the grill and it smells amazing. Lacey sets out bowls of pretzels and nuts, and I grab a handful of cashews.

"Hey, you guys hear what happened to our mascot last weekend?" Noah asks. He plays for the Eagles' farm team, the San Diego Hawks.

Riley starts laughing. Apparently, she's heard.

"What?" I ask.

"He was at some kids' event and decided he was going to run at the glass window. He thought it was like the glass on the ice, and he could just throw himself at it and bounce off it. But he smashed the glass."

"Oh my God!" the women all exclaim.

We're all laughing and shaking our heads.

"Is he okay?" Lacey demands.

"Yeah, he's fine. The costume protected him, I guess. It's on video. Wait, I can find it." Noah pulls his phone out and we all gather around to watch the big hawk throwing himself through a glass window while the kids all freeze in shock.

"That's hilarious. Who's in the costume?"

"Guy named Ian." Noah shakes his head, grinning. "He's a nut, so this doesn't surprise me."

The shared laughter has totally changed the vibe, and I don't even care that some of it was at me. Everly's right—family's important.

"Okay," Gary, our strength-and-conditioning coach, announces in the dressing room after our morning skate Sunday. We have a game tonight against Florida. "We're trying something new, starting tomorrow."

"Oh shit," Scotty says. "Now what? Some new kind of torture?"

Gary grins. "Yoga."

Some of the guys groan, some stare in disbelief, others shrug.

"I can do yoga," I say. I've been to a couple of classes.

"Yeah, me too," Bellsy adds. We exchange mirthful glances, remembering our experience.

Gary spouts off about the benefits of yoga. "Never mind the woo-woo stuff," he says. "There won't be any meditation and aligning your chakras."

I snort out a laugh.

"It won't be like that. This is about increasing your balance and flexibility. Lots of you guys are hurting this late in the season. We need to try to gain every advantage we can heading into the playoffs."

Ugh. I'm not sure I buy it, but whatever. I know other teams are trying it.

"Tomorrow morning, in the weight room, nine o'clock sharp."

I make a face as I toss my practice jersey to Joe to add it to the laundry. Great, even earlier start time. But what the hell. They want every advantage we can get, and so do I. If a yoga class is part of it, so be it.

I'M PICTURING THE WEIGHT ROOM WITH DIM LIGHTS AND some kind of new age music playing softly when I arrive at the Coliseum the next morning.

I'm tired and sore and haven't managed to down my giant Starbucks coffee yet. We won last night again, but it damn near killed us. We let things slide in the second period and got down by two goals. I was pissed and lectured everyone else before the third period because I wasn't about to give up, and somehow we pulled it off with three unanswered goals, the last one with five minutes to go. That last five minutes was intense; the Panthers were throwing everything at us. It was a taste of what playoff hockey will be like. After coming back like that, there was no way I wanted to blow it in the last few minutes, so with grit and determination we hung on. Luckily Bergie was playing outstanding, making some incredible saves. Bellsy threw himself in front of the puck a few times and I bet he has the bruises to show for it. He's nuts. In a good way.

The good thing was, Coach moved me up onto the second line, playing with Eddie Rintala, our superstar first-round draft pick, and Pavel Volkov. I played more minutes, and it felt like the three of us could really read each other.

I walk into the weight room. A few guys are already there. Space has been cleared on the floor for us, and they're arranging colorful yoga mats.

I start toward the corner where Gary is talking to a woman . . . and I stop dead.

Arya. From Makara Yoga.

My mind blanks for a moment, thrilled to see her but not sure why she's here. Then it clicks. She's our yoga instructor!

Fan-fucking-tastic!

5

HARRISON

I've been thinking a lot about Arya since that disastrous class. I fucking hate that I pushed her into the water like that. It was a stupid accident, and I was so pissed at myself after. I couldn't really blame Bellsy, who made the damn smart-ass comment. It was totally my fault.

She looked so shocked, coming up with water streaming down her face, blinking those long eyelashes. Then the way she stared at me kind of made my balls shrink.

I probably didn't make a good impression on her the first time I went to her class either, when I deliberately knocked JP into the water. And I don't think she appreciated my yoga jokes.

I just wanted to impress her.

She's seriously gorgeous, just the type of woman I love. I know, I know, I have a type. I can't help it. I'm not saying I could never be attracted to a woman with a different appearance; I've gone out with all kinds of women. My last girlfriend actually had short, dark hair. We were together for three years. So it's not like I only date blondes. But I have to admit I'm attracted to them.

But it's not just the way she looks. It's the calm, confident way she gets in front of a bunch of people and leads them through the poses, obviously knowledgeable and proficient. She's clearly good at what she does, apparently with waiting lists for her classes. It's the way she regarded me, with glints of humor and a spark of interest in her eyes that encouraged me, even though she turned me down.

Anyway . . . here she is! It's a sign! And the perfect chance to make up for being an idiot.

I make a beeline toward her, smiling.

She glances up as I approach and her mouth drops open, her eyes widening.

"Hi!" I greet her happily. "I can't believe you're here!"

Her eyes pop wide open and she blinks. "Harrison. Uh . . . hi."

"You two know each other?" Gary looks back and forth between us.

"I told you I've been to yoga classes," I say. "Arya's a fantastic teacher."

Her eyebrows shoot up skeptically. "You've been to two classes. And you disrupted both of them."

I grimace. "Yeah, about that . . . I apologize again."

Gary closes his eyes and draws in a deep breath. "No disruptions," he snaps. "The team has hired Arya and you need to pay attention and do the class."

"Of course." I put on a serious expression. "No fu—" I stop. "No joking around."

"You play for the Condors," Arya says, still wearing a bemused expression.

She didn't know who I am.

"Yeah." I grin. I don't assume everyone knows who I am. California is a big state and a lot of people here aren't into hockey. I guess she's one of them.

I step over and pick up a mat, then walk over and lay it on the floor between Bellsy and Scotty.

"What a coincidence," Bellsy says in a low voice. "Of all the yoga instructors, in all the yoga studios . . ."

"Yep."

"She thinks we're idiots," he adds.

Dammit.

When I asked her out, it was only partly to try to make up for what I'd done. The very first class of hers I went to, when Everly dragged me there so JP wouldn't be the only guy, I was attracted to her. She didn't pay much attention to me, despite my attempts to show off. The second time, I knocked *her* in the water, but after her initial shock, it seemed like she found it funny. When I asked her out, I definitely felt a vibe like she wanted to say yes, like she was struggling. I just don't get why.

I scrunch up my face in frustration. I need to pay attention and focus on yoga, not the hot instructor.

Soon we're all there, sitting on the floor of the weight room. Arya and Gary move in front of us.

"This is Arya Ross," Gary says. "She has seven years of experience teaching yoga." He looks at a paper in his hand and reads haltingly. "She earned her RYT 200 Yoga Alliance certification five years ago, specializing in hatha and vinyasa. She's studied with some world-renowned instructors to further her education. She teaches at Prana Yoga in Venice and has her own stand-up paddleboard classes at Makara Yoga in Marina del Rey. She creates a safe, noncompetitive space for her students to find deeper meaning and inspiration. Her classes emphasize the importance of proper alignment, pranayama breathing techniques, and mindfulness." He looks up. "Welcome, Arya."

"Thank you, Mr. Jones." Arya smiles at him, then at all of us. "I'm honored to be here today. I know firsthand how much yoga can restore balance, awareness, health, and happiness—yoga was and still is a healing force in my life. I love bringing that to others. I have to be honest and tell you that I have never taught a class like this, to professional athletes. I know all of you are in top physical condition, but I believe that yoga can help fine-tune your bodies by optimizing any structural inefficiencies, improving your stability and range of motion. So, let's get started."

Music begins to play. The kickass sound system in the weight room usually blasts a lot of hard rock and rap music for us to work out to. I cringe, waiting for the tranquil sounds of some kind of new age music, but that's not it. The first song is slow, yeah, but it has a country music sound.

"Lie down on your mats," Arya instructs us. "Legs apart, palms facing the ceiling."

She teaches us how to breathe as we each lie there with a hand on our abdomen, feeling it rise and fall as we breathe deeply. "Breathe in new energy," she says. "Exhale and feel the relaxation."

Then she has us do a wide-legged Child's Pose, our foreheads to the mats. We did this one on the paddleboard.

"Take those same deep breaths," she says. "Right into your belly. Drop your hips down to your heels."

We stay like that for a while, the music playing, nobody talking. This is weird.

I know flexibility is important, and I force myself to stretch, but I've never really liked it. It's too . . . static. I like to be moving.

Eventually we move onto our hands and knees. This is good. Now I can see her. Today she's wearing cropped leggings and a modest tank top. She has us rolling our spines, arching our back then letting it curl down. I watch the way she moves, sinuous and graceful. And sexy.

I follow along. The music changes, becoming a little peppier, a guitar opening joined by a harmonica. This is cool. Soon she has us in a pose that's like a side plank, one arm in the air.

"Float your right leg up off the matt," she says.

Whoa. Okay.

I thought doing these poses would be easier on dry land than on the water. I was wrong. I really need to focus, as I'm balanced on one hand and one knee. On dry land, Arya has the benefit of being able to move around as we follow her direction and hold various poses, and she's apparently very picky, adjusting a foot, a hand, the arch of a back. But the way she describes how to perfect the poses is actually bang on—like, when she says to press firmly into one foot, it really does help with balance.

As I'm in what she just called Puppy Pose, she approaches me and, still talking in her serene voice, she places a hand on my back. "Keep your hips directly over top of your knees," she says in that mellow tone. "Your chest melting down to the mat . . . you should be feeling an opening in your armpits. Maybe your pecs."

Awareness jumps along my nerve endings. Her touch is gentle yet firm, and my skin tingles everywhere. If I keep screwing up, will she keep putting her hands all over me?

I can see her toes . . . I don't have a foot fetish, but they're really pretty, with shiny purple polish on her nails.

She moves away. "Keep pressing your fingers into the mat."

She stops by Bergie and murmurs, "Good work. You're really flexible."

Huh. She's praising *him*? Shit. I need to do better. I sink my hips lower.

The class lasts about forty-five minutes.

"Let's find Savasana," Arya says. "Final resting pose." She lies on her back again. "Stretching out our arms and legs, palms to the ceiling, eyes closed." Her tone has become softer, and the music is another gentle but still lively song.

Lying still is usually hard for me to do. I have a ton of energy, and doing nothing makes me antsy. But I let the music fill my head, focusing on what she says.

"Take note of how your body feels now, compared to when we started," Arya says. "Focus on your breathing. Take your time. When you're ready to get up, please do so slowly. Namaste." Then she lets things go silent, and this is hard too. I can sense the guys wanting to jump up and talk.

If anyone disrespects her, they'll have to deal with me. But it doesn't happen. Gradually some of the guys slowly sit up, then stand.

I stand and roll up my mat to take it to the corner of the

room. I drop it off quickly, then hustle over to Arya as she picks up a backpack. "That was a great class," I tell her.

She fixes her gaze on me and says nothing. My instinct is to fill the silence, but that hasn't gone so well in the past as I spout off stupid bullshit, so I make myself wait for her to respond.

Finally, she says, "Thank you."

"I have really tight hip flexors," I say. "I was surprised at how that one pose . . . the . . ."

"The Bow Pose?"

"Yeah. It felt great. Do you have other ones that would work on hip flexors?"

"I do. I'll be sure to include them in our next class."

"Oh. I was hoping you could show me . . ."

She shakes her head slowly, her lips pursing in a near-smile. "I'm pretty sure you have a practice to get to right now. But like I said, I'll include that in our next class."

She slings her bag over her shoulder and makes her way out of the weight room.

The other guys are shooting me looks as we head to the locker room to change into our gear. I lift my chin. "Listen up. That's the woman I'm going to marry," I announce. "Everyone else stay away from her."

A bunch of guys laugh.

"Riiiiight," says Scotty.

"I'm serious." I pull open my locker door and yank my shirt off over my head.

"Not sure how to tell you this," Bellsy says. "But I don't think she's into you."

"Not yet." I shove down my shorts. "She will be."

"Pretty sure of yourself, Harry," Jabber says.

"What's not to love?" I grin, stretching my arms wide, standing naked.

"Uh . . . does she have small hands?" Meals on Wheels —Milo Foster—asks.

I frown. "What? Why?"

"Small hands make your dick look bigger."

The guys hoot and I ball up my T-shirt and chuck it at him. He ducks, laughing.

"Joke all you want. You'll see."

I've never believed in love at first sight, but I do now. Obviously, the first time I met her, I thought I was merely attracted to her, but now . . . pretty sure I fell in love.

6

———

ARYA

That went okay.

I have to admit I lost my composure for a moment when Harrison approached me.

He's a hockey player. For an NHL team. So is Wyatt, who was at class with Everly that day.

I don't know why I'm so surprised. I guess it's because I think professional athletes are all big, entitled jerks. These two guys seem pretty regular and easygoing. And yeah, they're big, but not like a pumped-up bodybuilder.

And damn, Harrison is cute. He's kind of a goof, but in an appealing way. His smile is big and endearing, and creases up his face into adorable dimples. I noticed how attractive he is before, but now seeing him in his own environment, he seems even more . . . adorable.

He's also still flirty.

I'm struggling with this, because . . . I like it. But it also makes me nervous.

I stop in Gary's office as he asked me to, to debrief.

"I think it went well," I say, setting my bag on a chair.

"Good, good. I'll see what the feedback is from the guys. Some of them weren't enthused about it, but oh well."

"I've had one request for more poses that work on tight hip flexors."

"Great. What about hips? And low back? Those are areas a lot of players have tightness."

"I'll definitely work on those too."

"Excellent. See you Thursday morning."

My bike is locked up inside the arena, near the players' entrance. The security dude jumps up to open the door for me so I can wheel it outside. "Thanks, Luis." I give him a wave and push off to ride to Prana. I'm early for my next class there, but it's not worth going home and I can lock up my bike and walk down to Steeps on the corner.

When I'm seated on the little patio at Steeps with my lychee peach green tea in hand, I lean back in my chair and turn my face to the sun. I've always loved the sun. I find the warmth on my face so soothing and relaxing, yet energizing.

I was nervous about that class, but it went fine, despite the surprise, and once again I can tell myself—*I am capable of anything.*

A small swell of pride surges inside me. I smile and sip my tea. Yum.

They're also paying me damn good money to teach those classes. Not sure how I got so lucky, but I'll take it. And now, in spite of my earlier misgivings, I want to do this. I want to do well at it. Maybe I can have some small part in making this team better. I love that idea.

I send a text to my mom. I told my parents about the opportunity after I met with Gary Jones a few days ago.

Mom's excited for me and I know she'll want to hear about it.

I miss my parents.

But I'm doing this.

Now I just have to make sure I don't screw things up next class.

I ENTER THE LIGHT ROOM ON THE SECOND FLOOR, CALLED that because of the big, high windows on three sides of it, for my Wednesday class. The class is full, which is usual. I've been gratified that since I started here, my classes have become really popular. Everyone is lying quietly on their mats, arranged in neat rows. Ceiling fans twirl lazily above us.

I walk to the front of the room where my mat is already laid out. I set my water bottle on the floor against the wall and turn to the sound system to start one of my playlists. Finding great music for my classes is a fun pastime when I'm not teaching. I like lots of different sounds, and I think my music also sets me apart from other instructors.

The first song is by XXYYXX, "About You." It has a cool, sort of laid-back lounge feel.

"We'll begin today's class in a Child's Pose," I say, sitting on my mat. Everyone sits up.

That's when I see him. Harrison.

What the duck fuck?

I don't let my attention linger on him, as I have a class

full of people. "Bring your knees either wide or together, with your big toes touching. Press your hips to your heels and relax your forehead down." I survey everyone as they shift into place. The soft music fills the space. "Let everything settle down, right into your mat." I stand to move through the class, my bare feet silent on the smooth wood floor. "Also let yourself settle mentally." I stop behind one woman and set my hands on her back, gently pushing her hips lower. "Float in your head and begin to tune into your breath."

I pause at Harrison. His head is down, so I can't meet his eyes. His hips are *not* on his heels. Swallowing a sigh, I lay my hands on his lower back and do the same for him, gently pressing down, a little more . . . a little more . . . feeling his tight hips relax somewhat. My feet are spread and braced on the floor, using my own body weight to ease his lower.

His body is big. Warm. Strong. Pulsing with energy that transfers into my hands and arms.

I imagine myself draping over him, my arms going around his body, pressing my face to his back . . .

Focus.

"Breathe in and out of your nose, creating that sound in the back of your throat . . . like the ocean."

I move on to the woman beside Harrison.

What is he doing here?

"Keep your breath smooth and steady for the entire practice," I say.

I slowly pace back to the front of the room and get into my own Child's Pose, using this moment to refocus my breathing, my energy.

"Next . . . inhale . . . and come to a Tabletop, on your hands and knees." I slowly move into position.

I continue the class, ignoring Harrison other than when he needs some adjustment of his poses.

The music changes to "World on Fire" by Louis the Child. The beat is up-tempo, the singer's voice soft and sweet, with some piano riffs. I love this song.

We get into some more challenging poses later in the class. "Back to center," I say.

So far, Harrison has been a model student—silent and compliant.

"Hands on your knees and breathe in." I pause. "Then relax your head and neck down. Rise to standing. Arms float high. Exhale, palms together in front of your heart. Take a moment to close your eyes, adjust your stance, your breath . . ." I stroll between the mats, giving them time. Alina Baraz sings "Electric." This song is super sexy, and I have a hard time not imagining being tangled in sheets, wrapped up in a man's arms and legs, as she croons, "Kiss me." I glance at Harrison and our eyes meet. Khalid's raspier voice joins in the song.

I pull in a slow breath through my nose and break the eye contact.

Kiss me.

Dammit, why did I use this playlist today, with steamy songs that make me think of sex?

"Shift your weight to your left foot and bring your right foot up for Tree Pose." My own hands are pressed together in front of my chest, and I put my weight onto my left foot. "Bring your foot to your calf or your thigh . . . lift your belly button . . . for an extra challenge you can reach up, and even look up." Everyone lifts their arms, including Harrison, but he wobbles and touches his foot down. He resumes right away, though.

I move over to him to turn his knee more outward. "Just don't rest your foot on your knee joint and possibly move it out of place. Lengthen your tailbone toward the floor. Press this foot against your inner thigh . . ." I touch his bare foot, which feels very intimate. "Resist with your left leg. Gazing at a fixed point in front of you on the floor will help with the balance."

He smells good.

God.

I let them all hold the pose on that side, then the other, then softly tell them to lower their arms, their foot, and shake out their legs.

We move into Triangle Pose. "Feel like there's a wall behind you, and lean into it. Nice, Stella. Find your strength."

The only reason I'm paying more attention to Harrison is because he needs it, so I make myself move around to be sure I'm getting to everyone who needs assistance, but I return to him to adjust his hips. I grab a yoga block for Harrison as I instruct further.

"Thanks," he murmurs, placing his hand on the block.

"You're welcome. Lift your right leg . . . stack your hips and your shoulders . . ."

They're balanced on one foot and one hand. Harrison wobbles a bit again. "Reach your right arm to the sky. It's fine if you fall, don't worry." I pause. Nobody falls. "Energize your fingers . . . flex your toes . . . and keep breathing."

We end the class with Happy Baby, which is not a pretty pose. I drag my eyes away from Harrison's rounded butt and massive thighs. Wow.

We then move into savasana. The song playing is another Alina Baraz song, "Down for You," again with a chill vibe. I like to leave people relaxed but energized. I guide them through relaxing, then I quietly leave the studio, allowing them to rest as long as they want.

In the empty teachers' lounge, I drop onto a chair and blow out a long breath.

I was definitely distracted by Harrison's presence, but I don't think anyone else in the class noticed anything.

I'm done teaching for the day, so I grab my backpack. I check my cellphone for any messages. A Snapchat from Janey, a text from Taj telling me he won't be home for dinner. So I can do whatever I want. It's only five o'clock. I'll jump on my bike and head to the beach.

I run down the stairs to the retail area. Hazel and Willow are working there, a few customers looking at clothing and accessories.

And Harrison is there.

He lifts his head and spots me. A smile breaks across his face. "Hi."

I walk toward him, my heart doing a jitterbug in my chest. "Hi."

He holds up a pair of men's shorts. "Do you think I need these?"

I have to smile. "You have shorts."

"Yeah, but, uh, things move around."

I bite my lip and take the shorts from him, trying not to

think about things moving around in his shorts. Gah. "These have a special liner."

"Yeah. I think that would be good."

"These also have flat seams, so no chafing. And they were designed by a man."

"Good. I'll take them."

"We also sell underwear." Oh God. Why did I say that? He's not just another customer.

He grins. "I can always use more."

I lead him over to the table with the performance boxer briefs. The image of his legs and his ass floats through my mind as I show him the garments. "The fabric is breathable and sweat wicking."

"It's really soft. I'll take a three pack." He grabs a size large.

I swallow.

The model on the front of the package is lean and muscled, but what I wouldn't give to see Harrison wearing these briefs. Heat sweeps from my hairline down to my chest. I'm probably turning fire-engine red.

Then he says, "Oh, sorry. It looks like you're on your way out."

"Yes. I'm done for the day here."

"Great! I can buy you a drink." He moves toward the counter to pay for his items.

"Oh my God, you don't give up, do you?"

"I wouldn't be a professional hockey player if I gave up."

"Why are you here?" I ask him.

"I wanted to learn more. And I wanted to see you again."

My chest squeezes. Well, at least he's honest. I don't get a creepy vibe from him, but still . . . those words freak me out a little. "How did you know I work here?"

His forehead furrows. "Gary said it when he introduced you the other day."

"Oh. Right." I eye him.

He pulls out a credit card and hands it to Willow with a smile. She smiles back, clearly finding him attractive.

As do I.

Most women would be enjoying this. A gorgeous professional athlete who seems nice, if a bit goofy, who's clearly attracted to me and is asking me out. And I'm attracted to him. I can't deny it. But . . . I'm not most women.

I nibble my bottom lip. I'm so tempted to let him buy me a drink. But I'm also nervous.

I am brave.

He turns away from the counter with the brown paper shopping bag containing his purchases. "So? Where should we go?"

Okay. I'm doing it. "There's a place a few blocks down the street . . . Bottles and Bites. We could meet there."

"Okay. Sounds good. Which way?" We step out onto the sidewalk. I point toward the beach.

I push my arms through my backpack straps and move to the bike rack to unlock my bike. I'm not sure where he parked, but I'll probably get there before him since it's not far and he'll need to find parking again.

Sure enough, I am there before him, but I'm just locking my bike again when he walks up. "Do you bike everywhere?"

"Pretty much." I straighten. "I don't have a car."

"Huh. Really? LA is such a car city."

"I know."

He opens the door of Bottles and Bites and gestures for me to go in ahead of him. I walk in. I look at him when the hostess asks if we want to sit inside or outside, but he lets me decide. "Outside," I say. "It's a beautiful day."

The patio is nearly full. I guess it's happy hour. It's shady and cool, with lots of greenery. Wooden tables and wrought iron chairs sit atop the red brick patio. We're led to a small table in the corner, which happens to be right by the window. I drop my backpack on the patio and take the bench seat.

"Nice." Harrison looks around. "I haven't been here."

"It's kind of local, I guess."

"Yeah."

We each pick up the menu we're handed.

"How about food?" Harrison asks. "I'm a little hungry after that workout."

I purse my lips in a smile. "I'm sure you work out a lot harder than that."

He grins. "Well, yeah. But seriously, I feel those moves."

"Good."

"Let's get a couple of things to share," he suggests. "What do you like?" He pauses. "You're not vegetarian, are you?"

"What's wrong with being vegetarian?"

"Nothing! I was just asking." He shifts on his chair.

"I'm not. But I don't want the octopus. I don't care much for seafood. I guess I'm a prairie girl at heart."

"Huh?" He tilts his head. "Okay, how about the meatballs? And crispy broccolini?"

"That sounds good."

Our server arrives and we order drinks and food. I order a cocktail called Crimson and Clover, and he asks for a beer.

Wow. I'm on a date. I guess. My stomach does a little flip and I slide my fingers together to keep them from trembling. It's fine. It's totally fine.

"Prairie girl?" he asks. "You look like a typical California girl."

"I do?"

"Yeah. Blond, tanned. Hot."

I huff out a laugh. "Thanks."

"Really." He nods.

"I'm from Fargo, North Dakota."

"Jeez. Seriously?"

"Yep." I smile. "I moved here about a year ago."

"Wow."

"The blond hair comes from my Scandinavian roots. My ancestors moved to North Dakota back in the eighteen hundreds."

"Huh. That's cool."

"What about you?"

"I was born here. But my family is Canadian."

I grin. "That's why you're a hockey player."

"That's right."

The server arrives with our drinks. This conversation is easy, so far, not awkward or painful.

I sip my drink. "Mmm."

"What's in that?"

"Orange juice, rosé wine, and a bunch of other booze."
He laughs.

"Want to try it?"

"Sure, if you don't mind." I push the glass over to him.

"Oh yeah, that is good. Okay, so how did you end up here?"

"My friend Taj lives here. I wanted to leave Fargo and he offered me a place to stay. So here I am."

"You live with a guy?"

"Yes." I tip my head. I'm not going to mention that Taj is gay. Yet. "We're friends."

"Okay." He doesn't seem put off by this.

I relax a little. "So, have you lived here your whole life?"

"No." He shakes his head. "But most of it. I played college hockey in Michigan for two years. Then I got drafted by the Condors and came home to California."

"That must have been a lot different, living in Michigan."

"Fucking cold." He smiles. "Like North Dakota, I guess. But I survived."

"You'd think hockey players are used to cold. You play on ice."

"Well, my dad grew up on the prairies, one of those guys who learned how to skate on an outside rink. They'd go out and play no matter what the weather. I *have* skated on outdoor rinks . . . when I was a kid we used to visit family in Winnipeg and Montreal. But I'm pretty spoiled by growing up in indoor arenas."

This is interesting, hearing about his family in different places. "I've been to Winnipeg lots of times."

"Yeah?" He cocks his head and his eyes crease up as he smiles at me. "I bet we were there at the same time once."

I choke on a laugh. "Right."

"No. I feel it." He lays a hand on his heart.

"I guess it's possible."

"Undoubtedly."

He's entertaining, I'll say that.

"So, you haven't bought a car yet," he says. "Or you don't want one?"

"I don't need one. Right now. It might be nice someday. Taj's place isn't far from the yoga studio. On Saturdays I can go with him to Makara. He owns the paddleboard place and lets me teach my classes from there."

"Ah."

"And he lets me use his car the odd time I need to. Biking is good for me. And better for the environment."

"That's true."

Our food arrives, and it looks delicious. The meatballs are beef with soft pitas and tzatziki, yum.

"Were you a yoga instructor in Fargo?" Harrison asks a moment later, after devouring a meatball.

"Well, I was, but it was a part-time thing. I started teaching in college to make a little extra money, and kept doing it on the side after I graduated. My full-time job was at Optimal Health in human resources."

It sounds so basic and boring, but I liked my job. The apartment I shared with my friend Leah. My other friends. I sigh.

"What's wrong?" He eyes me, concern etching a notch between his brows.

"Oh, sometimes I miss home." I pick up a piece of

broccolini and make myself smile. "But I love it here. When I moved here, I decided to see if I could make a living teaching yoga. I'm not rich, but I'm doing okay."

He nods.

"I went to college at UND in Grand Forks. A guy I went to school with plays in the NHL now—Grant Forrester."

"Oh hey. He got drafted in the same year as me. How old are you?"

"Twenty-six."

"Me too." He shakes his head. "See? We're just meant to be."

I freeze. I stare at him, my stomach contracting so hard it hurts. For a moment I'm not seeing Harrison, I'm seeing someone else. Terror grips me, making my skin cold and my mouth dry. Time stretches out. I can't breathe.

"I-I'm sorry. I have to go." I push back my chair, grab my backpack, and bolt out of the restaurant.

7

HARRISON

I GAPE AS ARYA VANISHES. FOR A MOMENT I'M TOO STUNNED to do anything. Then I stand too, tossing my napkin down on my chair. I catch the server's eye. "Be right back," I mouth at her. She nods.

I hasten outside and catch up to Arya, who's crouched down trying to unlock her bike with shaking hands. My gaze lands on the small tattoo on the back of her neck, a delicate black symbol of some kind.

"Hey." I keep my tone soft and I don't touch her, even though I want to. "Hold up, Arya. What's wrong?"

"Don't. Don't talk to me. Just . . . just leave me alone."

I frown, my stomach knotting with worry. How can I leave her alone like this? But I say, "Okay. I will. I just want to make sure you're all right."

"I'm fine."

"I upset you. Or offended you. Would you at least tell me what it was?"

Crouched beside her bike, she closes her eyes. "We're not 'meant to be.'"

We sure as hell are. I'm convinced of it. "Okay. I'm sorry. I was joking. I didn't know that would offend you."

"I'm not offended." She stands and pushes stray strands of hair off her face. Her hair is still in a ponytail from class, and she's still wearing leggings and a tank top with a loose blue sweater wrapped and tied around her narrow waist. "I'm . . ."

I want to jump in but hold myself back to let her finish.

"I'm . . . triggered."

Okay, there's a word that gives me anxiety. This means something terrible happened to her and I just reminded her of it. The fucking last thing I want to do. But also . . . something terrible happened to her.

Or did it? I went out with a woman who used that word for everything. She was "triggered" when someone talked with food in their mouth. If I disagreed with her about something, she was "triggered." When she didn't like someone, she found them "triggering." Once I asked her, "Found them triggering of what?" She didn't know what to say. We didn't go out together long.

"I'm sorry," I say again. "I had no idea."

She sighs. "Of course you didn't. I'm sorry too."

"Please come back in." I like her a lot, and I was having fun getting to know her better, and I want her to be okay, and I know I shouldn't push, but . . .

You don't get what you wish for, you get what you work for.

I'm not giving up on her.

She hesitates, studying me. "All right." She takes a deep

breath and follows me back inside. "Hopefully they don't think we dined and dashed."

"I let the waitress know I'd be back."

She sits across from me again. Pink stains her cheeks and her eyes are bright. She sets her backpack down and stares at the table. "I'm sorry."

"It's okay." I want to reach across the table to touch her hand, but I stop myself. "Do you want to tell me about it?"

She lifts her eyes to meet mine. "No."

"Fair enough." I smile, holding her gaze, hoping to ease her anxiety, whatever it's about. I'm not going to push her. Someday she'll tell me.

"Tell me about your tattoo," I invite, picking up my beer to take a big swallow. "I noticed it outside."

"Oh." She lifts a hand behind her head to touch her neck. "It's an unalome."

"Say what now?"

She smiles. "Unalome. It's the symbol for the journey to enlightenment."

I blink.

"I like it because it shows us that the journey isn't always a straight path. We make mistakes and learn lessons along the way. Sometimes we go sideways or backward."

I nod. "Can I see it again?"

She turns in her chair and lifts her golden ponytail. I study the swirling lines and understand what she means.

"I get it," I say. "My journey is like that too. I mean, I don't think I'm heading toward enlightenment." My lips quirk.

"Maybe you are."

"Maybe. But I have a goal and that's how it feels . . . sometimes things go sideways. Sometimes I feel like I'm going backward instead of forward."

"Yes." Her eyes are steady on mine. "What's your goal?"

"I want to play in the NHL."

Her eyes crinkle up and her forehead creases. "You do play in the NHL."

"Yeah, right now. I got called up from the farm team a couple of weeks ago because they have a bunch of injuries. When everybody's healthy again, I'll probably get sent back down."

"Sent back where?" she asks quietly, then sips her drink.

"Pasadena. Not far. But yet, so far." I smile. "It's just frustrating being called up and sent back down, when younger guys are making the team and staying there. I'm getting so old, they won't want me anymore." I pause. "That sounds pathetic. I don't really feel that sorry for myself. But I have a pretty high-achieving family and I always assumed I'd play in the NHL."

"Ah. I understand."

"Right now, I'm trying to do everything I can to make them want to keep me. Even going to yoga classes." I give her a half-smile.

"That's why the yoga interest?" Her eyelashes flutter.

"Well, you're *part* of the yoga interest." I hold up a hand. "I mean that sincerely and I think you already knew that. But if doing yoga will make me better, give my game an edge . . . I'm all in."

"I see." She nods thoughtfully. "Well, I admire that."

"Thanks. I've been working out hard, practicing hard."

"Yoga's not something you go hard at."

I grin. "I know. But I want to be as flexible as Bergie."

Her eyebrows lift.

"He's our goaltender. You told him he was really flexible and doing great."

"Oh. Right." She tips her head. "Yoga's not a competitive sport."

"Ha ha. *Life* is a competitive sport in my family." I roll my eyes. "I know it isn't, but I want to do my best. I appreciated it when you corrected me during that class. I could feel the difference, even when it's just a subtle thing."

"You're very strong. And actually pretty flexible, for a guy."

My shoulders go back. "Thanks. Those balancing poses are tricky."

She smiles, her features loosening into relaxed lines again. Goddamn, she's pretty. Her blue eyes are big and expressive. Her mouth has a sweet curve to it, even when she's not smiling, her lips just the right amount of full and soft. And when she smiles, her face lights up and her eyes glow. "They can be. But balance is something you can train."

"Yeah. Even when you told me to focus on a spot on the floor, that helped. *You* make it look easy."

"When I'm not being dumped into the water."

"Aaah. You had to bring that up."

She's laughing, and I have to laugh too. "It's okay. I've let it go." She places her palms together in front of her chest. "Inhale the future. Exhale the past."

I'm still smiling, but her words hit me in the chest. "Yeah. Words to live by."

"I try."

I'm curious about her past but I won't ask more questions. She said she doesn't want to talk about it.

"I need to remember that," I say. The meatballs are gone and I offer her the last piece of broccolini. She shakes her head, so I take it. "Just because I've been sent back to Pasadena every other time doesn't mean it will happen this time."

"Exactly."

"And the guy I'm replacing is out for the rest of the season, and we're in the playoffs, so I should be playing for a while. Assuming we can go deep."

She lifts her eyebrows.

"I mean, make it through a few rounds of the playoffs."

"Ah."

"This team hasn't made the playoffs in years. This is a big deal. We really want to do well." I shrug. "Some would say it's impossible, but we want to win the Cup."

"Nothing's impossible." She studies me with warm eyes. I love how her interest seems so real. I mean, it is real. I think. She seems like a very honest person. And she makes me feel like I'm fascinating. Like I'm not just one of the famous Wynns—I'm me, I'm Harrison, and I matter. "Is it hard to stay motivated when you know the games don't matter?"

"Well, they do matter in that we want to get home-ice advantage."

"What does that mean?"

I ponder this. I know what it means, but in my life, so does everyone else. "Well, each round of the playoffs is seven games. If you have home-ice advantage, you play four of the seven games at home, assuming you play all seven. You travel less, you don't have to stay in hotels, and you get to play in front of your fans."

"Ah."

"Also, the home team gets last change."

She looks at me blankly.

Right, this is another thing I assume everyone knows. "So, when there's a stoppage of play, the visiting team has to put their lineup on the ice first, and they can't change it until play is resumed. That gives the home-team coach a chance to see who's out there and put the players on he wants to match up against them."

"Oh, okay. So, if there's a player who's a good goal scorer, the coach would want to put someone out who could stop him."

"Yeah." I beam at her. "Basically that. So, we need to have more points than the team we play against to get home-ice advantage. But also, we play for our pride."

"You know, don't dismiss the mental edge that yoga could give you."

I scrunch up my face. I don't want to be dismissive of something that's important to her, but I'm skeptical about stuff like that.

"Really. I once took a class with a yoga teacher who's also a psychotherapist, and it was very educational. Yoga teaches us about how our emotions affect our behavior and our minds." She must read my expression because she grins. "I'm not all that much into spirituality and a higher consciousness. I'm a basic bitch from North Dakota."

I laugh.

"I do focus more on the physical aspects of yoga, and I

think my classes are popular with a lot of people who like that, who don't want a lot of meditation and talk about seeking to become aware of the spirit within."

I nod.

"Some say that without those aspects, it's only a superficial yoga practice. Without the spiritual side, you could just go to the gym or stretch. And I get that. But I do believe that yoga can help us get to know ourselves and build self-trust."

"So, what are the mental benefits?"

She smiles again. "I could talk for an hour about that. I'm sure you don't want to hear it all."

"Maybe some other time you can tell me more."

She doesn't respond right away, then shrugs. "Maybe."

"Do you have any superstitions?"

She blinks. "Uh . . . maybe."

I grin. "Tell me. Don't worry—I have lots of stupid ones."

"Well, I always make a wish when I see a falling star."

I nod gravely. "Of course."

"And when I was a kid, I wouldn't kill spiders because that causes rain."

"Only daddy longlegs spiders."

"Yes. Those other kind that look like tarantulas . . ." She shudders. "I kill those mothers."

I bark out a laugh. "What else?"

"My grandma always made us throw a pinch of salt over our left shoulder if we spilled some." She wrinkles her nose. "I still do it. Just in case. I also have a piece of rose quartz that I hold when I'm feeling . . . negative."

"Rose quartz?"

"Yes. It removes negative energy and replaces it with loving vibrations. It helps you learn to love yourself, accept yourself, and forgive yourself."

"That sounds like that spirituality stuff you said you don't practice." I say it teasingly.

"You're right." She smiles. "I know it's silly, but . . ." She lifts one shoulder. "It helps."

"I get it."

"What are your superstitions?"

"We have little rituals we go through before every game. A secret handshake, a hug, that kind of thing. I also have to wear hockey socks to the arena for every game."

"Hockey socks?"

"Not the ones we play in. Ha, that would look hilarious with a suit. I mean, I have a collection of socks that have hockey themes on them. Some are Condors socks, others just have a hockey stick and a puck, or a face-off circle."

She grins. "I like that."

"And I'm a superstitious dresser. I always dress right to left, so I put on my right shin pad then my left, my right sock then my left, and so on."

I like that she doesn't laugh at my superstitions or mock them. I like that she has her own. It's like a connection we have.

"Do you go to any Condors games?"

She shakes her head. "I haven't. Although I used to like going to hockey games in college."

"Right, right. UND. They have a good hockey program." Something strikes me. "Not only were we probably in Winnipeg at the same time, I bet you watched me play hockey."

She laughs. "Oh my God."

"No, really. If we're the same age and you went to games that Grant played in, they must have played against us at some point. You were probably there!" This idea gets me revved up again. I need to chill, though, because I scared her last time I got excited about us being fated mates. Ha ha, okay, we're not living in a Kresley Cole novel.

She taps her lips. "You could be right, actually."

"See? It's practically like we already know each other." I grin to make sure she knows I'm joking.

She shakes her head, smiling. "Sure. Okay."

"Would you like another drink?"

"I better not. Cycling while drunk is not a good idea."

"True."

We talk more, until the server brings the bill. I take care of it, waving off Arya's attempts to contribute, and then we leave. It's dark outside now.

"Are you okay to ride in the dark?" I ask, not liking the idea of her biking home in the dark.

"Of course. I have lights and reflectors, and a helmet. I do it all the time. And it's not far."

"I could put your bike in the back of my car and drive you."

"No need. But thanks."

"Okay." I hesitate. "I'd like to see you again. I mean, outside of yoga class."

"I don't know." She sets her hands on her handlebars. "I'm not really into dating, or relationships. That's not fair to you."

"It can just be casual. Hang out at the beach. Go for a bike ride."

I can see the conflict on her face. She wants to see me again, which is good. I just don't understand what the problem is. Other than I triggered her, somehow.

Fuck.

"We'll see."

"Would you give me your number?"

"No." She answers without hesitation, deflating me. "But I'll take yours."

"Okay. Sure." I give it to her, she enters it into her phone, then pushes off and pedals away with a wave.

Well. I'll see her tomorrow, because tomorrow is our second team yoga class. So I don't feel totally blown off.

I stroll to my car, parked just around the corner. I pull out my phone to check for any messages as I walk. There's one from my sister, Everly. It's a chat group she created for us, with the whole younger Wynn family.

Mom and Dad went to the doctor today.

I stop short. My gut tightens. I tap back,

And???

I don't know any more than that yet, but at least they went.

Okay, true.

I get in my car and head home. By the time I'm there, the chat has expanded with everyone asking questions and weighing in.

I'll try to talk to Mom tomorrow.

Everly replies to all.

Ash is home and also got the message.

"Hey, where were you?" he asks. "Thought you'd be home from practice ages ago."

"I went to yoga class."

He stops in the act of stirring something on the stove. "What?"

I smirk and grab a bottle of water from the fridge. "Yoga class. They're making us do it as a part of our conditioning program, so I decided I'd do an extra class."

"The one on water?" His eyes widen.

"Nah. Dry-land yoga. Ha ha."

He narrows his eyes at me. "Huh."

"What are you making?"

"Ginger beef. Can you stir that rice?" He gestures to another pot.

I grab a spoon and lift the lid. "Why don't you use the rice cooker?"

"You have to make a ton of rice in that thing."

"Leftovers are good."

"Yeah, but it's a pain in the ass hauling it out. This works fine."

"Whatever. That smells great."

"Have you eaten?"

"I had a couple of snacks and a beer after class, but I can eat more."

We talk about Everly's message about Dad as we eat on the couch in front of the TV watching a sports news network. We're both worried. My mellow mood from yoga is fast disappearing.

So I think about Arya. That cheers me up. We had a

few bumpy moments, but I really like her and I feel pretty confident that she likes me too. Will she go out with me again? With my usual impatience, I wish I could text her and tell her I enjoyed spending time with her, but I don't have her number.

I guess I'll just have to wait and see. Damn.

8

ARYA

My second yoga class with the California Condors is making me even more nervous than the first one.

Okay, maybe it's actually Harrison Wynn who's making me nervous.

Confession time: I googled him.

I had no idea who his father is, and that his father owns the team he plays for. When he said he has a high-achieving family, wow, he really meant it. I can understand better now why he feels so pressured to be a success.

There wasn't a lot about him online, to be honest, which could be good or bad. At least there aren't horrible stories about him drunk driving or abusing his girlfriend, although those could be buried. I see pictures of him in Pasadena with a boy who's his little brother through Big Brothers, and him participating in a charity event to help the homeless. He's a little pushy, a lot flirty, and making comments about us being "meant to be" panicked me. But those stories and a lack of anything negative reassure me and even make me like him more.

I don't know how to handle this. It's been almost two years since my life was shattered, and I haven't been interested in dating since then. Guys have asked me out, sure, but it's been easy to say no. I prefer being on my own.

But Harrison tempts me. I don't know what to do about that.

I didn't even tell Taj about him coming to class yesterday and then going out for a drink with him. I'm afraid Taj will think that sounds very stalkerish and I was stupid to go out with him. Maybe it was. But I'm fine.

I got a definite tingle in my girl parts yesterday during class, a combination of the sexy tunes and Harrison's body. And it continued into our, uh, date. My belly was flip-flopping and my inner muscles clenching, thinking about being naked with him.

Vibrators are great and all, but sex with a real live man? Nothing better.

It's been a while.

Anyhoo, here I am back at the Coliseum in a room full of muscles, deep voices and testosterone, and I only have eyes for Harrison.

He's wearing his new shorts, which hopefully are keeping his kibbles 'n bits nice and secure. Oh God. Now I'm hot.

He catches my eye but doesn't come over to me this time. He bends over to roll out his mat and my gaze lands on his bootylicious behind. Damn.

I am capable of anything.

I go inside myself to find my focus before beginning the class.

"This time we'll work a little harder," I tell the team. "You guys are all big and strong, so we'll focus on some specific things, like balance and range of motion. In yoga, you're using your muscles in ways that are different than hockey, which helps with strength and stability. We'll also be releasing tension and stiffness, keeping you loose and open. Improved stability and better range of motion means more efficient performance. Does anyone have any questions before we start?" I look around.

One player lifts a hand. "How often do we have to do these before we start seeing results?"

I smile. "Yoga isn't like the other kinds of training you do. It's a practice. Your focus should be on being present, and not so much on the end result. Over time, your practice will change as you become more flexible and stronger. So don't worry about results or competing with each other."

Another man raises his hand. "I heard yoga is good for sex. Is that true?"

Everyone else laughs. I smile and open my mouth to speak.

"Jesus, Archie." Harrison speaks up.

I look over at him. He's scowling at his teammate.

"That's not appropriate," he adds.

I blink.

"Well, I think flexibility would help with a lot of different sex positions," Archie says. "Right, Arya? I bet you're really flexible."

My eyes fly open wide when Harrison jumps up from

his mat, takes two giant steps over and gets right in Archie's face. "Apologize for that."

"Jesus man, what the fuck?"

The atmosphere in the room changes, thickening, a few guys muttering.

"Chill, dudes." Wyatt also stands but stays on his mat.

Harrison is giving Archie a stare down and I'm a little worried he's going to punch him. This is not good.

"It's okay, Harrison," I say in a soothing tone. "It's actually a legitimate question."

"Not the way he asked it," Harrison growls, not looking at me. "Apologize."

"Sorry, Arya," Archie says.

I try to act unfazed. "Of course yoga can help improve your sex life," I say, as if this is a natural topic for me to be discussing with twenty-some men. If better sex convinces them to participate, fine. "Not just the flexibility, but energy levels. Being present in the moment. With a clear mind, it's easier to be truly intimate with someone. All right, let's begin. Harrison, you can return to your mat."

Still frowning, he sits on his mat and we start the class.

Now I'm really going deep for focus. I need to compartmentalize and set aside what just happened to think about later. Yoga has helped me do this in the past, paying attention to my body, being in the moment.

We end with reclining Bound Angle Pose.

"This is great for opening up the hips," I tell the men, padding between mats to observe them. "If you have a groin strain or this feels hard on your knees, just slide your feet out and make the diamond a little bigger." I adjust one player's feet. "Can you move them in a little closer?" I help him with that.

I slide blocks under Archie's knees to support them.

"The longer you lie like this, the more your body will relax into the stretch. You can also use some blankets under your back and head to make it more comfortable."

Today's music is classic rock, so I let them relax into this pose to "Wild Horses" by the Rolling Stones.

I pass by Harrison and crouch beside him. I shouldn't look, but I do. There's a lovely bulge in his shorts. I yank my gaze away from there. "Okay?" I murmur.

"Yes." His eyes remain closed.

We end the class with Jeff Buckley's rendition of "Hallelujah."

"When you feel ready, get up slowly and continue your day. Namaste."

I remain in Savasana a moment longer, then roll to my side and rise. Some players are rolling up their mats, other still relax on the floor. Harrison is lying, eyes closed, his face peaceful.

I breathe in slowly. I was attracted to him before, but that was nothing to how I feel now, having seen him confront his teammate about his somewhat inappropriate comment to me. He defended me. I want to jump him.

Sweet jumping Jesus, what is happening to me?

I had met briefly with Gary before class to see if I needed to make any changes to what I'm doing, so I can leave now. I store my mat in the special pouch of my yoga bag.

"Arya."

I look up to see Archie.

"I hope I didn't offend you," he says, not making eye contact, all awkward. "I apologize if I did."

It'd be easy to say "it's fine" or "don't worry about it." But I've learned some lessons. "I guess you didn't think that I might feel uncomfortable talking about sex in a room full of men."

His cheeks redden. "Uh, no, I didn't."

"Let's keep the class to more appropriate topics."

"Yeah, yeah." He nods and bolts.

I pick up my bag and start out of the room. Harrison steps in front of me. "Thanks for a great class," he says. "Sorry about Archie."

"He just apologized again. I clarified my expectations."

"Well, good." He smiles, his eyes warm.

We look at each other for a stretched-out moment, neither of us saying anything. Heat slides through my veins. I feel a compelling tug of attraction drawing me to him.

"Well, see you," he says. "You have my number."

He walks away.

I blink a few times as I watch him, bemused.

Okay, then.

I turn and leave.

I do have his number. I just don't know if I have the nerve to use it.

AFTER MY CLASSES AT PRANA, ENDING AT SEVEN, I MEET UP with Janey for dinner at Buttons. They have the heaters going on the patio, so we sit outside.

I've just taken my seat when I hear my name. "Arya! Hi!"

I look over a couple of tables and see Everly, Taylor, and their friend who came to one of my SUP classes. The infamous dunking SUP class. I smile and lift a hand.

Everly stands up and approaches the table. "How are you?"

"Good, you?"

"I am great. Would you like to join us? We have room for two more at our table."

"Oh." I glance at Janey. She smiles in agreement. I'm not so sure, though. This is Harrison's sister. "Uh . . . we don't want to intrude."

"Oh, you won't be. The more the merrier, right?"

"Okay, sure. That's nice of you."

She leads the way over to a bigger, round table. I introduce Janey to Everly and Taylor, but I don't remember the other woman's name.

"My friend Lacey," Everly says. "Well, she's my friend but she's also my niece-in-law."

I laugh. "Okay. That sounds complicated."

"Right?" Lacey grins. "I'm married to her nephew."

"Who's a year older than me," Everly adds. "Our family is weird."

And, thanks to Google, I know who her family is now. "Speaking of family," I say casually, "I'm teaching your brother and your, uh . . . boyfriend?"

Her eyes widen. "Wyatt? Yes, he's my boyfriend."

"I'm teaching the hockey team yoga classes."

"Oh! That's awesome."

"Yes, the team hired me to teach classes a couple of times a week, depending on their schedule."

"It'll be so good for them!"

"That's fabulous," Taylor adds. "Uh, hopefully not on the water, though."

I laugh. "No, I'm doing the class in their training room at the arena."

"Good, good."

They've already ordered drinks, but a server approaches and takes drink orders from Janey and me. "Margaritas are on happy hour special," he tells us. "Any flavor."

"Sounds good to me. I'll have a . . . blackberry margarita."

"Great choice." He turns to Janey, who orders a pomegranate one.

"So, how long have you been teaching yoga?" Everly asks me, dipping her straw in and out of her margarita, which appears to be classic lime on the rocks.

I give them a bit of my bio, similar to what I told Harrison yesterday.

I haven't mentioned that Harrison came to one of my other classes and we went out after. I feel I'm hiding something, but I'm not sure I should make it into a big deal.

We chat, learning more about each other. I learn what Everly does with the Condors Foundation, Taylor's speech pathologist career, and Lacey's fascinating work as a makeup artist doing movies and styling for a few up-and-coming stars. Janey tells them about her job as a veterinary assistant.

"Oh!" Everly exclaims. "We needed you at Christmas!"

She tells a story about Taylor's dog eating chocolate and

being sick, which is hilarious but only because the dog is okay, thankfully.

"We were all freaking out," she says.

"*You* weren't," Lacey puts in. "As always, you were cool, calm, and collected."

"Inside, I was freaking out."

"Chocolate can be so dangerous," Janey says. "Thank goodness he was okay."

"It's amazing Taylor forgave JP," Everly says, leaning her shoulder into Taylor's. "She loves that dog so much."

"So does he," Taylor says. "He felt terrible."

"JP? He was with you at that stand-up class?" I ask.

"Yes."

I nod, remembering everyone, noting their names.

"He's also my nephew," Everly says.

"How do you keep the family straight?" I ask Taylor and Lacey with a smile.

"It was weird at first, but I've got it down now," Lacey says.

"Harrison mentioned that he had a complicated family," I say.

Three sets of female eyes laser in on me. "Oh. Did he?" Everly says.

"We, uh, went out for a drink together yesterday. After class."

Three pairs of eyebrows shoot up. Janey grins, enjoying the reaction. She already knows about this.

"Well," Taylor says.

I divide a tentative smile between them. "Is that a problem?"

"No!" they all say at once.

Our drinks arrive and I grab my margarita. Everly lifts her nearly empty glass. "I think I'm gonna need another one of these."

"Of course." The server looks at Lacey and Taylor.

"Bring 'em," Lacey says.

I smile.

"Not a problem at all," Everly assures me. "We're just . . . curious."

"It was nothing," I say. "Just a drink." I don't tell them about my embarrassing freak-out.

"I thought you had a boyfriend." Everly says.

"No." I blink at her.

"That guy at the paddleboard place . . . where you have your classes . . . what's his name?"

"Oh, Taj! No, he's just a friend. And my roommate. We live together."

"He is freakin' gorgeous," Lacey says.

"He's also gay," I add. "So definitely not my boyfriend."

"Ah. Okay, then." Everly nods.

Their drinks arrive, we order food, then Lacey says, "Okay you guys, I have to tell you about this new pillow I got."

"Pillow?" Taylor tips her head.

"It's a sex pillow."

"Whaaat?" We all gape at her.

"Not even kidding. It's amazing!"

"What does it do?" I ask curiously.

"It helps get you in the right positions. It's made by this company, Femme Products. Have you heard of it?"

We all shake our heads.

"The owner of the company, or I should say one of them, is married to a hockey player. Former hockey player."

"Who?" Everly asks.

"Jared Rupp. He used to play for the Chicago Aces."

"Oh yeah. How about that."

"They make sex products just for women."

"That's very cool. Tell us more."

"It's kind of small, and soft, and sort of wedge-shaped." She uses her hands to demonstrate. "You can put it under your hips, and it tips things up so you get, ah, maximum contact where you need it." Lacey grins. "Or you can put it under your armpit . . ." She gestures. "If you're lying on your side and he's behind you. All kinds of positions."

Everly sighs. "I guess I better just get over hearing about my nephews having sex."

Janey and I laugh. "That must be weird," Janey agrees. "I need this pillow."

"You can order it online," Lacey says. "It's called the Cush."

I make a mental note of this; not sure why. As I may have mentioned, I haven't had sex in ages. But I've been thinking about it the last little while . . .

With Everly's brother. She probably doesn't want to hear that either.

"So, back to you and Harrison," Lacey says, leaning forward and looking at me. "Are you going to see him again?"

"I haven't decided."

"So, he asked you out again?" Taylor pounces on that.

"Well, yes." I suck my bottom lip between my teeth. "I'm not really into dating, so I didn't commit to anything."

"Not into dating?" Everly eyes me with sympathy. "Bad relationship?"

It would be easy to agree and let it go. But I like these women and I feel comfortable with them, and making friends and building connections with people means being honest. "Not exactly," I say slowly, glancing at Janey. She knows what happened to me, but she also knows I don't talk about it much. "A few years ago, I went out with a guy I met on a dating app. He seemed really nice and fun, and I agreed to see him again. But he got . . . weird." I drop my gaze briefly, then look back up to see all the women regarding me with somber expressions, as if they know what's coming. "He dropped by my apartment before we even went out again. I'd let him pick me up on our first date, which was a mistake. It creeped me out a bit, but I was also sort of flattered. I thought he really liked me."

I sip my drink as everyone nods.

"We went out again, but he came on so strong and it made me uneasy, and I told him I didn't want to see him again. He was pissed. He turned into a stalker, phoning me and texting me, showing up at home and at my work."

"That's so scary," Everly says quietly.

"Yeah. It was. He started getting threatening. He slashed the tires on my car."

"Oh my God." Taylor's eyes widen. "Did you call the police?"

"Yeah, but they didn't take it very seriously, even though I told them he was following me everywhere."

"Fuck," mutters Lacey.

"Then he . . ." I pause, take a breath, and say, "One

night after work I was on my way to the gym and he followed me and attacked me with a knife."

Their mouths all drop open in horror. Everly presses her hand to her lips, eyes dark. "Oh no."

"I was lucky, someone called the cops. I had a lot of cuts on my arms and hands from trying to defend myself, and I ended up in the hospital." I haven't told this story many times, but this time it feels easier. I feel stronger. I straighten my shoulders and attempt a smile. "That's why I moved here to California. I needed to get away."

"He better be in prison," Everly says fiercely.

"He is." I nod. "The trial was short because he pled guilty, but it was still excruciating, and . . . I'm glad he's locked up, but still, I wanted to get away from the memories."

"You're amazing." Taylor reaches out and squeezes my hand. "We had no idea you've been through something like that. You're so composed and . . . at peace."

I make a face. "I don't always feel that way. But it's getting better." My smile is genuine now. "My life is good."

"That's why you don't want to see Harrison again?" Everly asks quietly.

I bite my lip, nodding.

"He's not like that." She holds my gaze. "Really. He's a goof, but he's a good guy."

"Okay. Thanks." She's his sister. She knows him. "Don't tell him about this."

Her eyebrows pull together. "Why not?"

"It's . . . a lot to deal with."

Her lips push out, her eyes shadowed, but she moves her head up and down in agreement. "Okay."

As Janey and I leave, standing on the sidewalk outside the restaurant while I unlock my bike, I say, "I hope that was okay that we joined them."

"Sure! They're all really nice. It's fun meeting new people."

"Oh good."

"Small world, though, that you just went out with Harrison and then meet up with his sister."

"I know. I wasn't sure what to say about that."

"Are you going to see him again? I feel like you want to."

"I do."

She squeezes my hand, her silky black hair blowing in the breeze off the ocean. "You need to do what you're comfortable with."

"Thanks." We hug and then I set off for home on my bike.

Taj is out when I get there. I toss my bag onto my bed and pull out my phone. Then I sit on the couch and stare at Harrison's name and number.

9

HARRISON

Sunday. Day off. We had a home game Friday night and played in Long Beach last night. Last night's game was another Beach Barn Battle. I know a lot of the fam was there watching again—Mom and Dad and Théo, Everly and Ash, and Matthew and his wife, Aline. I played against JP again, Mark coaching, obviously.

We lost, sadly. A loss against the Eagles is always painful, but especially for me, with my whole family watching.

Mom has texted all of us—me, Asher, Noah, and Everly—and said she wants to get together, so I'm getting ready to head over to Mom and Dad's place for lunch. I'm dreading what we're going to talk about. I know if it was good news Mom would have just told us all.

Ash and I drive together again in his car. He parks on the street in front of the house we grew up in—a big, Spanish-style, two-story house not far from the arena in Santa Monica. Ash and I climb out of his Mazda and saunter up the brick sidewalk to the front door.

I don't know about Ash—we didn't talk a whole lot on the way over here—but my stomach is a churning mess. I'm trying to act cool and unconcerned, like a manly man would. But that's bullshit, because I'm terrified.

I'm a twenty-six-year-old man and I'm terrified that my dad is dying.

I feel like a child again and I hate it.

We enter without knocking and step into the cool interior, out of the bright sun. "Hello!" I call. The house is quiet. Maybe they're out back on the patio.

Mom appears from the kitchen. "Who's that? Hi, boys." She smiles but it's not a happy smile. "Noah isn't here yet. Everly and Dad are out by the pool. Come on out."

We make our way through the house and out the patio doors. The sun sparkles on the turquoise pool, surrounded by paving stones and an immaculate green lawn. Palm trees, shrubs, and flowers line the perimeter of the yard. Dad used to pay a gardener to look after everything, but now he just has someone cut the grass and he looks after the flowers himself. How long will he be able to do that?

Everly's face looks as stiff as mine feels, though she's smiling too. Mom has drinks out here and pours us glasses of lemonade. Ash and I take a seat on the wicker chairs arranged around a coffee table. Dad's on the big sectional.

I study his face. Is it my imagination, or does he suddenly look older?

Christ, this is awful. I'm afraid I'm going to puke. I rub my mouth. "Yard looks great, Dad."

He nods. "Yeah. Look at that hibiscus . . . isn't it amazing?"

I don't know what a hibiscus is, but I agree.

"Hey Harrison, guess who I had dinner and drinks with the other day?" Everly says.

I sip my lemonade, hoping my stomach behaves. "Who?"

"Arya Ross."

My head jerks. "Say what? My Arya?"

She smirks. "*Your* Arya?"

"You know what I mean." My face heats.

"Yes. Yoga instructor Arya. She said you two went out."

I feel my jaw loosening and my heart jolts. "Uh, yeah. We did."

"You didn't pester her into going out with you, did you?"

My mouth drops even more open. "What? Pester her? Hell no!"

"Good," Everly says, with a firm nod. "Because no means no, right?"

What the hell? My sister is lecturing me on consent. "I know that!" Then I think back on my interactions with Arya. Was I a little pushy?

"What's this?" Dad asks. "New girlfriend?"

"I wish," I mutter.

"She doesn't know if she wants to see him again," Everly tells Dad. "I guess he didn't impress her that much."

I roll my eyes.

"Oh, I hear someone at the door. That must be Noah." Mom jumps up and disappears.

"You didn't mention this," Ash says to me.

"Nope."

He shakes his head. "Is she the yoga instructor the team hired?"

"Yes."

"Also the one he dumped in the water," Everly adds helpfully.

"Never gonna live that down," I mutter. "At least *she's* gotten past it."

Everly laughs. "I put in a good word for you, doofus."

I eye her skeptically. She probably told Arya about the time she caught me watching porn when I was fifteen. I'm never going to hear from Arya again.

Noah and Mom come out, we do all the greeting stuff, Mom gets Noah a drink and he sits down, and . . . a two-ton hush settles over everyone.

Mom looks around and her eyes are shiny, the corners of her mouth tight. "You are the best kids in the world," she says a little shakily. "I love all of you so much."

Jesus. Now I'm gonna cry. "Love you too, Mom," I choke out, as do the others.

She glances at Dad, sitting next to her on the love seat, and takes his hand. I never really paid any attention to the age difference between them, growing up. They were adults and I was a kid. But right now, I see it . . . Mom in her early fifties, still youthful, Dad looking grayer and sad. My chest aches.

"You know we went to the doctor last week."

We all nod.

"We actually have been to the doctor about this already," she continues.

We all frown at each other.

"A couple of doctors, to be honest."

"Mom . . ." Everly starts.

Mom holds up a hand. "Let me finish." Her voice

quivers. "I know you all have started noticing problems lately, but I noticed it a long time ago." She takes in a breath and lets it out. "We were referred to a neurologist. They did a bunch of tests. A lot of them are to rule out other problems. But last week we were told that almost certainly Dad has Alzheimer's."

I close my eyes. I did not want to hear those words.

"You should have told us," Everly says quietly.

"I wanted to be more certain. I'm sorry. I know this is hard and I didn't want to worry everyone if there was some other reason." She presses her fingers to her mouth.

"I'm fine," Dad says gruffly. "Nobody has to worry about me."

But I can tell . . . *he's* worried. Maybe even scared.

My dad. My role model. The man I've always counted on for support and advice and help with anything.

My throat thickens and I take a quick sip of lemonade.

Tears are running down Everly's face. She gets up and goes over to Dad to crouch in front of him. She takes his hands. "I love you, Daddy."

"I know, Evvie." He smiles at her.

I stand too and move behind the sectional. I set my hand on Dad's shoulder and squeeze. "Love you, Dad."

He pats my hand. "I love you too. All of you. Like your mom said, you're the best kids."

Dad has two other sons, and his comment makes us acutely aware that they're not here and are still fighting with Dad over money.

I get now why Everly did what she did. Everything else seems stupid and meaningless in the face of this shitty news.

"So, what's the plan?" I ask Mom.

"We have a medication that may help slow the cognitive decline," she says. "Other than that, we can only take things as they come. We're exploring options for the future. Dad says he doesn't want to be a burden on me . . . or anyone." Her voice breaks. She leans her head on his shoulder, eyes closed. For a moment, she can't speak.

I feel like a hippo is standing on my chest. This fucking sucks for everyone.

My mom is strong. I know she is. But she always had Dad with her, backing her up. Now she's going to have to do this alone.

But she's not alone. "Mom, we're all here for you," I say. "For both of you."

"I know." She lifts her head. "Thank you."

I'm filled with emotions battling inside me. I don't even know what I feel. Anger. Sadness. Denial. Confusion. My father is dying. It's going to be hell watching him decline, seeing everything he's losing. And *we're* losing *him*.

I don't know if I can deal with this.

I turn and walk over to the edge of the pool to stare at it.

I hear the conversation continue behind me . . . "How long does he have?" "Maybe years. We don't know what will happen or how fast it will progress."

I cover my mouth with one hand, my lungs burning. *Fuck.*

I turn back to the group. I meet Ash's eyes. He and I are twins and we've always understood each other without words. It helps to know that he's feeling exactly the same.

When Dad goes inside to the bathroom, Mom tells us more.

"I've been driving him to and from work as much as I can," she says. "I'm not confident about his driving anymore."

"Shit," I murmur.

"You need to take his keys away, Mom," Everly says, grasping Mom's hand. "He can't drive if he's a risk to others."

She nods. "I know."

"Is that why you've been at the office with him so much?" Ash asks.

She frowns. "How do you know that?"

"Théo."

"Oh." She sighs. "That, and also I need to know what's going on. He doesn't remember everything."

I slowly move my head from side to side and sink back down into my chair. "Théo's got things under control, Mom."

"Yes, he does. And I'm so glad it's him. I trust him."

She trusts him. Even though his parents have never trusted her. Fuck, she's amazing.

"We all trust Théo," Everly says. "What else can we do, Mom?"

"I'll let you know. I will. You all have lives to lead." She smiles. "I'm happy for you and Wyatt. And you do a great job with the Foundation." She turns to me. "You keep playing. Your dad is so proud of you."

"He is?"

"Of course. He's proud of all of you. Ash, you're such a great writer. Noah . . . you're the only goalie in the family."

He shakes his head. "Only *male* goalie, Mom."

We all smile at his defense of Riley.

"Right, of course." Mom shakes her head. "I meant in the NHL. She's done amazingly well." My niece played for the US women's national hockey team before becoming a goalie coach for the Hawks in the AHL.

"Can you convince Dad to retire?" Everly asks. "He should relax and enjoy his life now. He's worked so hard."

"I don't think he can totally give up hockey. But we've talked about it. We're thinking of going on a trip this summer. And next season . . . we'll see."

Dad returns and Mom bustles into the kitchen to get lunch. I go in to help carry out a platter of sandwiches, a couple of salads, and veggies and dip. When everything is outside on the big dining table on the patio, I stop her in the kitchen. "Are you okay, Mom?"

She meets my eyes, hers going glossy again. "No."

I pull her in for a hug. "I know."

"We'll get through it," she mumbles. "Thank you for being here."

"Of course. We'll always be here for you."

She squeezes me, pulls back, dashing away tears, and smiles bravely. "Okay, let's go eat."

Monday morning, we have a practice and another yoga class before. The guys who were skeptical about yoga are coming around, saying they feel better when they get on the ice after the poses and the focus.

And everyone's in a great mood because Vancouver lost

last night, and right now, we're ahead of them in the standings.

I feel happy about it, in a distant sort of way.

Today nothing much seems to really matter. I'm struggling with the news we got yesterday. Even though we'd suspected for a while, it's hard having it confirmed. Even so, I keep thinking, maybe the doctor is wrong. I know it's stupid denial, but I can't help it.

When I see Arya, my mood lifts. She's so sweet and pretty, all golden and glowing. And there's a serenity about her, in her soft voice and calm demeanor. I always try to focus on what she tells us to do, but today I'm really concentrating on it, trying to get the most benefit I can from this session.

"Yoga moves us from the fight-or-flight state, to the rest-and-digest state," Arya says as she moves among us. "Breathing deeply calms the nervous system. Your body starts to turn off arousing nerve chemicals like adrenaline. It stops releasing fatty acids and sugar into the bloodstream, and sodium leaves the inside of the body's cells. This slows the rate of nerve firing and relaxes your brain . . . your heart . . . your muscles."

I go with it, focusing on my breath. Arya stops next to me as I balance in Tree Pose. "Feel like you're pushing your right foot through the mat," she says. "Use your hand to bring your left foot even higher."

I shift my foot higher on my thigh, trying to focus on balance and not on her.

"Big inhale . . . and reach your hands up." She lifts her own arms up.

We stand like this for I don't know how long. The music

is Pink Floyd's "Breathe," which is appropriate but surprising. I really like the music she chooses for these classes.

"Let's try a variation on this today," Arya continues. "Bring your hands up again . . . on the exhale, bring your left hand down and touch your fingertips to that knee . . . shift your weight slowly as you reach your right hand over your head to the left . . ."

I wobble. I breathe. I find my balance.

She touches my right side. "Create a nice big opening here . . . that's it."

She moves on. "And bring your right arm back up . . . palms together . . . and down to heart center."

We repeat the pose on the other leg. I try to make it perfect. Breathe. Balance. Focus.

After class, I head to the locker room to change. Remarkably, I do feel in a better place than when I arrived at the arena. My head feels clearer.

On the ice in our practice jerseys, Coach starts off with a lecture about how just because we've made the playoffs doesn't mean we can slack off. We know we'll be playing against Vancouver, and there are things we have to work on to beat them. Meantime, we still have four regular-season games to work on those things.

He gets us skating our asses off in some drills, the whistle blowing, working on 3 on 3 D support, which works on quick transitions, give-and-go passes, and swinging to become a passing option. This is a hard workout for us forwards, but I'm a lot more aware of transitions now.

We end the practice with a small-area game. The nets are set up on the sides of the ice, at one end. Playing in a small area forces us to be creative since we have a limited amount of space. We have to be in control of the puck and use our teammates, and it gives everyone a lot of puck touches, meaning it's fast and fun. And competitive. I'm intense, going hard for the puck, shooting at Bergie and making him work hard too. I even get it past him a few times.

At the end, we're all breathing hard and laughing.

I'm laughing.

I shouldn't be laughing. My dad is dying.

I close my eyes briefly as I glide across the ice, stick in my hands. I can't think that way. Life is still happening all around us.

I coast toward the gate and my eyes widen when I see Arya sitting in the stands right behind the bench. Gary's talking to her about something, and she nods, and stands, since practice is over. I hop off the ice and stop as she walks down the steps.

"Hey," I say. "You're still here."

"Yes. Gary thought it would be good for me to watch you guys on the ice." Her face is animated, eyes bright. "That was really cool." She pauses. "You worked hard."

"Yeah. It felt good."

We stand eyeing each other, me sweaty and stinky in my gear, her golden and bright, separated by plexiglass. She's never going to use my number that I gave her. I want to push . . . *you don't get what you wish for* . . . but I don't.

"Well," I finally say. "I better go shower."

She tips her head to one side. "Is everything okay?"

I frown. "Why do you ask that?"

"I don't know . . . you just seem . . . different."

Huh. Different. "I got some bad news yesterday. I'm dealing with it."

She nods slowly. "I'm sorry to hear that."

More guys are coming off the ice behind me. I need to move. "See you." I head down the tunnel to the dressing room.

I get on a bike to cool down, stretch, and then hit the shower. Dressed in my athletic shorts and T-shirt, I grab my phone from my locker and stroll into the players' lounge to see what's for lunch today. I swipe my thumb over my screen and my feet stop.

There's a text. From Arya.

Yes. I'll go out with you again.

10

***

ARYA

I watched Harrison during the yoga class. His usual smile was absent. His mouth is perpetually tipped up at the corners, giving him that boyish, carefree look, but today it just isn't there. He barely even looked at me. He did focus on class, though. His big strong body is getting more flexible and graceful with each session. All these guys are amazingly fit, but I do love watching Harrison.

After class, I was excited to observe the practice and see the guys in action. I guess I could go to a game, but this is a different perspective, and it's really up close. Gary explained some of the drills they were doing and what they were working on. I don't understand a lot of the hockey skills and strategy, but it's fascinating.

As in the class, I have a hard time taking my eyes off Harrison. On the ice, he's different again—powerful and intense, his every move deliberate, his face austere and focused.

To be honest, it turned me on.

Yikes.

Okay, if I'm being honest, everything about him turns me on. And this has been the problem.

I watch him interact with the coaches and his teammates. There are moments where they kid around and laugh. The coaches yell at everyone to work harder but give them words of approval. I can see the respect and camaraderie among all of them and it's impressive. Kind of . . . loveable.

Likeable, I mean.

Then he tells me got bad news.

That's the reason his smile is missing.

I hope it's not something serious. Maybe he's being sent back to Pasadena. I hope he's okay.

After he leaves the ice to shower, I make my way out of the arena, picking up my bike near the security booth. I lean it against the concrete wall and tip my head back. I remember the class where he came to my defense over an inappropriate comment. I remember how concerned he was when I dashed out of the restaurant. I remember Everly's obvious affection for her brother.

I pull out my phone and find Harrison's number. I blow out a breath, then tap in a message to him.

There.

I don't even know if he's still interested. Today he barely looked at me. Only said a few words to me. Maybe he's given up and moved on.

I tuck my phone into the pouch inside my yoga bag and walk my bike outside. Another sunny day in California. I love it. I tip my face up to the sun and prepare to mount my bike when I hear my phone buzz.

If it's Harrison telling me "never mind," I don't want to see it. I'll check it later.

I grab my phone. So much for self-discipline.

It *is* Harrison, replying to my text. One word.

Now?

I laugh out loud. Relief lightens my limbs. I guess he's still interested.

I have classes this afternoon.

He answers right away.

Dinner?

I can't stop smiling.

That would be nice.

I can pick you up, if you tell me where.

I scrunch up my face. That's not happening, but I don't want to seem weird about it.

I'll meet you . . . where?

After a moment, I'm about to get back on my bike, when I get his text.

Noir. 7:00?

I tap back my agreement and, still smiling, jump on my bike and pedal off.

It's not far to the beach and I get onto the path that follows the shore. It's an easy, pleasant ride to Rose Avenue. I pass the Golden Fish and head up Rose toward Prana.

Excitement bubbles inside me, thinking about seeing Harrison again. I had fun talking to him the day we went out. I haven't been able to stop thinking about him. It's crazy.

I don't want to let myself ponder what happens after that. I get a tight, anxious feeling in my stomach when I contemplate how things could go, so I'm going to push that away, focus on right now, because I have classes to teach and my students deserve my best.

My last class is at four, so I have time to go home and change, thankfully. Last time I went out with Harrison, I was still in my yoga gear. I hardly ever dress up anymore, since my life is yoga and biking and running, and my friends don't care what I look like when we go out. But tonight, I'd like to look a little more put together.

I already let Taj know I'm going out, so he went to the Golden Fish to hang out with Ziggy.

I'm even going to splurge on an Uber so I don't have to ride my bike. This makes a skirt or a dress and heels an option. But I don't want to look like I'm trying too hard. And I don't have a big wardrobe to choose from.

Yeesh! It's been a long time since I've been through this pre-date dilemma.

I decide on a dress, wash my face, and reapply makeup. I usually only wear eye shadow, mascara, and lip balm, and all I do tonight is use a darker eye shadow and a lip gloss with a bronze shimmer. I leave my hair down, also unusual.

Oh my God, it doesn't matter!

When I get to Noir, I walk in peering around, uncertain if Harrison's here yet. "I'm meeting someone," I tell the hostess. Then I spot him. My heart jumps in my chest. "Oh, there he is."

I make my way to the table, conscious of Harrison watching me.

He seems to approve. He stands to greet me. "Hi."

"Hi." I smile, our eyes meeting and holding. Heat shimmers over my skin.

"You look amazing."

"Thanks."

He pulls out my chair for me, which I love—Mom would approve!—then takes his own seat again. He looks pretty damn good too, wearing narrow beige pants, a white shirt with the collar open, and a black cotton blazer over it.

"This place is lovely," I comment, dragging my gaze away from him to survey the small restaurant. "I've never been here."

"I'm glad you like it. Do you like wine? I don't even know that."

"Sure."

"They have a lot here. It's a wine bar. I guess you know that."

I smile at him. Is he as nervous as I am? Another thing that makes my heart go squishy. "It'll be fun to try different things."

"Yeah."

"So, your season's almost over."

"Four more games. Tomorrow we leave for Vancouver and Calgary, and then two home games next week. Wow." He shakes his head. "It goes fast."

"You play a lot of games, though."

"Yeah, we do. Things get even tougher now." He pauses. "Will you still be doing yoga classes for us in the playoffs?"

"We haven't decided yet. They wanted to see how things went and if you guys feel it helps."

"Well, I'll put in a good word for you. It hasn't been long, but I feel really good. Physically."

His eyes shadow. I remember the bad news. Should I ask about it? I don't want to be a downer.

"That's good, I'm glad to hear it. I think there are benefits, and for the playoffs not getting injured and being able to focus are very important."

"Yeah, for sure. How were your classes today?"

We make small talk while we look over the menu. They have a three-course wine dinner plus dessert, each course paired with a different wine, which we decide to have.

"No seafood, right?" Harrison says, looking at the menu.

"You remember."

"Sure."

That's so . . . nice.

Dinner starts with a salad of greens with cranberries and sunflower seeds, served with a delicious Spanish rosé brut.

"If the team doesn't hire you to do more classes, I'm going to keep coming to your other classes," Harrison says.

I tense briefly, make myself relax. "Sure."

"Today it really helped clear my mind and focus."

"That's good." I'm still curious.

"It was also you," he says. His words should alarm me, but he says it in such a low, quiet tone, not even looking at me, I'm touched rather than scared. "Just your . . . I don't know." His cheeks redden. "Your serenity. And your voice. You're so calming."

"Oh. That's so nice to hear."

"I needed that today." He looks up and meets my eyes, his smile crooked.

"I kind of got that."

"You're really perceptive."

"I guess. I try to read the group and feel what's going on."

"I think you're good at that."

"Thanks." I pick up my wine and take a gulp. The bubbles tingle all the way down my esophagus. "I enjoyed watching you practice. Seeing you interact with your teammates. I think you're good at reading them too."

"Yeah?" He tips his head, eyebrows elevated. "Cool." He pauses, then says, "I wish I'd known you were there. I would have shown off more."

I laugh. "I was impressed enough."

He straightens. "You were?"

"Sure. You guys are some of the best hockey players in the world."

He purses his lips. "Oh. You mean you were impressed with the team."

I chuckle again. "Okay, I was impressed with you."

"There we go." He smiles. He lifts his wine flute and

holds it up to me. I clink mine against it in a little toast, and we both finish off our glasses.

The next course is pasta—tagliatelle with cremini mushrooms, tomatoes, spinach, and peas. It's a small serving, the perfect size. The wine is a California Roussanne blend. "Delicious," I say after taking a sip.

"I've always wanted to do a winery road trip," Harrison says. "It sounds so cool. I left here when I was eighteen and since I've been back, it's never happened. I'd love to drive up to Napa Valley."

"Oh, that would be amazing! I haven't seen much of California since I've been here, but I love it."

"Why'd you leave North Dakota? Tired of the winters?"

"Something like that. I needed a change."

"That's pretty brave, coming this far and starting over."

"It *is* scary," I agree. "Luckily I knew Taj. He moved here after college and has made friends here, so that really helped. I wasn't totally alone."

"Oh yeah." He frowns, his fork poised over his plate. "The roommate."

I smile. "Yes." I twirl some pasta ribbons around my fork. "You should meet him. His boyfriend owns the Golden Fish, right near the beach."

"Boyfriend?" Then he smiles. "Ah. Yeah."

My insides warm with the knowledge that he was a little jealous. Except jealousy can actually be a dangerous, ugly thing. I didn't get that from Harrison, though.

I don't know. I don't trust my instincts anymore. I don't trust myself. Apparently, my judgment is flawed when it comes to men, and trusting the good in people is naïve. So maybe his jealousy of Taj should be a red flag to me.

I just don't know.

I sigh.

"What's wrong?"

"Oh. Nothing. Sorry. Just a busy day."

Conversation flows a lot more easily through dinner than when we started out, both of us relaxing. The third course is a chicken breast with pesto, accompanied by glazed fennel and baby carrots with a Pinot Noir from Oregon, and then dessert is a lemon bar served with a Sauternes.

"I get why they serve this for dessert," I say, after sipping the wine. "But it's a bit sweet for me."

"It goes nicely with the lemon, though."

"We sound like we know what we're talking about."

He laughs. "We will, after we do that Napa trip."

Oh. That sounds so amazing and fun. And impossible. We barely know each other. My heart beats a little faster.

Don't do this. Don't ruin a lovely evening with a freak-out.

I excuse myself to use the ladies' room, do some deep breathing. *I breathe in courage and breathe out doubt.* I'm okay. I touch up my lip gloss and smile at my reflection.

I really am okay. I'm doing this.

After dinner, Harrison suggests walking to the beach, which is only a couple of blocks away. I'm in heels, and I'm not used to wearing them, but I've been sitting for nearly two hours so I can handle it.

Once we cross Ocean Avenue, south of the pier, and reach the beach, I slip off my shoes and carry the sling backs hooked over a finger. The ocean is vast and dark, the sky an ombré from baby blue at the horizon to midnight above us. The bright neon and glittering lights of the pier glow in the distance.

"Beautiful," I say with a sigh.

"Are you warm enough?"

"I have a sweater. Um, can you hold my purse?"

"Sure."

He's a keeper. I remember my mom saying any man who will hold a woman's purse without complaint is a keeper. But that's not a reliable way to judge a man.

God! Why do I keep analyzing things? Why am I trying to judge him, assess his character? I should just be enjoying the moment, because this is a spectacular moment. I'm on the beach, next to the ocean, a lovely breeze in my hair, and a handsome man holding my purse while I put on my sweater.

There are people all around us, even though it's dark. It's fine.

A couple walking toward us has a dog on a leash that reminds me of Roxy, my parents' French bulldog. "Oh, look!" I smile at the people. "A Frenchie! What's your dog's name?"

They smile back at me. "Leo."

"He's so sweet! My parents have a dog almost like this. Her name's Roxy. I miss her."

Leo lets me rub his ears then wistfully stroke down his back a few times. I give him a final pat, then stand to continue walking.

Harrison slants me an amused glance. "You like dogs?"

"I love dogs! I miss Roxy so much. I wish I could have one, but it's Taj's place. Someday."

"Yeah." We walk in silence for a few seconds. Beneath

my bare feet, the pavement is still warm from the sun. "So, remember I said earlier I got bad news?"

"Yes."

"I didn't want to bring it up at dinner, because it's kind a bummer."

I turn my head up and sideways to peer at him. Without my heels on, he's a lot taller than me. "You can talk about it if you want."

"You noticed something was off."

"Yeah, I kind of did."

"That's why I said you're so good at reading people."

Huh.

"I found out yesterday that my dad has Alzheimer's."

"Oh. Oh no." My heart squeezes. "That's awful."

"Yeah." He sighs. "We've been suspecting it for a while. But they've done testing and ruled out other things, and it seems that's what it is."

"How old is he?"

"Almost seventy-three."

"Oh." My eyes widen.

Harrison smiles. "I know what you're thinking. My mom is Dad's second wife. He was married before. His two sons from his first marriage are in their fifties. That's how I have nieces and nephews the same age as me."

"Right."

"He didn't have us until he was a lot older. So. It's not like he's young. But still. It's hard to deal with."

"I'm sure it is."

I don't know how, but my hand has slipped into his as we walk. I give it a squeeze.

"I've been thinking about it so much, since yesterday. I don't know why I'm having such a hard time with it."

"I think that's normal. He's your dad."

He nods.

"I still have both my parents. I can't imagine what it will be like."

He sighs. "I can't either. He's always been my biggest supporter, from the time I started skating. My biggest fan. I suddenly thought about playing without him watching and it feels like . . . playing for no one." He pauses, then adds quietly. "I've wanted to play in the NHL my whole life, and it feels like time is running out. Not only because I'm getting older . . . but because if it does, my dad won't be around to see it."

"Stop." I squeeze his hand. "You *do* play in the NHL. You *have* shown your father you can do it. It doesn't matter if you have some contract or whatever. I don't think anyone is ever guaranteed they're going to always going to play for a certain team. Right?"

"I guess."

I don't know a lot about how professional hockey works. I guess the very best players in the world would never get sent down. But still . . . maybe it could happen.

"I'm sure he's proud of you."

One corner of his mouth lifts. "I hope so. He's never been the kind of dad who pushed us to play. He let us do what we want. My brother Asher never even tried to make it into the NHL. After college, he decided to write about hockey instead of play it. And Dad was fine with that."

"See? I think you're putting the pressure on yourself."

"You're probably right. But even so . . . I want him to see me make it."

"I understand that."

We approach a bench and Harrison slows and turns to sit on it, tugging me gently with him, my hand still clasped in his. His is big and strong. His knuckles are rough and reddened. My heart melts a little at seeing that.

"And I'm also a selfish dick," he says.

"What? Why?"

"I need his advice. My coach had a talk with me when they called me up, and . . . and I need my Dad's take on it. But I don't feel I can do that right now. He's got enough problems."

I study his face, the set of his jaw, and his firm lips. "I bet he wouldn't agree. I bet he'd love to give you advice."

He tips his head. "You think?"

"I think parents live to give their kids advice." I laugh softly. "Even when they *don't* ask for it."

"Thanks for letting me yak about it," he says. "I don't want to be a downer."

"You're not. It's a major event in your life. It will take time to work through what it all means, and in a way, I think, you've already started grieving. That's a hard process."

He purses his lips and nods. "Yeah. I didn't think of it that way." He stares out at the dark ocean for a moment. "My family—my extended family—is kind of messed up. This might be something that brings everyone back together."

"Yes. Adversity can do that."

"Or maybe make everything worse." He slants me a crooked smile. "Maybe this will show us who everyone really is."

11

ARYA

"I'm sorry you're going through this."

Harrison turns to face me more directly. "Thanks. I shouldn't have dumped it on you."

Truthfully, I kind of like it that he did. "I don't mind. Talking can be helpful."

"It was. So thanks. Should we head back?"

"Okay."

We rise and stroll back the way we came.

"Do you have brothers and sisters?" he asks me.

"I do. I have an older sister, Grace. She's married and still lives in Fargo. I miss her."

"Yeah."

"And I miss my dog sister."

"Dog sister?" He grins. "You mean Roxy?"

"Yeah." I smile too. "She's so funny. And you have a brother you mentioned, and Everly . . . and another brother?"

"Yes. Noah. He's younger. He plays hockey in San Diego."

"And your nephews . . . they both play hockey?"

"Not exactly. JP—who you met—plays for the Golden Eagles. Théo used to play, but now he's the general manager of the Condors."

"Huh. He's your boss?"

"Yep."

"Couldn't he just give you a permanent gig on the team?"

He laughs. "He could. But he won't, unless I deserve it."

"Harsh." I pause. "I'm teasing. I'm not really a proponent of nepotism."

"I get it. But our family has been involved in hockey forever—my dad played too, way back. Nobody ever got ahead because of our name. And none of us would want that."

"That's really . . . admirable."

Christ on a cracker. I'm liking this man—and his family—more and more. "What did you mean when you say they're messed up, though?"

"Long story. My dad remarried not that long after his first wife died. My mom's twenty years younger than him. That caused some bad feelings for Mark and Matthew—his sons from his first marriage. They've never liked my mom."

"Oh no. That must be hard."

"Yeah. I wasn't totally aware of it all when I was a kid, but as I got older I clued in. That caused tension between all of us, for a long time. Then . . . well, I might as well tell you, it's not secret. The media had a feeding frenzy when it happened. My dad apparently borrowed money from Mark and Matthew, from the trust fund they inherited from their mom. He was supposed to pay it back and he hasn't, and now they're suing him."

"Oh my God. Okay, yeah, that could cause some family drama."

"You have no idea." But he smiles.

"Do you think . . . his Alzheimer's has something to do with that?" I ask hesitantly.

"I do now. We've been working on trying get this mess figured out. Funny, yesterday, at my parents' place when they gave us the news, we never talked about that. But Mark and Matthew need to know too—he *is* their dad."

We arrive back at the street where we crossed Ocean. I stop to brush sand off my feet and put my shoes back on. He offers me an arm to steady myself.

Mother of cake. I *really* like this man.

"How did you get here?" he asks. "Can I drive you home?"

I don't answer while I think about this and we walk toward Ocean Avenue. I really like him. He seems like a good guy. But I don't trust my instincts anymore. "I'd rather not. I took an Uber here. I'll take one home." I pull out my phone.

"That's crazy," he says. "That could be dangerous."

"I'm careful." Although he's right, I also know the danger of giving out my address to someone I don't really know that well. I bring up the app.

"Seriously, just let me drive you. It's no trouble."

Pushing doesn't make me feel any better. "Please. This is what I prefer."

He goes silent and when I glance at him, he looks . . . hurt. "Okay," he says slowly. "I get it."

He doesn't get it. At least, I don't think he does.

A car will be here in a few minutes. Perfect. We stop at the corner.

"Thank you for dinner," I say. "It was amazing, with all the different wines. And thanks for opening up about what's going on with you."

"Thanks for listening."

We stand on the street corner shadowed by a big tree as traffic passes by. Neither of us says anything else as our eyes meet. He moves a little closer. I want him to kiss me.

A car pulls up at the curb. It's my Uber.

I smile. "Gotta go. Thank you again." Since he hasn't made a move, I do, going on my toes to brush my lips over his.

I check out the car, slide into the back seat and have the driver say my name, then wave at Harrison as we pull away.

I lean my head against the side window. I should have let him drive me home.

No. He may have been hurt that I didn't trust him, but my safety is more important than his hurt feelings. I can't get sucked into stupid decisions by worrying about how others feel or what they think of me.

Except I'll probably never hear from him again because of it, and damn, I like him. I like him a lot.

I dig through my purse and find my phone. Might as well deal with it now.

I type in a message to Harrison.

> Thanks again for a really nice evening. I had fun.

He doesn't reply. After a few minutes, I tuck my phone away and sigh, staring at the city lights flashing by outside the car.

At home, Taj is there, watching *Disasters at Sea* on TV.

"Hey," he says, looking up. "How'd your date go?"

"Well." I drop my purse, then hear my phone buzz. "It was good. Until the end."

I pull out my phone. Now Harrison has replied.

> Did you really?

I sink down onto a chair.

> Yes, really.

> Honestly? I thought you were brushing me off.

I nibble my lower lip. I knew he thought that. I don't want him to think that.

> Honestly? I wasn't.

He sends me a smile emoji.

> Okay, then. When can I see you again?

Before I can answer, I get another text.

Shit, I'm going out of town. We're back
Saturday.

I tap in my reply.

So . . . Saturday, then?

Another smile emoji.

Great.

A big smile tugs at my lips. I look up to see Taj watching me with raised eyebrows. "Everything okay?"

"Yeah." I set my phone on the coffee table. "It is now." I grimace. "I didn't want him to drive me home, and he was a little . . ."

"Pissed?"

"No." I shake my head. "If he'd been pissed about it, I probably wouldn't see him again."

"Good girl."

"He was more hurt, I think. He thought I was giving him the brush-off, and I wasn't, I was just being careful."

"He doesn't know about what happened."

"No. And I'm not going to tell him. Anyway, I texted him to let him know I did want to see him again. So we're going out on Saturday. He's away on a road trip until then."

"You really like this dude?"

"I do. I mean, we're just getting to know each other. He seems great." I purse my lips. "I'm just still . . . gun-shy, I guess." I pause. "He told me about some bad news he just got about his dad. We talked about it and I felt touched that he would open up to me about that. But then I thought, what if it's a big story designed to soften me up and make me feel sorry for him?"

Taj squints. "Ah, Ary."

"I know, I know. I can't help it, though."

"I get it. Just take things slow . . . there's no harm in going out and having some fun. It's up to you how far it goes."

"Right." I nod. "Good advice. Well. I'm going to bed. I have a ten o'clock class tomorrow."

I wash my face and get ready for bed. Then, in the dark, under the covers, I relive nearly every moment of our date, remembering the way Harrison looked at me, how he seemed nervous at first, which I was too, the vulnerability he revealed when he talked about his dad.

I want to believe in him. I really, really do. I just don't know if I can.

12

―――――――

HARRISON

WE WIN IN VANCOUVER, LOSE IN CALGARY, A HORRIFIC SIX-one loss. Calgary's out of the playoffs, which makes it even more humiliating. I'm a little annoyed actually, because I feel like I've been playing so well on the line with Pavel and Eddie, and tonight Coach moved Eddie up to the first line to give Jimmy a break and made Pavel a healthy scratch too. So was playing with Scotty and Olle, who are great but different. But it's not about me and what's best for me—it's what's best for the team.

Anyway, Calgary's coming to our town next week and we'll have a chance at redemption. The games are meaningless for us, but like I told Arya, now we're playing for our pride.

I've had a lot to think about this week. The news about Dad, going out with Arya, the way she acted at the end of our date, and then taking off on a road trip.

The guys would laugh at me if they knew, but I did some yoga in my hotel room, since we had extra time. I use it to relax my body and turn off my mind. Of course yoga makes me think about Arya. I can't wait to see her again on Saturday. What should we do? I don't want to do another restaurant thing. So I ask my teammates for ideas when we're out for a team dinner the night before the game at the steakhouse in the Westin in downtown Calgary.

"Okay you guys, I'm taking my future wife out on a date on Saturday and I need ideas."

"Future wife." Bellsy shakes his head at me. "You need to slow your roll, dude."

"Don't worry, I haven't told her yet." I smirk at him.

"Dinner at Rossignol," he suggests. "I took Everly there. We saw Tom Hanks."

"Don't want another dinner date." I cut into my perfect medium-rare steak. "We've done that. I want to do something fun and different."

"Take her on a hike to the Hollywood sign," Bellsy offers. "I did that with Everly too."

I roll my eyes. "I don't want to go on the same dates as my sister, thanks."

He snorts.

"How did you get her to do that, anyway? Did she hike in her Prada heels?"

"Yeah, of course," he says. "Dumbass. It was *me*. She wanted to be with me."

"Uh-huh."

"How about a movie?" Bergie suggests. "Chicks like rom coms."

I consider that. Sitting beside Arya in silence for a couple of hours doesn't sound that appealing. Although maybe we could make out in the back row of the theater . . .

"Griffith Observatory," Jabber suggests. "You can look at the stars. Very romantic."

"Huh." That's a possibility.

"You two could hang out with us," Nicky says.

"Ha. I'm not bringing her around you guys."

"What? Why not?" Nicky looks offended.

"She sees enough of you at yoga class. Besides, that's too high pressure. I might as well take her home to meet my family."

That gets a bunch of laughs.

"She's going to have to meet them at some point," Jimmy points out. "If she's going to be your wife."

"Yeah, at some point. But she's already met my sister. And Bellsy here."

"Aw. Am I family now?" he asks. "I'm honored."

I shrug. "Sort of. Also JP." I grin, remembering knocking him into the water at the first SUP class we went to.

"Take her shopping," Scotty says. "Buy her something expensive."

I stare at him incredulously. "Seriously?"

"Lots of women like that."

"If that's how you have to get women to date you, that's sad."

He flicks his middle finger my way. "Fuck you."

"I'll figure something out." I shake my head.

"Don't ask Archie," Bergie says with a grin. "He has the worst luck with dates."

"It's true." Archie rolls his eyes. "Remember my blind date?"

I shake my head. I haven't heard these stories.

"I met this girl at a restaurant. She didn't say a word the whole time we ate dinner. Seriously. Not. A. Word. After I paid the bill, she just got up and left."

"What the fuck?"

"Yeah. Then I checked my phone and discovered a text from the chick I was supposed to meet, saying she couldn't make it."

I crack up laughing.

"Still don't know who the hell I had dinner with." He shakes his head, grinning.

"How about the time you texted your date that you wished you hadn't asked her out?" Nicky asks.

"Ha! I was trying to text *you*. Right in the middle of the date, I accidentally texted her. She looked at her phone, then looked at me. Awkward!"

We take our time at dinner because we're going to a dance club that doesn't even open until nine-thirty. We pile into a bunch of cabs the valet at the entrance of the hotel waves up for us. This place supposedly has great DJs, and on a Thursday night, should be hopping.

Not that I care. I'm not feeling the club vibe right now. I want to get home and see how Dad's doing and take Arya out on a date and maybe go see my half brothers, Mark and Matthew, and give them shit.

It doesn't take long for women to notice us. Nicky and Jimmy order bottles of wine and pour them drinks, and a bunch of guys are dancing with girls in short, sexy dresses. I catch the eye of a hot blonde. She smiles. I look away and sip my whisky.

I'm used to this, although the cities I usually travel to are smaller and the bars not quite as plush as this one. Wherever we are, women always seem to notice the hockey players. Tonight, I'm not interested. I lean back on the banquette where I'm sitting and think about Arya . . . her toned body, how her soft hand felt in mine as we walked on the beach, her pretty mouth, and how she helped me process what's happening with Dad.

It's been a while since I had a girlfriend. I forgot what it's like to have someone to talk to, someone you can share that kind of stuff with and not feel like a complete dork. I *haven't* forgotten what sex is like, though, and I'd really like to know how that is with Arya too. I bet it's spectacular. I was all pissed at Archie when he made that comment about Arya being flexible, but I have to admit I've thought of it too.

I start imagining the kinds of positions we could try . . . *No. Stop.* I'm getting a boner. Can't have that. Instead, I think about what's going to happen with Dad. And the team. And Mom. Yeah, that takes care of the ill-timed erection, all right.

ARYA WON'T LET ME PICK HER UP AT HER HOME, WHICH makes me sigh. It also makes me wonder why not. She lives with a man. She said they're just friends, and she said he has a boyfriend . . . but maybe that's not true . . . Is she hiding something from me?

I hate thinking things like that. I'm not naïve, but I like to think that people are mostly good and honest. And when I think of it, I wouldn't want my sister letting strange men pick her up at home. Not that I'm strange. Ha.

After a little texting back and forth, we agreed to meet at the Golden Fish, the bar owned by her roommate's boyfriend. As I near the place, I see her standing on the sidewalk outside.

A smile breaks out on my face.

Her hair is down again tonight, in long waves of all different shades of gold. She's wearing jeans—first time I've seen her in jeans—dark jeans that fit her slender curves perfectly, with a black-and-white graphic T-shirt and a tiny red leather jacket over it. On her feet are metallic gold flats.

I pull up to the curb and lift my hand. She spots me, and her spontaneous smile leaves no mistaking that she's happy to see me too.

Something inside my chest puffs up.

She slides in and pulls the door closed. We turn to each other, both smiling like jackasses eating thistles, as my Grandpa Clark says.

"Hi."

"Hi. How are you?"

"Good. Especially now."

Her eyes warm. "Did you miss me?" she teases.

"Like I'd miss my left nut."

She laughs lightly. "Okay, then."

I put my vehicle in drive, look over my shoulder, and pull away from the curb.

"Where are we going?" she asks, tugging her seatbelt across her body.

"Bowling."

"Whaaat?"

"Yep."

"I love bowling!"

"You do?"

"Sure."

"You're not just making me feel better for taking you on a lame date?"

Her lips curve upward. "I won't know if it's a lame date until later."

"Ah. Good answer."

I drive us to Freeze Frame, which is one of the oldest bowling alleys in Los Angeles. It's been refurbished and has a really cool retro vibe, with antique furniture, the original vaulted wood ceiling, and big framed vintage posters on the walls.

Arya is practically bouncing as we wait to get our bowling shoes, and she snatches hers from the attendant and heads to our lane. She plops herself down on an old leather couch and switches out her pointy-toed flats for bowling shoes. She takes off her jacket and tosses it onto the couch.

Her T-shirt says "ZEN AF."

I grin.

I watch in amusement as she tests out the shoes, then does a series of stretching moves.

"What are you doing?" I ask.

"Warming up." She jumps up and down on the balls of her feet.

I rub my jaw. "Okay."

Like a gentleman, I let her go first.

She holds the ball up in front of her, takes a few smooth steps, bringing her arm back and letting the ball roll off it. I stare as it zooms down the center of the lane and takes out all ten pins.

She laughs with delight and pumps her arms in the air. "Strike!"

"What the . . ."

She turns and skips back toward me. "I used to bowl in a league when I was younger."

"Uh-oh." I pick up a ball. "Why do I have a feeling I'm about to get my ass kicked?"

"Oh, come on." She nudges me with her shoulder. "You're a professional athlete."

I purse my lips and focus as I aim my ball up the middle. It looks good at first, but somehow I put some curve on it and it hits the gutter when it nears the pins. "Damn!"

"Maybe you should have warmed up," Arya suggests helpfully.

"Ha ha."

"My team was named the Ball Busters," she informs me.

I choke. "Okay, good to know."

My next ball takes out a few center pins, leaving one on the left and two on the right.

"Split happens," Arya says cheerfully. "That's a six-seven-ten split. Would you like to know what my strategy would be?"

"I'm flattered that you think I have the ability to carry

out any strategy," I say. "My goal is basically to not end up in the gutter."

She laughs again and stands next to me, leaning in. She points. "Go for the ten pin." She nudges me over. "Line your body up with the ten pin . . . like so. But look at the right side of the six pin."

I don't have the heart to tell her I don't know which pin is which.

She steps back to let me take the shot. "This is a hard shot for anyone."

As expected, the ball rolls right through the empty space in the middle.

Also as expected, I lose. Who knew she was a kick-ass bowler? Usually I'm super competitive, but tonight? I don't even care about losing because she's having so much fun.

As we make our way to the bar for a beer and pizza, she pats my back. "Don't feel bad. Bowling takes balls."

I snort-laugh. "Funny."

"I was going to tell you more bad bowling puns, but I thought I'd spare you."

I laugh. "Enough!"

She grins. "Sorry. I'm pretty sure I know every bowling joke there is."

God, I love it that her eyes are sparkling and her lips are tipped up in a happy curve.

13

ARYA

I haven't bowled in so long! This is really fun. I didn't actually bowl that well, compared to how I used to play, but it was enough to beat Harrison. He's being a good sport about it, despite his grumbling at the beginning. I'm pretty sure he likes to win at everything, so it touches me that he seems happy for me.

Did I mention it's been a while since I had sex?

There's no other explanation for the fact that watching Harrison bowl is turning me on.

He may not be the best bowler in the world, but he's athletic and coordinated, and watching him move is a definite turn-on. His jeans stretching over his thighs and butt when he threw the ball . . . muscles flexing under his T-shirt . . . biceps bulging the sleeves . . . I'm hot and twitchy.

Not to mention his sense of humor. I love a guy who can make me laugh.

"What would you like to drink?" he asks in the bar. We have a table, but we have to order at the bar.

"I'll have a beer. Whatever you're having as long as it's not IPA."

He grins. "Okay. And any preference for the pizza?"

"Anything except shrimp."

He gives me a thumbs-up and heads to the long antique bar.

I settle onto the high stool and look around, taking in the ambience in the dimly lit bar overlooking the bowling lanes. This place is so cool, a bowling throwback. Amber lights illuminate all the bottles behind the bar and antique bowling balls sit on display.

Harrison returns with our beers and a numbered card. "They'll bring our pizza," he says, setting one glass in front of me.

I take a sip of my beer. "Ah. That's good."

"So. How old were you when you started bowling? Two?"

I grin. "A little older than that."

He shakes his head. "Good thing I didn't plan this date to impress you."

I lean forward. "You know what? You *did* impress me."

He tips his head. "How so?"

"You're a good sport. I love to bowl and I'm having fun and you're not mad that you lost." I meet his eyes. "That impresses me."

Our gazes hold. The air thickens around us and that little ache deep down inside me intensifies. I squeeze my thighs together.

"I'm having fun too," he says softly, also leaning forward.

I study his face—his thick, straight eyebrows, his square

chin dusted with stubble, his imperfect nose. Arousal slides through me, slow, liquid heat, pooling low inside me. "Good." I drop my gaze a little shyly. "So, um, how was your road trip?"

"Long. Only two games, but we had two days between. Went shopping for cowboy boots."

My eyebrows lift. "Really? Did you buy some?"

"No." He grins. "But apparently you're supposed to do that in Calgary. We went to a club one night, but I wasn't into it. I was kinda distracted."

"Oh." I bite my lower lip. "Thinking about your dad?"

"Er, yeah."

"Any more news?"

"No." He holds his beer with two hands and looks down at it. "I'm going over to see them tomorrow."

"That's good."

"Yeah. I need to check in with Everly and my brothers. Everly's in charge of all this." One corner of his mouth lifts. "I'm not sure what happens next. Mom and Dad are supposed to meet with Mark and Matthew—my half brothers." He grimaces. "I don't know how that's going to go."

I've been thinking about this too. It's not even my family, but I hurt for Harrison that his dad has this terrible disease. After the night we walked on the beach, I could tell how it's affecting him. It must be so hard. On top of that, there's this huge rift in the family over money. That really sucks.

"I'm sure everyone will want to work things out now," I say, reaching across to lay one hand on top of his. "Like you said, this could help bring everyone together."

"Thanks. Let's not talk about depressing shit. How was your week?"

I smile. "It was fine. I missed teaching hockey-player yoga, though." I've gotten used to doing that two or three times a week, but this week with their travel schedule there was only one class. "But I'll see you guys Monday morning."

"Confession? I did yoga in my hotel room while I was away."

I straighten. "Really?"

"Yeah. Like I said, I was distracted by a bunch of stuff, so I did it to try to focus and relax."

"Well." I blink. I'm not sure if I believe him or not. "That's great."

Why don't I believe him? He seems sincere. He seems like an honest guy. I hate being like this!

I pull in a slow breath through my nose, then tell him about the work we're doing at Prana to collect items for a women's shelter. "They always need toiletries, baby food . . . lots of things. So I set up a place in the studio where everyone can contribute things. I'm taking over our first donation on Monday."

"That's awesome. Where did you get that idea?"

"Ummm. I think I saw something online about them needing things."

"If you need any help, I'm free Monday afternoon."

I consider that. I was going to ask Taj if I could borrow his car, but if Harrison could drive me, I wouldn't have to bother Taj. "Okay," I say slowly. "That would be great, actually."

His face brightens. I think he thought I was going to say no. "Okay! Good."

Our pizza arrives, and we dig into the pie topped with pepperoni, bacon, mushrooms, and green peppers.

"Oh, this is good!" I capture a string of mozzarella dangling from my piece with one finger. "Spicy!"

He watches me slip my finger into my mouth to pull off the mozzarella, his eyes darkening. My belly flutters.

I take another bite of my pizza, trying to control my attraction to him, and we both eat for a moment. Then I ask, "Would you rather be the best player on a terrible team, or the worst player on a great team?"

One of his eyebrows shoots up. "Where did that come from?"

"Just making conversation."

He nods. "Well . . . seeing as I like to win, I guess I'd rather be the worst player on a great team. As long as by worst, you mean no talent. Not worst because I'm lazy." He appears to wince slightly. "Because you can overcome being lazy. But if you have no talent and you work as hard as you can, that's all you can ask."

I feel like a might have hit a nerve there. Interesting.

"How about you?" he asks.

"I can't argue with what you just said. But maybe if you're the best player on a terrible team, there's a chance you could influence them to be better . . . lead by example?"

"True."

"If you could only eat one food for the rest of your life, what would it be?"

"Aaaah. I can't answer that! I love food."

"Me too. But I'd say pizza." I nod at the pan on our

table. "Because there's so much variety, it would be hard to get tired of it."

"Good point. I'm also partial to broccoli. Can't get enough of the stuff."

"Really?" My chin jerks down.

"No." He grins. "I eat it because I have to."

"It's really good roasted. Pretty much any vegetable is good roasted. Roasted cauliflower is like vegetable candy."

"I don't know if I'd go that far, but yeah, roasted veggies are good. Even better battered and fried."

I laugh. "Yeah, I'd eat pretty much anything deep-fried."

"I ate deep-fried beer once."

"No!"

"Yeah."

"How do they do that?"

"It's in a dough. Like a pretzel. Really weird. Can't say I'm a big fan, although I do like beer."

"Hey. What about deep-fried pizza? That would be good!"

"Oh hell yeah. We should try that."

"We'd need a deep-fryer. I don't have one."

"Me either. But I could buy one. We could deep-fry all kinds of things."

"For about a year, until we have massive heart attacks."

He laughs. "Yeah."

We talk easily until the pizza is gone and our beers are finished. It's nearly midnight. I'm having so much fun.

"Where to now?" Harrison asks.

I hate to say home, and as usual, I don't want to give him my address.

Yet.

Gah. What am I thinking?

I don't want the evening to end, though. "How about we go back to the Golden Fish where you picked me up? We could have a drink and you can meet Taj. He said he'd drive me home from there."

He nods slowly. "Sure."

Maybe I shouldn't have said that, about Taj driving me home. I've kind of killed the fun mood.

We enter the Golden Fish and find Taj seated at one end of the bar laughing with Ziggy, who's standing on the other side. The place is packed, even the patio, a song by The Killers playing from speakers mingling with chattering voices and clinking glasses.

Taj spots me and lifts a hand. "Hey, beautiful."

I lead Harrison toward him. "Hi, guys. How's it going?"

"Good, good." Taj's gaze lands on Harrison.

I make the introductions, Taj and Ziggy both giving Harrison appraising looks.

Harrison shakes their hands with a firm grip and an unfazed smile. "Hey, good to meet you."

"What can I get you to drink?" Ziggy asks.

"I guess I could have one more beer," Harrison says, looking over at the chalkboard listing beers on tap. "How about a Shock Top."

"You bet. Arya?"

"Can you make me one of your hibiscus tea cocktails?"

"Sure thing."

Ziggy sets about getting our drinks.

"Hibiscus tea?" Harrison arches a brow.

I smile. "It's delicious." I turn to Taj. "We went

bowling!" I hang my purse on the hook under the bar and hop onto a stool. "It was so fun!"

Taj barks out a laugh. "How the hell did you know she loves bowling?" he asks Harrison.

Harrison shrugs, taking the stool on the other side of me. "I had no idea. Lucky coincidence. Good thing my ego can stand being hammered, though. She's totally a can of whoopass."

Taj laughs again. "That she is." His smile is warm and affectionate.

Harrison takes note of this.

"What'd she do?" Ziggy calls.

"Kicked his butt at bowling," Taj calls.

Ziggy grins.

"I didn't really bowl very well," I say. "It's been a while."

"Christ, I'd hate to play against you on a good day, then," Harrison says.

"But you'd be happy to play *on* my team." I smile at him.

Our eyes meet. "Yeah," he says softly. "I would."

We study each other, the air about to ignite around us. I want to touch him . . . see if his hair is as thick and silky as it looks, feel his beard stubble on my cheek, stroke a finger over his lips . . . heat builds between us, and when his gaze lands on my mouth, electricity jolts through me.

Taj clears his throat. "Glad you had a good time."

Right, right. "We did."

Harrison sets a hand on the back of my stool, leaning forward so he can see and talk to Taj, which brings him right up close to me. I breathe it in the scent of his cologne. God, I love the scent of men's cologne. Well, not all; Harrison's is light, yet warm and sexy. I'd like to bury my nose in the side of his neck and inhale him. Like, forever.

Ziggy serves our drinks and the four of us chat. Ziggy has to disappear into the kitchen to deal with something, but he comes back in a while. Harrison charms them with self-deprecating bowling stories, then answering their questions about hockey.

I can literally see Taj and Ziggy falling under his spell.

I don't know if this is good or bad. Taj has solid judgment about people, so I guess . . . it's good? I want him to like Harrison.

An hour flies by and it's last call. Harrison looks at me. "Guess I should get going." He shifts his gaze to Taj and gives him a penetrating stare. "You're going to see Arya safely home?"

"Of course."

"Walk me out?" he says to me, standing.

I slide off the stool and follow him outside onto the sidewalk. The crisp, damp ocean breeze tugs my hair, and I shake it back out of my face. We move a few steps away from the entrance.

"Thanks for coming tonight," Harrison says in a low voice, stepping closer.

I don't move back. I want this. I want him closer. Closer. I tip my head to meet his eyes, as he's so much taller than me. "Thank you. I had a lot of fun."

"I always have fun with you," he murmurs, moving another strand of hair off my face. Then he gathers my hair into a tail and holds it in one hand at the nape of my neck. I feel his body heat, waves of male warmth, smell his cologne . . .

"Me too."

His eyes meet mine again, and he slowly lowers his face toward mine, keeping the eye contact. He gives me lots of time to back away or say no . . . but I don't. My eyelashes flutter down just as his lips touch mine.

Ohhhhh. Lush heat fills me, pooling low down. I fall into a haze of sweet, hot desire, quivery sensation rippling through me. I slide my hands up his chest and then over his shoulders. Our bodies press together, chest to thigh. I love how he feels, strong and solid. His hand twists my hair then cups the back of my head, tilting it for a deeper angle, while his other hand slides around my hip, pulling me closer still.

I don't want this to end.

We kiss and kiss and kiss, until I'm breathless and aching. My breasts feel full and heavy, my pussy squeezing with need.

Then he pulls back and smiles. His eyes have darkened, his lids heavy with arousal. "Wow."

I can only give a tiny nod.

"See you Monday," he says softly.

I'm lost for a few seconds, then I nod again quickly. "Yes. Right. Monday."

"We can talk about delivering your donations."

"Yes." I try to breathe.

He kisses my forehead, and slowly releases my hair. "Good night."

"G'night."

He walks me back to the door, then lifts his hand and strides down the sidewalk to where he parked his car.

I can't move. I stand, fingers pressed to my lips, my body pulsing, wishing he wasn't leaving, or wishing he wasn't leaving without me.

I drift back into the bar like I'm full of helium, and glide onto my stool. I pick up my empty glass, peer at it, then set it down.

"You okay, Ari?"

I turn to Taj. "Mmm. Yeah."

"You look like you were just kissed into next week."

A smile pulls at my lips. "Pretty much."

"You really like this guy, huh?"

I regard him contemplatively. "I do."

He nods.

"What do you think?" I lean in earnestly. "I need to know, Taj."

"I don't know him."

"I know, but first impressions are important."

Annoyingly, Taj hedges. "He seems like a good guy."

"I know that!"

He lowers his head, then looks up. "I'm not going to be your trust-o-meter when it comes to men."

My mouth drops open. "What?"

He gives me a look like someone's pulling his toenails out. "I get that you're cautious."

"I have to be!"

"I know, I know. But you also have to learn to make decisions on your own."

My bottom lip tries to push out. I suck it back in, but my chest fills with hurt. "I thought you were my friend."

"I am your friend. That's why I'm not going to tell you whether to fuck this guy or not."

I gasp. "That's not what this is about!"

"Isn't it? You two were practically setting the air in here on fire."

I shove a fingernail between my teeth and bite down. "Um . . . we were?"

"Fuck, yeah. You two have chemistry. I'll weigh in on that."

"But . . ." I don't know what to say. I was counting on Taj to either tell me Harrison's a good guy or an asshole. Heat flushes through me and my heart speeds up. I narrow my eyes at him. "Well, thanks for that." I jump off the stool and grab my purse. "Ready to go?"

He sighs. "Yeah. Sure. Let me find Ziggy and tell him we're out."

14

———

HARRISON

"My balls are sagging."

I freeze and stare at my locker instead of looking at Scotty. "I don't want to hear about your balls while I'm naked." I finish drying off and grab my boxers from my locker. "In fact, I don't want to hear about your balls, ever."

"But, like, really," Scotty says. "Is it normal?"

"Of course it's normal," Nicky replies. "Your testicles need to stay cool."

"Probably because you're getting old," Jimmy adds. "Everything sags when you get old."

Scotty snorts. He's twenty-one. "You should know."

"There's surgery for that," Nicky adds. "You can get a scrotal lift."

"Shut the fuck up!" Jabber gapes at him.

"No shit." Nicky shrugs and rubs his hair with a towel. "It's a thing."

"Huh." Scotty purses his lips.

"Jesus. The idea of having the skin around my 'nads

145

sliced open is terrifying," Jabber says. "Who would do that?"

"Lots of people," Nicky replies. "But you can't have sex for six weeks after."

"How the hell do you know so much about it?" Jabber demands.

I'm dressed now. "This conversation is done. If you're really worried, Scotty, go to a doctor."

I play with a lot of young guys in Pasadena; for some reason I didn't expect to be having stupid conversations like this here in Santa Monica.

"I guess you don't want to hear about my manscaping accident," Jabber jokes.

I wince. "Nope. Come on, let's grab lunch."

We just finished practice Monday morning, after Arya's yoga class. I feel really good. I had a bit of a hammie strain after the last game, but it feels fine now. I'm going to give Arya the credit for it not being worse . . . all those stretches probably helped.

We take advantage of the team lunch with some healthy options they've set out on the buffet in the players' lounge. I pause at the tortellini with pesto sauce.

"What?" Jabber says. "What's wrong with the pasta?"

"Major garlic. I'll pass." I move on to the chicken parm.

"You don't want the Caesar salad then either, I guess."

"That's a no."

"Hot date?" Jabber smirks, loading his plate with tortellini.

"Sort of."

"The future missus?"

"Yep."

"She know about this yet?"

"The date or the wedding?" I grin as I ladle vinaigrette over the salad which has nutritious avocado, dried cranberries, and pine nuts.

"Ha ha. Either."

"She knows about the date. Not the wedding. Too soon."

"Well, at least you know that."

"I'm not an idiot."

"Hmmm."

I roll my eyes. "Don't you believe in love at first sight?"

"No."

Bellsy joins us at a table, his plate also filled with garlicky goodness.

"Did you fall in love with Everly the first time you met her?" I ask him.

He squints, pops a tortellini in his mouth, and chews. "No. She annoyed the hell out of me. I wanted to argue with everything she said."

I grin. "I can relate to that. She was an annoying sister."

"I think it's a little different," Jabber points out. "I think by 'argue,' he means 'bang.'"

"Ugh."

"Fact," Bellsy agrees with a smirk. "What's up with you and the yoga teacher?"

"I'm helping her take some donations to a women's shelter this afternoon."

They go silent and stare at me.

"What?"

"Jesus. You really *are* going to marry her," Jabber says.

I shrug and spear a chunk of avocado. "You'll see."

Today, I'm meeting her at Prana. Once again, I don't get to see where she lives. I'm starting to wonder if she's in a kinky threesome with Taj and his boyfriend. Nah. I didn't get that vibe when we were all together at the Golden Fish the other night. The important thing is that she got home safely.

They seemed protective of her, but it felt more like they were big brothers. I definitely felt they were checking me out. Hopefully I passed whatever their test was. I can only be myself, though, and if that kiss was anything to go on, pretty sure Arya likes me.

Not kiss. Kisses. Plural. Scorching-hot, mind-scrambling kisses. Christ, it was hard to walk away from her that night. I wanted to pick her up, throw her in my car, and take her home with me.

I feel impatient, but I have to remind myself we haven't known each other that long and have actually only been on a few dates. Not sure if this afternoon counts, but maybe she'll let me buy her dinner after, or something.

There's a loading zone in front of Prana, so I park there and put my flashers on before I head inside. Arya's there with a few other women who all appear to also work there, about her age, all pretty and wearing exercise clothes.

"Hi!" Arya greets me with a luminous smile. She's wearing a pair of cropped black leggings and a neon-pink tank top. Her hair is in a long, thick, messy braid that hangs over one shoulder.

"Hi." I return the smile.

"We got things packed up." She waves a hand at the cartons piled on the floor.

"Great." I bend and pick one up. "I'll get these out to the vehicle."

"We'll help," Arya says.

"Eh. How heavy are they?"

"Only a couple are heavy."

The girls pick up boxes and follow me outside. We load them into the back of my SUV. I make a couple of extra trips with the heaviest containers.

"Thank you so much for doing this," one woman says to me.

"Oh, I'm sorry, I should introduce you all," Arya says. "Ivy, Hazel, Willow—this is Harrison Wynn."

"Great to meet you, ladies." I flash them a grin and dust my hands off. "This is a great thing to do."

"All Arya's idea," Ivy says. "She organized it."

Arya smiles diffidently, lifting her shoulders. "It wasn't that much. I guess we have everything?"

She and I climb into my vehicle and she pulls out her phone to give me directions to the women's shelter.

"Is it a homeless shelter?" I ask.

"It's for women who are victims of abuse, who need somewhere to go to get away from their abuser."

"Ah." I frown. A knot forms in my chest. "That's, uh, good they have a safe place to go."

"And they can bring their children," she adds. "Hence the big packages of Huggies. Aurora House offers other services too . . . counseling, a crisis line, support groups. It's hard for women to leave an abusive relationship if they don't have anywhere else to go."

I fucking hate thinking about women being abused.

"How do you know so much about it?"

"I did some research."

I frown and tighten my hands on the steering wheel. "Were you . . . ?"

She shakes her head. "No. I haven't used a shelter myself. But . . ." She trails off. After a short pause, she says, "It's an important service."

"Yeah." I like it that she's doing something like this. It impresses me that she got the idea and did the research and made it happen.

When we get there, they're expecting us, and a few people come out to help unload the boxes. We carry things inside. It's homey—a living room, kitchen, dining room with a long table. I can see into an office, and a hallway leads to what I assume are sleeping rooms or bedrooms. Kids are playing in a corner of the big living space with a bunch of toys there.

Arya makes another introduction, this time to one of the women helping. "Harrison, this is Karen King, the Executive Director of Aurora House. Karen, Harrison Wynn."

"You play for the Condors," Karen says immediately, taking my hand and shaking it. "Thank you so much for helping today."

"My pleasure."

A lot of hockey players do various community work. Everly manages the Condors Community Foundation, so her job is probably similar to this woman's. I've helped Everly out with fundraisers, and I've been involved with Big Brothers in Pasadena for a few years, but this season I was getting called up more and I haven't actually been mentoring a little brother for a while. I forgot how good it feels to do something like this.

Karen gets one of the other staff to take a picture of her, Arya, and me in front of some of the boxes. "For our blog and newsletter," she says. "I hope that's okay."

"Sure."

We chat with the people there a bit, as they start unpacking things. Karen holds up a package of diapers to show a woman cradling a tiny baby, and she gives a small smile of gratitude, though her face is tired and drawn. My chest tightens.

I catch Arya's eye and I can tell she's moved too. I move over to her and slide my hand up her back as she talks to Karen.

"Okay, I guess we're done," she eventually says to me.

"Thank you again," Karen says.

"We'll be back," Arya replies. "Everyone at Prana was eager to help out. We gathered all these things in only a couple of weeks."

"It's greatly appreciated."

Back in my vehicle, I turn to Arya as she fastens her seatbelt. "Thanks for letting me help."

"Thank *you* for helping."

"Do you have classes to teach today?"

"Nope. I'm done for the day."

"Me too. Want to do something?"

She tilts her head. "Like what?"

"Make out?"

She chokes on a laugh.

"Just kidding. I really do want to kiss you right now, though."

In the small, enclosed space we eye each other. The air around us vibrates. She's so goddamn beautiful, her eyes liquid, her lips parted. A fierce ache burns from my belly to my balls.

"I want to kiss you too," she whispers.

I lean over and press my lips softly against hers. Once. Twice . . . then more firmly, opening my mouth, opening her to me, licking over her bottom lip.

My dick thickens, heat sliding through my veins. She lets out a little moan.

I lift a hand to slide it over her cheek, her jaw, her neck, cupping it as our mouths move together, and she curls a hand over my forearm. I want to touch her everywhere. Taste her everywhere. I can't get enough of her.

I draw back. We're parked on the street in a public place so we should probably stop. Still close enough to see every one of her long eyelashes, some of them coated with dark mascara but tiny ones at the corners still a pale gold, close enough to see the flecks of silver in her blue eyes, the texture of her plump lips, I breathe in her fresh floral-citrusy scent.

"We could go for a walk on the beach." I suggest, contrary to what I really want to do. "Or we could go to my place and I could, um, make us mojitos on the patio."

I await her response. I know what I want her to say. She's been so guarded with me at times, I expect her to opt for the beach.

Finally, she answers. "Let's go to your place."

Perfect.

My heart leaps into a galloping rhythm.

I want to break all the speed limits on the way home,

but I force myself to act casual and drive appropriately. My insides are jumping around like popcorn.

I park on the street. I have no idea what Ash's schedule is like. He works from home a lot, but he's covering the Dodgers this summer and he's been going to a lot of games.

Luck is with me, and we're home alone. The alarm beeps when we walk in and I enter the code to disarm it.

"I share this place with my brother," I tell her. "I guess he's out."

"You haven't said a lot about the rest of your family." She follows me in, looking around. "Nice place, by the way."

"Thanks." I'm uncomfortably aware it's messy—books, magazines, newspapers, and golf equipment litter the living room on our left. The dining room on the right is tidier. She peers up the oak stairs with the wrought iron railing, then moves into the living room.

"Love the fireplace." She trails her hand over the oak mantel.

"Yeah. I'll show you around." I lead her past the stairs and down the hall. "Ash's office is that room, and my bedroom is the next one. He has the whole upstairs—the master suite is really nice."

"How come he gets it?" she asks teasingly.

"Because he lives here all the time, and I'm only here part-time. I have an apartment in Pasadena too, that I share with a teammate."

"Ah."

I turn into the kitchen, cringing at what it might look like. I left early to get to the arena.

Luckily, Ash must have put the dishes in the dishwasher

and it's not bad. "Kitchen," I announce unnecessarily. "A little out-of-date, but okay. Now for mojitos. We need mint."

I open the back door, which leads out into our tiny yard. There's a patch of mint growing like crazy right near the door. I pluck a few sprigs and step back in.

"Can you grab two glasses from that cupboard?" I nod.

Arya gets the glasses while I rise off the mint then muddle it in the glasses with sugar. I retrieve a couple of limes from the bowl on the counter and the bottle of rum from another cupboard, and soon we have our drinks.

Arya sips hers. "Yum. Good job."

"Thanks. Let's take them outside."

It's a nice warm day, the sun shining right on the seating area out back.

"Oh, pretty," she says, following me.

The yard is tiny and there's no grass, but curved red brick outlines a few flower beds containing shrubs, and the red brick patio holds modular patio furniture with thick, gray cushions. We sit on the couch.

"This is so nice!" Arya looks around.

I point upward. "There's a deck off the master bedroom up there."

"Cool."

"I think Ash sunbathes in the nude there."

She laughs. "I really didn't need to know that."

"Fuck. I'm such an idiot." I rub my face.

She sets her glass on the outdoor coffee table, turns to me, and leans in. My body electrifies in shock as she kisses me.

When she eases back and meets my eyes, I blink. "Um . . ."

"I'm nervous too."

"Jesus. You'd think we're a couple of virgin teenagers." I pause, my eyes widening. "Oh . . . is that why you're nervous?"

She laughs softly. "No. I'm not a virgin."

"Okay. I mean if you were, that would totally be fine. I don't have a virginity thing. One way or the other, I mean. And I'm not either. A virgin."

She lays her soft hand on my cheek. "Somehow I didn't think so. But why are you so nervous?"

"Because . . ." I clench my teeth briefly. I can't tell her why. She'll run screaming. "Because I really like you."

"I like you too." She caresses my face, my stubble rasping against her hand.

I set down my drink too, cover her hand with mine, and turn my face so I can kiss her palm. I watch her carefully. Her lips part, her eyes are half closed, and a pulse flutters in her throat. "We can just take things slowly."

"Yes."

With a hand on her hip, I bring her closer and kiss her. She makes a little noise in her throat, opening for me. Our tongues slide together. She tastes fantastic. I want to devour her.

Easy.

I touch my fingertips to the side of her neck so gently, my thumb brushing her jaw, our mouths moving on each other in slow, lingering kisses. Her hand curves over my shoulder, around to the back of my neck, caressing me. I suck on her bottom lip. For a moment we pause, my nose resting alongside hers, our eyes flickering open to peer at each other. Heat swells inside me and shimmers around us.

I dive in for more kisses, hotter, faster. I slide my mouth down to the side of her neck and suck gently. Leaning her forehead on my shoulder, she shivers, then she tips her head back giving me access to her throat. I glide my tongue over her smooth skin and kiss her there too. She's panting and making needy little sounds, and a groan climbs my throat.

I shift her closer to the arm of the couch and lean her back onto it. She lifts one leg up onto the couch. Now I'm on my knees, our hands all over each other.

She toes off her flip-flops, letting them fall to the patio, grabbing at my shirt to tug me closer.

Okay, then!

I slowly slide my hand down from her shoulder over her collarbone. Watching her face, I wait for any resistance as I linger there, then leisurely cup her breast.

"Ohhh." She sinks her teeth into her plush bottom lip, her eyes fluttering closed. Her back arches, pushing her soft flesh into my hand.

"Christ," I mutter, gently squeezing, then kissing her again. "You feel so good . . ."

"Yes . . ."

We make out for a long time . . . kissing and touching, licking and sucking. I want to feel more skin, and it seems she does too, as she slips her hands beneath my T-shirt to explore my back.

I lift my head, panting. "This isn't exactly private." I jerk my head toward the next-door neighbor's house. We're on a corner, so there's only one, but still . . .

"Yeah." She gives me big blue eyes.

"Inside?"

She nods.

I take her hand and help her stand. Then I hesitate. "Um . . . wait right here. Just a minute."

She slowly sits, watching me, luckily her lips curved in a half-smile.

I dash to the door that leads to my bedroom. At the back of the house, it also has a door onto the patio. I don't have my fucking key. Argh!

I hustle back into the kitchen, down the hall, and through my room. It's a generous-size room, having been two smaller bedrooms at one time, with shiny oak floors, a big white-covered bed against the wall between two windows, and another door to an en suite bathroom. The room is dim, with the blinds on the two windows still closed, the only light coming through the frosted panes of the French door to the patio.

I scoop up the socks and underwear lying on the floor and shove them in the hamper, grab two towels and hang them in the bathroom, and kick a pair of shoes under the bed. Other than that, the place isn't too bad. Thank God I made my bed this morning.

I fling open the French door and step outside.

Arya's sitting, sipping her mojito, her face flushed.

She stands.

"This is my room," I explain. I hold out a hand for her to climb the two steps up and inside.

"How convenient," she murmurs, taking my hand.

"Right?" I smile and remove her drink from her grasp. I set it on the dresser and turn to her. "I, uh, just had to tidy up a bit."

Her eyebrows lift. "Oh." Her smile is so sweet. "Are you a bit of a slob?" Her fingers tease the back of my neck again.

"Just a bit." I hold up my thumb and forefinger about a half inch apart.

She laughs softly. "I am too."

"Whew."

I bend my head to kiss her again, wrapping my arms around her and gathering her up against me.

15

ARYA

I'M TREMBLING, INSIDE AND OUT, ACHING WITH NEED. My mouth opens to Harrison's and I love how his tongue feels against mine, sliding in and out of my mouth. He cups the back of my head, his other hand cradling my ass, while I basically try to climb him. I can't get close enough. I need more.

I let out a squeak when he hoists me up by my butt, and grip him with my thighs. He carries me over to the bed, which I'd noticed immediately upon entering the room. It's huge, king-size, with a crisp white duvet and white pillows, except the big square ones against the headboard, which are gray—charcoal gray—as is the suede headboard and all the walls in the room. It's masculine and seductive.

Not that I need much more seducing. Making out on the patio has me wet and throbbing.

He lays me down on the bed, tugging a pillow under my head, then stretches out next to me. With one arm beneath my neck, his other hand rests on my belly as he kisses me again. I want him to feel my boobs again, oh God, I want it. My nipples are hard, my breasts full and tender.

Then, praise Jesus, he glides his hand up to cup my breast. His hand tangles in my hair, our mouths sliding together in slow, lush kisses. My blood is on fire.

"Can we get rid of this?" He plucks at my tank top.

"Yes."

He works it up and over my head, leaving me in a pink lace bralette. "Sweet," he murmurs, kissing my chest. "Sweet and sexy."

I can tell the moment his gaze lands on my scar.

He touches it gently just above my right breast with his fingertips and lifts his gaze questioningly.

I say nothing, rolling toward him, pushing him down, climbing nearly on top of him.

His mouth curves into a smile before I kiss him again, his hands gripping my ass as I wriggle against his erection. Dear God, he's hard. And big. I love it. I want it. All of it.

I find his skin again, under his T-shirt, sleek and hot, then he rolls me onto my back, jackknifes up to sitting and tugs the back of his shirt over his head. He tosses it aside. My chest fills with air that won't exhale as I stare at him. He's perfect . . . smoothly muscled, tanned, and solid.

I trail my index finger down between his pecs.

"I think this is first base," he says.

I peek at him through my eyelashes. "No, no. Kissing is first base."

"Oh. I'm doing better than I thought, then."

I laugh and kiss his chest. "You're doing *great*." I finger the button of his jeans, but then I can't resist palming his cock. I give it a firm rub up and down.

He closes his eyes, groans, and falls back into the pillows. "Oh yeah."

I caress him there, enjoying the thick, firm length of him. Then he rolls me over onto my back, going onto his knees. He slides one hand under my butt, the other clasping my ankles and lifting my feet in the air. Curling his fingers into the waistband of my cropped leggings, he meets my eyes. I nod.

He drags them off me, past my knees, then over my feet, still in the air. When they're off, he runs his hands up my legs. "Gorgeous," he says hoarsely. He cups my pussy with one hand and leans down to kiss me again. He kisses my mouth, my jaw, my throat . . . down my chest. He kisses my scar. I lift my hips to press myself into his hand, needing more pressure there.

"Yeah," he murmurs, rubbing me. "So hot. I want to make you come."

"Ohhh. I want that too."

He tugs aside the lace cup of my bralette and kisses my nipple. My skin tingles and tightens, lust flipping low in my belly, and when he closes his lips over the tight peak and sucks, sensation darts right down between my legs where he's rubbing me.

He tugs at my nipple, presses on my clit, and I come, in a burst of sparks and rippling heat. I cry out, fingers clutching the duvet, my head going back.

He lifts his head and gives me a wicked smile. "There's one orgasm."

"I, uh . . . what?" I can barely breathe.

He eases up the bralette over my head, then pulls my panties off. His big hands land gently on my thighs and push them open. I'm quivering everywhere, my heart thumping.

"Christ, so beautiful." He's studying me so intimately. Heat flushes from my face down to my chest. "So pink and wet. I want to taste you."

"Ungh . . ." I've lost the ability to speak actual words. But I part my legs wider for him.

"Yeah . . ." He moves to kneel between my legs and lowers his head there.

Oh. My. God.

My body jolts as he licks me. Fire rips through me, lighting me up. He glides his tongue up and down my outer lips, which is lovely, then kisses me there, licking where my thigh joins my hip on one side, then the other. He's taking his time, and I'm dying.

Using his thumbs to part me, he licks deeper, slowly, as if he's savoring me. Tension builds inside me again, making me tremble. He makes appreciative growls, and then sweeps his tongue over my clit.

I nearly lurch right off the bed. I'm still so sensitive from that orgasm only moments ago. He presses me down with his hands on my hips, tonguing my clit, then slides his hand up my body to cover my breasts. He stretches out on his belly, settling in, tweaks my nipples, rubs my clit. Sensation swirls inside me, spiraling into a tight, almost painful coil that builds higher, stronger . . . and higher still. "Oh my God!" I shout as another orgasm bursts inside me, white-hot sensation sliding down my legs, spreading from my pelvis through my body.

He sucks my clit, drawing out the pleasure almost

unbearably, until I reach down for his head to push him away. "I can't . . . stop . . ."

He lifts his head with satisfied smile, then lays kisses over my quaking stomach, up between my breasts, and then onto my mouth. Rising up on his knees, he unfastens his jeans and shoves them down to his knees.

I'm still gasping for air, barely able to focus, but wow, what a vision in front of me—male perfection, all sculpted muscles, sleek skin, and sweet Jesus . . . his cock is magnificent, thick and ridged, the head smooth. My lips part, my chest rising and falling.

He moves to get his jeans all the way off, reaches for something from the drawer of the table beside the bed, then returns to his position between my legs. He holds up the condom, then rips it open and rolls it on.

"Thank you," I whisper, my shaking lips trying to smile.

His hands on his thick cock are so erotic . . . both big and solid. Powerful and yet gentle. In the quiet, dimly lit room, sunshine filtering between the blinds on the window, I feel like I've been transported to another reality, somewhere sensual and wanton and dreamlike.

My pussy is aching again. "Those orgasms were amazing," I say, my voice throaty. "But I need you inside me."

"I'm going to be," he rasps out. "I need it too. Arya, Jesus, watching you come like that . . ."

I don't know what my O face is like, but apparently it wasn't hideous.

He kisses me again, his fingers on the slippery folds between my legs, probing deeper this time. "Yeah," he murmurs. "So ready."

"Oh my God, yes." I pull up my knees as he grips his sheathed cock and finds my entrance.

It pinches at first, just a bit, and I wince.

He stops immediately. "Okay?"

I nod, biting my bottom lip. "You're, um, big."

"I'll go slow." He works his way in, inch by inch, and my body stretches and accommodates him. The sensation of him filling me is exquisite . . . I try to relax, but I'm so wound up, so ready to come again. It's crazy.

He strokes loose strands of hair off my forehand and gazes into my eyes. "Still okay?"

"Yes . . . oh yes . . ."

He's all the way inside, his groin pressed against mine, and the pressure on my sensitive mound is intense and erotic.

He's up on his knees, sliding out of me, then back in. Pleasure torches me, burning through me body. He touches my stomach and I grip his hand, my body rolling to meet his strokes, shocked gasps falling from my lips as he fills me so deeply. So completely.

He falls forward onto his fists and lowers his mouth to mine, swallowing my panting breaths. I rub the back of his neck and pull my legs up, my feet sliding along his hips. Nose to nose, eye to eye, we move together. It's heat and light, sunshine and fireworks, sweetness and enchantment.

My hands move everywhere—cupping his face as we kiss, caressing his hair, gripping his biceps. His strokes get faster . . . harder. Sensation builds in my core, a hot, throbbing glow. The bed bounces wildly.

He rears back up onto his knees, one hand on the inside of my knee, the other clasping my breast. I watch his face . . . oh God, so beautiful. Intense. Concentrated. Focused on me. My inner muscles tighten. I find my clit and circle it with my middle finger, and he groans.

"Do that," he rasps. "I'm close . . . want you to come again."

God, I want it too, so much. I rub faster, slicking up my arousal, and I topple into acute, all-pervading ecstasy, clenching on the thick flesh filling me.

"Yeah," he growls. "Fuck, that's hot. I'm there too, baby . . ." He lowers himself over me again, burying his face in the side of my neck. I wrap my arms and legs around him and hold him as he pounds into me with his powerful hips. the inside of my body so sensitive I feel like I'm still coming in wave after wave of pleasure.

He emits a long, raspy groan as he comes, muttering in my ear delicious curse words about how good it feels.

We're wrapped up in each other's arms, both of us panting and shaking and sweating. I press my open mouth to his shoulder in a long kiss, my heart quaking. This was amazing, more than anything I've ever experienced. It's almost frightening, it's so intense.

Neither of us move for a long time, holding on tightly to each other. Neither of us says anything. I'm shattered.

Eventually I feel Harrison's body relax a bit and his weight bears down on me. His breathing is heavy in my ear. I grip his shoulder. "You asleep?" I whisper.

He grunts. "Sorry. Am I crushing you?"

"It's okay. It feels good, but if you relax all the way I might not be able to breathe."

Slowly he lifts his head and smiles down at me. "Jesus. I think you destroyed me."

I drag my bottom lip between my teeth, my heart squeezing. "That's how I feel."

He eases out of my body, holding the condom on, and rolls off the bed. "Be right back."

I can't move. I can barely think.

He returns a moment later and lifts me off the bed

"Eeek!"

He holds me against him and yanks down the covers, then settles me back on the mattress before joining me. We move together like magnetic puzzle pieces, naturally fitting and fusing. I'm floating, drunk on pleasure and hormones and Harrison.

We doze a little. The next time I open my eyes the room has darkened, although it's still light outside the French door. This feeling of being held so snugly against Harrison's strong body, his hair-roughened legs twined through mine, his arms around me . . . I can't even describe it. I haven't felt this secure and safe in a long time. I never want it to end.

I study his face, my eyes moving over the faint bump on his nose, the scar on his eyebrow.

My heart thumps.

Harrison's eyes flicker open, his short, thick eyelashes lifting to reveal his beautiful blue eyes. This close I can see glints of cobalt and icy blue. The corners of his wide mouth lift. "Hi."

"Hi."

His hands move on me in leisurely strokes that both soothe and excite.

"I'm hungry," he says.

I blink, then grin at his unexpected statement. "Worked

up an appetite?"

"It *is* dinnertime."

"What?"

"It's six-thirty."

"Holy shit."

He chuckles. "I'll order something in."

"Um . . ." Should I leave?

"You're not leaving," he says, apparently reading my mind. "I have to feed you."

Okay, then. I smile. "All right, then."

"How about sushi?"

I don't move. Uh . . .

"Kidding," he says with a grin. "Thai?"

"No shrimp."

He gives me a thumbs-up and reaches down over the side of the bed. He rises with his phone in his hand. "Hang on . . . let me open the app."

After a moment, he shows me a menu. "Spring rolls . . . the fresh ones. We can get vegetarian."

"Okay."

"And . . . pad kee mao. With chicken?"

"Sure."

"This is my favorite—khao soy, with beef."

I read the description. I've never had either of these dishes, but they sound delicious.

He places the order and sets his phone down. Stretching out on his side, head propped on his elbow, he studies me.

Heat suffuses my body. The way he looks at me . . . like he wants me again . . . slays me. This is heady, feeling so desired, the sole focus of his intense attention.

"You're beautiful," he says. "Inside and out."

"Oh." I blink rapidly. "Thank you." I set my hand on his chest. "I think you are too."

He covers my hand with his and holds it there. His heart thumps in a slow, steady rhythm against my palm.

"I know you weren't interested in me at first," he says.

My forehead tightens.

"But I'm glad you finally agreed to go out with me. Maybe we could . . . keep going? Give this dating thing a shot?"

I'm still apprehensive and hesitant, but I want to be brave enough to go for something I want. *I am brave.* "Maybe we could."

He nods.

"And just for the record, it's not that I wasn't interested. Okay, maybe the first couple of times I thought you were a big joker, making fun of my class."

He closes his eyes. "Sorry. That wasn't my intent." He opens his eyes and holds my gaze. "The truth is, I was so attracted to you, I was trying maybe a bit too hard."

My lips tip upward. "Oh yeah?"

"Yeah."

"Well, I was attracted to you too. But I haven't dated for a while, and I'm a little nervous about it."

The corners of his eyes tighten. "Bad experience?"

I hold his gaze and nod slowly.

"Okay. I get it." He lifts my hand to his mouth and kisses it. "We'll just take it easy. Have fun. Okay?"

Now my heart is thumping too, and my veins are filled with an excited fizziness. I really like Harrison, and like he said . . . maybe we can give this dating thing a shot.

16

HARRISON

I'm probably crazy to be doing this. I'm supposed to be focused on hockey right now, on proving that I can play well enough for the team to need me, and keep a spot on the team permanently. Proving that Coach was wrong—I haven't been coasting. I'm supposed to be working my ass off.

Also, my dad is dying. I should be spending time with him.

Not starting a relationship with someone.

But I can't *not* do this. More than ever, I'm convinced that Arya and I are supposed to be together. I won't make the mistake of telling her that again, and I'll respect her hesitation if she's getting over a bad relationship, but I still believe it. I can do both . . . can't I? Play hockey and prove myself, and prove myself to Arya?

I hope I can.

Now that I've had Arya in my bed, now that I've been inside her, now that I've made her come with my fingers and my tongue and my dick . . . there's no going back. I'm not letting her go.

I have to let her go, though, to answer the door when our Thai food arrives.

I roll out of bed and pull on my jeans to answer the door, then unload the food onto the small kitchen table. Arya joins me, dressed in her leggings and tank top. She skipped the bra, and I approve of this, as I enjoy the sight of her nipples through the thin cotton. My dick also enjoys it.

I hand her a plate and a pair of chopsticks, and we sit and eat together.

"Delicious," she pronounces after a few bites of the khao soy.

"This is my favorite. I could eat it every day."

"I see why. I think I could too."

She looks around the kitchen as we eat, taking in the bowl of fruit, the blender that I use to make protein shakes, the double wall oven, and the extensive collection of utensils hanging behind the cooktop. "Who cooks? You or your brother?"

"We both do." I pick up a piece of beef. "He eats more junk food than I do, but he still likes to work out and eat healthy. He still plays hockey in a rec league."

"That's good. Is he working tonight?"

"Guess so. He doesn't always keep my informed of his whereabouts."

"That reminds me, I should text Taj and tell him where I am."

"I'd be happy to take you home later," I say. "If you're okay with that."

Her fingers go still on her phone. "Okay," she says slowly.

"Don't worry, I'm not a stalker," I joke.

She stares at her phone, and once again I feel like I just said the wrong thing. But she smiles and says, "Good to know." Then she taps in a message to her friend.

A while later, she sets down her chopsticks, pats her stomach, and groans. "I am so full."

"Yeah." I lean back in my chair. "So worth it, though."

"I love food."

I grin. "Me too. What's your favorite food? I know it's not shrimp."

She laughs. "I have too many faves. Pizza. Cake. Ice cream."

"Oh hell yeah. I *love* ice cream. What kind of ice cream?"

"I'd eat pretty much anything, but there's a little place not far from Prana—Leo's Creamery—and I love everything they make. English toffee. Lemon curd. Matcha green tea. They make everything themselves."

"Sounds amazing."

"I'll take you there."

I fucking love the sound of those words. I want to pump a fist in the air and cheer. "Sounds good," I say casually. "What are other favorite foods?"

"I love burgers and fries. And . . . okay, you might think this is weird." Sparkling blue peeps up at me through long eyelashes.

"What?"

"My favorite comfort food if I don't have ice cream is sweetened condensed milk. Out of the can."

I stare. "What?"

She grins. "Don't knock it until you try it. Just open up the can and get a spoon. It's delicious."

"I'm open-minded. I'll try anything once."

"That's good to know." She sounds flirty.

"I hope you're thinking about the athletic sex positions I've been fantasizing about us trying out."

She chokes. "Uh, well. I wasn't, but . . ." Her lips twitch. "I'm open-minded too."

I lean forward and say softly, "Good to know."

I reach for her hand and pull her out of her chair. "I think we need to start researching."

She laughs and lets me tug her down the hall and back into my bedroom.

WE PRACTICE TUESDAY, AND IT'S A PRETTY LAID-BACK, EASY practice with lots of joking around. Everyone's feeling good as we head into the playoffs, even though we got our asses handed to us last game.

I laugh my butt off when Scotty and Eddie are bitching at each other, apparently about Eddie's lack of dental hygiene, but then it's my turn to get pranked. I pick up a bottle of Gatorade, tip my head back, and squeeze it to direct the beverage into my mouth. We don't touch the bottles with our mouths, since we all share them. But when I squeeze it, the cap pops off and Gatorade spills all over my face and down onto my practice jersey. Some asshole had loosened the cap.

This cracks up a bunch of guys, of course, Nicky falling down on the ice he's laughing so hard. "Come on, that's not even original," I grouse at him.

"Still funny, though."

Coach calls me out when I'm skating around in my own little world when we're supposed to be working. "Fucking pay attention!" he yells at me.

"He's thinking about his future wife," Scotty says.

Coach frowns.

Shit.

I need to focus. We have two home games left to play. Tomorrow night we're motivated to salvage our pride by beating Calgary, then our last game is against the Long Beach Golden Eagles, ending the season with a Beach Barn Battle. With the intense rivalry between the two teams, it will be a good game to end the regular season. We've both made the playoffs, though, and could face each other in the second round depending on what happens in the first round.

I convinced Arya to come to the game. She's going to bring a friend, maybe Janey, who I haven't met, or Taj. The game is ostensibly sold out, but there are always tickets for the players. The ones we don't use are released for sale to the public on game day.

Wednesday after our morning skate, I go see Dad in his office. I don't do this very often, but I haven't seen him since that day Mom told us about the diagnosis. I need to go home for my nap, but I have time to check in on him.

I find Dad in his office with Théo, talking about meeting up with Vancouver in the first round and our potential travel schedule.

"Hey, come on in," Théo says, waving a hand. "You here to see Grandpa?"

"Yeah." I feel shitty keeping stuff from Théo. Of all the family members, he needs to know what's going on. He needs to make sure Dad's not making bad decisions or doing anything to embarrass the team, like forgetting the name of the commissioner of the league or publicly calling him an asshole. I need to talk to the rest of the family about this, especially Mom, I guess. "How's it going?"

"Good." Dad smiles at me. "How was your morning skate?"

"Fine. We're feeling good about the game tonight."

"I hope so. They killed us in Calgary. What the hell happened?"

I grimace. "No excuses."

"You didn't seem all in," Dad says, frowning. "Is everything okay?"

I stare at him. No, everything is *not* okay. Jesus Christ. My heart drops to my feet. I try not to look at Théo.

"Rumor has it there's a new woman in his life," Théo says.

"Ha!" Dad crows. "I knew it! Who is she?"

Now I slide my gaze over to Théo and lift my eyebrows.

He grins. "Tell us, man."

"It's just . . . we've only gone out a couple of times," I mumble.

"I heard it's serious."

I narrow my eyes at him. He's yanking my chain. And fuck the guys who are gossiping about me to my nephew. Ah. I know who it is. Bellsy. He lives in the same building as

Théo, and Everly and Lacey are friends. I'm gonna punish him. Maybe the old cutting-the-skate-laces trick

"Have I met her?" Dad asks.

That stops me short. I close my eyes. He doesn't know. I clear my throat. "No, Dad, not yet. She's coming to the game tomorrow night, but you won't see her then."

"My birthday's coming up," Dad says. "Your mom is planning a party."

"She is?" I don't know if this is a good idea. "I'll talk to her about it."

"She's here," Dad says. "She's with Kate."

"Oh." I remember Mom's been coming to the office with him so she can drive. Has she taken away his car keys? Ugh. That could be another disaster, if he was driving and got in an accident . . . or, God forbid, killed someone. We *do* need another family meeting to deal with some of these issues. And when are they going to talk to Mark and Matthew, so we can tell everyone else? Especially Théo. "Maybe I'll see her before I go." I force a smile. "Need my nap."

"You're the most superstitious of my kids," Dad says, shaking his head. "Make sure you wear your lucky cup."

Jesus. That was when I was eight years old. Now I wear lucky socks. "Okay, Dad." I turn to the door. "I'll see you guys later." They'll both be at the game tonight and Thursday's season finale.

Instead of looking for Mom, I go to Everly's office. I find her and Bellsy all snuggled up there. Well, not literally. He's there and they're talking in low voices, heads together.

"Hi."

Everly lifts her head and smiles. "Hey, guy. What's up?"

"I just checked in on Dad. What's happening?"

Her smile fades but doesn't totally disappear. Bellsy watches her with a look on his face that's sympathetic and protective. He rubs her back.

It's weird seeing him with my sister like this, but I have to say I'm really happy for her. She's always been so perfect, so on top of things, I always wondered what guy would ever take her on. I never thought it would be a party animal like Bellsy who grooves through life without a care. Yet he seems different too, more settled and less . . . frantic. Not that I know him that well.

"They still haven't talked to Mark and Matthew."

Mom and Dad asked us not to say anything to others until that happened. Then we'd all figure out how we're going to deal with it. Obviously, we want to maintain Dad's privacy.

"Damn."

"Yeah."

"What's the holdup?"

"Honestly, I think it's just the season." She runs a hand through her hair. "Everyone's so focused on hockey and the playoffs right now."

"True. And that's not going to end for a while."

"Yes. It's fine, I guess. It's not like . . ." She swallows. "Like Dad's going to die tomorrow."

I nod. "Yeah. But . . . there are serious things we need to figure out."

She bites her lip. "Do you think we need to talk about it sooner?"

"I don't know." I blow out a frustrated breath. "We don't need any more shit hitting the news."

"I'll talk to Mom."

"Dad says she's here again."

Everly nods. "She's here almost every day now."

"People are going to wonder why."

"I think most people here have figured things out. People that deal with Dad all the time. Théo's been really good at stepping in, though, and he's good with handling Dad."

I mention the birthday party.

Everly sighs. "Yes. But Mom's keeping it small. Just immediate family."

"Okay. Dad wants me to bring Arya."

"Do you think that's a good idea?"

"Everyone has to meet her sometime."

She gives me a weird look. "Things can't be that serious between you two already."

Bellsy snorts. "They're getting married, didn't you know?"

"Ahahaha. That's so funny."

"Shut up, Bellsy," I say mildly.

He grins.

Everly looks between us. "Getting married? What am I missing?"

"Nothing. Okay, I'm going home for a nap." I nod at Bellsy. "You should too, instead of molesting my sister in her office.

Everly laughs.

"I'm on my way," Bellsy says. "See you later."

WE MANAGE TO BEAT CALGARY TUESDAY NIGHT. Wednesday, we practice.

First, we have yoga class. It's almost getting to be my favorite part of practice.

But really, nothing will ever be as good as being on the ice, and probably a lot of why I like yoga has to do with Arya.

Now she's mine. We're really dating. I need to act casual about it, though. I don't want to embarrass her. We're both professionals.

This class seems a lot looser than others. I guess because we know we're in the playoffs and we only have one game left, everyone's pretty relaxed. Almost punchy.

"This is the Plow Pose," Arya says, to the chill tune she's playing. "Exhale and bend from the hips joints, and slowly lower your toes to the floor above and beyond your head."

Jesus, I can't breathe with my insides all squished up like this.

"You can continue to press your hands against your back, pushing your back up toward the ceiling . . . or you can release your hands and stretch your arms out behind you on the floor, opposite your legs."

"Did you just fart, man?"

After a couple of beats of stunned silence everyone cracks up. I fall over, laughing, and look at Scotty glaring at Bergie.

"Yeah," Bergie admits. "Couldn't help it."

"Ah! That's nasty!" Face screwed up, Scotty rolls away, waving his hands.

Bergy rolls his eyes, but he's still laughing. "Oh, come on, it's not that bad."

"You gotta stop eating those spicy burritos, man."

Arya is collapsed into a quivering heap up front, her face down on the mat so I can't see her laughing, but I know she is. She's a good sport.

She collects herself and rises to her knees. "Okay guys, if you haven't farted yet, you're not doing it right."

Everyone collapses into laughter again.

"Alright, let's do Prasarita Padottanasana," Arya says. "Wide-legged standing forward bend."

We all get to our feet. Hopefully Bergy has released all his gas. Truthfully, sometimes it's hard to hold it in, during some poses.

"Stretch your arms straight out to your sides and widen your stance until your ankles are directly below your wrists."

I shuffle my feet wider apart.

"Root your feet firmly in the mat. Make sure your weight is even between your big toes, baby toes, inner heels and outer heels."

I focus on the tiny adjustments I have to make, feeling all four points of my feet pressing into the mat.

We follow Arya's directions, hands on hips.

"Continue to lengthen your torso as you fold forward. When you're about halfway down, lower your hands and bring your fingertips to the mat beneath your shoulders. Move your weight slightly forward on the balls of your feet."

She talks us through it, and we walk our hands back, letting our heads hang, then resting them on the mat.

I hear a thunk behind me, a muffled curse, then another thud.

"Jesus Christ," Russ mutters, followed by a loud "oof."

With a sigh, I give up the pose to see what's going on. Three guys are lying on the floor all tangled up with each other. I move my head from side to side disapprovingly. "What the hell?"

"He started it." Russ points at Nicky.

"I lost my balance." Nicky tries to extricate himself. "Sorry."

"He knocked me over and I fell into Archie." Russ shakes his head.

Arya straightens to regard the mess. "It's like dominoes," she says calmly. "Are you all okay?"

They're lying on the floor laughing their asses off, so I think they're okay.

"This class is a little off the rails," Arya says. "I'll let it go this time, but next time, you're going to have to be in the right headspace to prepare for playoffs."

I meet her eyes, which are dancing with amusement. Damn, she's good.

I GET TO THE ARENA EARLY FOR OUR THURSDAY NIGHT GAME and sneak into the visitors' dressing room. My gaze roams over the cubbies until it lands on JP's jersey. I grab his gloves and stuff them with the Dubble Bubble gums I have in my pocket, pushing the wrapped gum right down into the fingers. I startle and glance around when I hear a noise, but it's out in the corridor. Quickly I finish up. I give the gloves a shake and nothing falls out. Perfect! I put them back just how I found them and slip out of the room, chuckling.

I go through my pregame routine, dressing the way I always do. When I'm dressed, I head out into the hall before everyone else and do my moves—some stick handling with no puck, lunges, a few jumps. Then Teddy opens the door and the other guys start coming through. I slash Bergie's knee, bump gloves with Scotty, bear-hug Bellsy and hold my stick butt end to the floor while Jimmy uses it to practice a couple of face-offs.

The atmosphere in the building is electric; it always is when these two teams play each other. A lot of Eagles fans travel to their team's away games here, so things can get a bit rowdy in the stands.

Glen, our announcer, calls out the intro. "And noooooooow, here they aaaaare, your California Condoooooooors!"

Lights are flashing, and there's smoke and deafening noise from the sound system and the cheering crowd as we all take the leap onto the ice and do a lap.

Glen announces the starting lineup, we stand for the anthem, and then Jimmy takes the face-off. And wins it.

17

ARYA

Janey and I arrive at the Coliseum. Harrison gave us directions yesterday about where to park and which entrance to use. I'm more familiar with the Coliseum since I've taught classes there, and I lead the way inside. Making our way through the crowded concourse, we find a small shop selling Condors clothing and memorabilia, and I purchase a Condors baseball cap. "In case someone gets a hat trick," the guy behind the sales register says with a grin.

I laugh. "Right!"

"Don't worry, if it happens, hats will be on sale after that so you can get another one."

"Good to know."

We pick up popcorn and beers and find our seats. They're in a corner, about the middle of the lower bowl, so they have a pretty good view. The players are on the ice warming up.

"Okay, where is he?" Janey asks, dipping her hand into the bucket of popcorn.

I scan the ice. It's hard to find him among all the Condors' jerseys and helmets, but I know he's number twenty. I spot him before I can see the number, though—I recognize the size and shape of him. "There. Number twenty." I point.

With "Jumpman" by Drake blasting through the arena, we watch the players skate around and shoot the puck at the net. It's been a while since I went to a live hockey game and I forgot how electric and exciting the atmosphere is. My head bobs along with the beat of the music.

I search out number thirteen for the Golden Eagles at the other end of the ice. "That's JP, Harrison's nephew," I tell Janey, pointing. "He told me almost his whole family will be here tonight, since they're playing each other. His half brother is the coach of the Eagles." I look at the bench, but I wrinkle my nose, as I don't know who he is.

I've told Janey a few things about Harrison's big, crazy family.

Harrison takes a lap around behind the goal, and as he does so, he looks up, right at me. A smile breaks across his face, a smile big enough for me to see behind his visor, and he lifts a big gloved hand as he glides around the curve of the boards.

"He saw you," Janey says. She bumps me with her shoulder.

"Yes." I tamp down my urge to squeal.

The horn sounds to end the warm-up and the players slowly start leaving the ice. Harrison takes one more shot at the empty net, hitting the back of it with the puck, then hops off the ice. I think he glances my way before he disappears.

I shove popcorn in my mouth and look around the arena as we wait for the game to start. "I wonder where the rest of Harrison's family is. Probably Everly is here. Oh, her boyfriend was out there too. I completely forgot about that. We have to watch for him when the game starts."

"I know nothing about hockey," Janey says. "You'll have to tell me what's going on."

"I don't know that much either. I went to games in college, but that was a few years ago."

I flip through the game-day program we were handed as we entered the section where we're sitting. There's Harrison, an unsmiling, official photo. He looks . . . fierce.

The game gets off to a fast and physical start, both teams immediately slamming each other into the boards. My eyes pop open wide when I see it's JP hitting Harrison. "Whoa."

Janey and I exchange looks of alarm.

They rough each other up a little bit, but it looks like . . . they're smiling. Then they slap each other's backs and skate toward their own bench.

"What was that?" I wonder aloud.

The play resumes, fierce and heated. The Condors are heading down the ice toward the Eagles net when two players collide. It happens so quickly, I'm not really sure who hit whom, but a Condor player is lying facedown on the ice. The whistle blows and every Condor on the ice converges around the Eagles player involved in the hit. There's a lot of pushing and shoving. The refs jump in and start separating people, and a guy from the Condors bench runs over to the player on the ice.

The fans behind us are shouting to "take that motherfucker out," I guess referring to the player who hit the Condors guy. Eeep. Bloodthirsty.

I watch, my breathing suspended, my attention darting from the guy on the ice (who I quickly determine is Scotty, dammit, I hope he's okay) and the mêlée of players near the net. Harrison is in that mêlée, and I chomp on my lip as I observe the scuffle. Eventually things settle down, Scotty gets up and skates off, and the coach of the Condors is standing on the bench, shouting.

The ref goes over to talk to him. I have no idea what they're saying but it's certainly a heated discussion. On the scoreboard, a video of the hit is playing, slowed down, and the crowd roars in disapproval as we all see the hit in slow motion. The Eagles get a penalty, which makes the crowd happy, but I'm still anxious about Scotty. He's on the bench, bent over, shaking his head.

"I hope he's okay."

"I forget that you know all those guys now." Janey leans into me.

"I know. I'm not sure this is good. I might have a heart attack before the game is over."

"It's really physical," Janey says. "I love it!"

The Condors score a goal on that power play, so yay! It's a goal by the young kid, Edvin Rintala, assisted by Harrison and Olle Larsson. Janey and I high-five each other as the fans cheer around us, nearly blowing the roof off the Coliseum.

I'm watching Harrison more than I'm watching the game. Even when he's on the bench, I'm fascinated, seeing one of the trainers hand him a towel so he can wipe down the inside of his visor, lean into the guy next to him—Nicky, I think—and gesture as they talk intently, then leap to his feet when his team gets control of the puck and flies toward the Eagles' goal.

The red light goes on, the horn blasts, the crowd cheers, and Harrison is celebrating with his teammate on the bench.

Seeing him like this reminds me of the day I watched him practice and decided I'd go out with him. He's so engaged in everything that's happening, so focused, and clearly very damn talented when he's on the ice.

And yet, off the ice . . . he's kind. Gentle. Thoughtful. Maybe a little overeager in some respects, but not aggressive. I want to believe that. I want to trust my instincts about him.

AFTER THE GAME, WHICH THE CONDORS WIN FOLLOWING AN overtime shoot-out, I'm exhausted.

Janey and I stop by the Golden Fish. We hang out with Taj and Ziggy, Arlo and Indigo, and have a drink. "I didn't even play the game," I say, laughing at how stressful it was.

"Imagine how the players feel," Taj says.

"Wow, no kidding. They work so hard." I'm in awe of their fitness and stamina, their toughness, both mental and physical. Can I really teach them anything? I'm questioning that now.

Taj is going to Ziggy's place tonight, so Janey drives me home.

"Thanks for inviting me," she says, her voice alive with enthusiasm. "I think I'm a new hockey fan!"

"Well, good. I'm glad it wasn't too boring for you."

"Not at all! We should go to the playoff games."

"Okay, great!"

Inside, I lock the door, turn on the lights, and pull my phone out of my small purse.

I send Harrison a text congratulating him on the overtime goal he scored. It didn't win the game, that was Rintala's goal, but still, he scored, and I'm happy for him. I don't know where he is; he probably had to do stuff after the game. Maybe he's out with his friends. It's a Friday night.

He texts me back to say thanks.

Then I ask,

Are you coming to SUP yoga tomorrow?

He's done a couple of water classes when he can.

Sorry, can't. We have a team meeting.

Okay, no worries.

I'll have a busy day tomorrow. Maybe we can have dinner?

Sure, sounds good.

After my Saturday classes, which end at two o'clock, I decide to ride down to the beach. It's definitely spring now, the sun stronger and warmer, the air soft. I pedal along the path, gazing across the wide expanse of pale sand toward the glistening ocean. Lots of other people are enjoying the warm weather too, sitting on the sand, walking, biking.

A vast feeling of well-being expands inside me and I smile as I ride. At this moment, I feel so lucky. Yeah, I've had some shitty shit happen in my life, but right now, I feel good. I have friends, I have—I guess—a new boyfriend who I really like, I have work that I love. And how can you be down when the sun is blazing in a clear blue sky and I'm at the frickin' beach?

I ride all the way to Santa Monica Pier and decide to stop at a little ice cream place for a treat. It's not as good as Leo's Creamery, but I basically love any kind of ice cream.

I study the menu, trying to decide between a waffle cone with toasted almond ice cream, or a s'mores sundae. Gah! Finally, I place my order for the cone.

Holding it, I wheel my bike over to a picnic table, where I take a seat facing the sun and turn my face up to the sky, before licking the ice cream. Absolute deliciousness—cold, creamy, sweet.

I enjoy people watching, especially at the pier, so as I eat my cone, I take in my surroundings, watching a teenage couple flirt, a family try to soothe a crying baby, and a girl with the cutest dog ever that I really, really want to pet.

Then I do a double take.

I stare at the couple standing across the wooden deck near the railing of the pier. I'm not that close, but . . . that looks like Harrison.

My stomach clenches as he laughs and leans in closer to

the woman. She's pretty—long shiny, dark hair, wow, killer long legs in a pair of short shorts.

He nuzzles her hair and . . . oh my God . . . kisses her cheek.

My mouth falls open and my head jerks back. Suddenly I feel cold.

Smiling, she turns her face to him so their mouths meet.

A rock lodges in my chest. It can't be him.

I lick my bottom lip, then bite it. I slowly stand and make my way toward the building that houses the ice cream shop. Staying close to the wall, I approach the corner.

Neither of them is paying attention to me, but still, I hug the corner of the building and peer around it.

Fuckety fucking fuck.

It *is* Harrison!

My skin tingles everywhere, and my head goes fuzzy. I can't think. What the fuck?

He had a team meeting . . . then said he'd be busy.

Oh yeah . . . he's getting busy all right.

I back up around the corner and lean my head against the wall, squeezing my eyes shut. My stomach is a mass of knots and tears burn my eyes. I don't understand this.

We agreed we're dating.

But I guess we never talked about being exclusive. Am I an idiot for assuming that?

Yes, apparently I am. Once again.

Fuck, I should have known better! I can't rely on my own instincts when it comes to judging character.

I need to get out of here. I feel like I'm going to throw up.

I toss my cone into a trash bin, grab my bike and jump onto it. Pedaling away, I blink back tears and grit my teeth.

Do I have the right to be hurt and angry? We just started seeing each other.

We had sex. That should mean something. Shouldn't it?

Maybe I'm a naïve little girl from the north, thinking that. Maybe it doesn't mean anything to him. Maybe he's seeing lots of other women. He never promised me anything.

But the things he said . . . how hard he tried to get me to go out with him. Why would he do that if he was still seeing other women?

My head is spinning faster than the tires on my bike. Legs pumping furiously, I turn away from the beach and head up Rose Avenue toward Taj's house.

Fuck Harrison Wynn.

Of course I have the right to be angry and hurt. I have the right to feel however I feel. And I'm fucking pissed.

I zig-zag through the residential streets till I'm home. I lock up my bike, stride into the house, and slam the door shut.

I'm not sure who I'm angrier at—Harrison or me, for being so stupid.

I retrieve my chunk of rose quartz from my bedroom, then sit on the living room floor in lotus position, palms in Jnana Mudra, a position known for its calming nature. The rose quartz will help with the negativity.

I close my eyes.

I use my failures as a stepping-stone.

I've learned from past mistakes. That doesn't mean I'll never screw up again. And I'll learn from this screw-up too.

Somehow.

No, I will. *I can do this.*

I focus on my breathing, still too fast. I try to observe thoughts as they drift through my mind without getting involved with them or judging them, trying to just be aware of each mental note as it arises. I know I've tended to quickly judge experiences as good or bad. I need to balance my thoughts.

Thoughts of Harrison. His smile. His words. The fun I had with him. That's a good thing.

We can learn from everything.

I sit like that for about twenty minutes, I think. Then I open my eyes. My mouth droops glumly. I feel better, but truthfully, I'm still hurt.

I could beat myself up over letting my guard down and getting hurt, but I knew what I was doing. I was nervous about it. Okay, terrified. I convinced myself to go out with Harrison because I had to move forward with my life. I knew there was risk involved. I accepted the risk.

I am capable of anything.

Now regretting the ice cream I didn't eat, I rise to my feet and head to the kitchen. In the freezer I find the tub of Cherry Garcia. When I pry the lid off, I'm disappointed to see it's nearly empty. Oh well. I grab a spoon and dig into the ice cream. When it's gone, I open the cupboard, hoping for a can of sweetened condensed milk. Score!

I eat that too.

What am I going to say to Harrison? What am I going to do?

He said maybe we'd go out for dinner tonight.

When the can is empty, I set it on the counter and go get my phone from my yoga bag.

There's a text from Harrison.

> What time should I pick you up for dinner?
> Anywhere you want to go?

My bottom lip pushes out sadly. Ending things by text is shitty. On the other hand, I don't really want to go for dinner with him.

> We need to talk.

Good, good. I'm a breakup cliché. I wait for his response.

> Okaaaay . . .

> I don't feel up for dinner, but maybe you could come by for a few minutes?

My phone rings.

I scrunch up my face, then answer it. "Hi."

"Hi, beautiful."

My heart bumps.

"What's going on?"

I don't answer right away. I haven't had time to figure out exactly what I'm going to say. I want to be honest, but it's hard to admit how hurt I am. Finally, I say, "I think we may have had a misunderstanding about this dating thing."

Silence.

Then, "I'll be over in ten minutes."

I swallow. "Okay."

I'm still in my leggings and tank top from my classes earlier. I look down at myself. I should change. But it doesn't matter what I'm wearing.

I change.

Wearing jeans and a pink T-shirt that says NAMASTE BITCHES on the front, I splash cold water on my face, then swipe on mascara and pink lip gloss.

A few minutes later, I open the door to Harrison. Wings flutter wildly in my belly, trying to climb up my esophagus.

He gives me a look—steady, inquiring, solemn. "Hi."

"Come in."

I twist a piece of hair between my fingers as I follow him into the living room. He doesn't sit but turns to face me. He tilts his head. "Misunderstanding?"

I drop my butt onto a chair, since my knees feel like pudding. "I saw you today. At the pier." I meet his eyes, studying his reaction.

His eyebrows pull down. "What? I wasn't at the pier."

"I *saw* you, Harrison." I sigh. "And the girl you were with. Kissing her."

His mouth falls open. "*What?*"

"It's okay." I take a deep breath. "Like I said, I think we misunderstood each other. I didn't realize you were seeing other people too. It . . . took me by surprise."

"I'm not seeing anyone else! Jesus. What the hell are you talking about?"

"You don't have to deny it. I don't like playing games. Just be honest."

"Are you accusing me of lying to you?" His eyes narrow.

I worry my bottom lip with my teeth. He seems genuinely confused. And getting angry.

"You *are* lying," I whisper.

He shakes his head, looks up at the ceiling, then back at me. "I'm not lying, Arya. We haven't known each other long, but I'd think you know I'm not a liar."

"You're right, we haven't known each other long. And I don't know what I know! Apparently, I'm a terrible judge of character. Look, I'm not . . . I'm just saying, I was surprised, I didn't expect that, and . . ." I stop, my throat thickening. "I'll admit it hurt."

"*I wasn't at the pier.*" His voice is low, his jaw clenched. "I had a team meeting. It went long. I hung around and talked to some of the guys for a while and had lunch. Then I went shopping for a birthday present for my dad. In West Hollywood. *Not* the pier."

My hands are shaking, my heart is banging. I don't know what to say. "I *saw* you."

He stares back at me, eyes clear and guileless.

I'm so confused! He seems sincere. But I know what I saw. I don't understand why he's lying.

Suddenly his eyes fly open wide. "Oh shit."

I blink. Did he just remember he *was* there? That's crazy.

He pulls out his phone and swipes and taps the screen, then holds it to his ear. "Hey," he says. "Where are you?" He listens. "On a date?" Again, he listens. "Who is she?" He nods. "What time did you get there?" Then he grins.

Now my jaw goes slack. Who is he talking to? I twist another strand of hair, watching him.

Harrison laughs. "Hey, take a selfie of you two and send it to me. No, really."

I squint at him incredulously. What is going on?

"Just do it. Okay. See you tomorrow, right?" He ends the call, then slowly walks toward me as he watches his phone. He crouches down beside my chair. His phone dings with an incoming message and he lets me see the screen as he opens it, then taps on the image attached.

I stare at the photo.

I look up at Harrison.

"I guess I never mentioned that my brother Asher is my *twin* brother."

18

HARRISON

Arya stares at me. "Twins?" She looks back at my phone where Asher is standing against the railing of the Santa Monica Pier with his arm around the shoulders of a woman I don't know. Her name is Camilla.

"Yep. Identical. He's older by half an hour or something." I shrug.

"That's . . . who it was." She closes her eyes. "You weren't lying."

"I don't lie, Arya."

She falls back into the chair, eyes still closed. "I'm so sorry."

Maybe I should be mad, but I actually find this kind of funny. I get why she thought it was me. It's happened before. "When we were teenagers, someone told my girlfriend she thought I was cheating on her. There was a big drama until everyone figured out it was Asher. One time I was going down an escalator in a mall and I saw Asher on another escalator and I started waving at him and yelling. I was waving at myself in a mirror."

She chokes out a laugh.

"We used to fuck up our hockey coaches all the time. It was hilarious."

She's smiling but her eyes are still closed.

"Arya. Look at me."

She opens her eyes and bites her lip in a cute and sexy way. "I'm sorry."

"It's okay. I get it. I'm not seeing anyone else. I don't *want* to see anyone else. I don't know how you could even think that."

She looks like she's in pain. "It's me. I'm messed up."

"We're all a little messed up. But it's not crazy that you thought Asher was me. It's happened a lot."

She rolls her head from side to side against the back of the chair. "I shouldn't have . . . I should have trusted you . . . I don't know if I'll ever be able to trust anyone."

I don't know what happened in her "bad relationship." Maybe someday she'll tell me. Obviously she's been hurt, and I fucking hate that.

I want her to trust me. I want that more than anyfuckingthing.

Pulling in a deep breath, I spy the pink rock on the coffee table. I pick it up and curve both hands around it. "Did this help?"

She gives me a reluctant smile. "Of course."

"Good."

"You should be angry," she murmurs. "I didn't trust you."

"Yeah. It does bug me that you didn't. If you'd gone up

to Asher and talked to him, you'd have found out the truth."

"Oh God! I couldn't have done that! I was mortified. I just wanted to get out of there."

"Yeah. I guess I understand that. And I'm sorry I never mentioned I have a twin. And you've never met him. But you'll meet him tomorrow." I set the quartz on the table.

Dad's birthday party is tomorrow, and I convinced her to come.

"You still want me to come to the party?" She eyes me doubtfully.

"Just to prove I'm not lying." I stick my tongue in my cheek.

She scrunches her face up.

"I'm teasing! Yes, I want you to come."

"I think you'd be better off without me."

"That's just crazy." I hold her gaze. "Okay? Are we okay?"

Her eyes get shiny and her lips push out, but she nods. "I am, if you are."

"I am." I rise up on my knees, slide a hand behind her neck and pull her down so I can kiss her. Her lips are soft and sweet, but she's trembling. After a few soft kisses, I pick her up, switch us around so I'm sitting in the chair and she's on my lap and we're kissing again, deeper and hotter.

I didn't know what the hell was going on when she sent me that ridiculous text about a misunderstanding. My mind went nuts thinking up crazy scenarios. I drove like a wild man to get here and find out what was going on. I'm so fucking relieved that the problem was something so easy to solve.

"Where do you want to go for dinner?" I ask, my lips against her jaw.

"I don't know." Her head falls back and I kiss my way down to her throat.

"Where's Taj?"

"Out." She sighs.

I want her so goddamn bad. My dick is hurting. "How hungry are you?"

Her lips curve. "Starving." She meets my eyes. "For you."

"Thank fuck. Me too. I promise you food after." I stand, hands beneath her ass. "Where's your bedroom?"

She directs me down the short hall to the room on the right. I kick the door closed behind us in case Taj comes home and set about taking off her clothes while kissing her. "I like this shirt," I say, tugging it up over her head. "Sassy."

She laughs softly and her fingers move at the button of my jeans.

I want her naked, but I also want to explore, dragging my hands over her shoulders and down her arms, up her sides. I cup her breasts through her bra, a barely-there pink number, then stroke up over her collarbones, neck, and cup her face as I kiss her again.

She reaches behind her and unfastens her bra, letting it fall down her arms, and I lift my head to pull it off, studying her sweet curves, her nipples puckered into gorgeous rosy buds. I brush my palms over them, back and forth, and she sucks in a sharp breath. With my fingertips, I tease them more, watching them flush an even deeper pink, a flush that spreads up over her chest and neck and into her face. "Like that?"

"Mmm. Love it."

She has my jeans undone now and they drop to the floor. Hers take more work to get off. "Much as I love your ass in these tight jeans," I mutter, "they're kind of hard to get off."

She huffs out a laugh and drops to the side of her bed. "I know."

I peel them off, leaving her in pink lace panties. I'm about to reach for her to hoist her farther onto the bed, but she curls her fingers into the elastic waistband of my boxer briefs, and tugs them down, freeing my straining, aching cock.

"There," she murmurs, curling her soft fingers around my shaft, right at her face level.

My body goes electric. She teases her fingers over my groin, my thighs, dragging them through the pubic hair at the base of my cock, all the while studying my cock. It pulses in her hand, eager for more, for any scrap of attention she wants to give it. I grit my teeth in anticipation, my body tensing. She kisses the tip, then, and my dick jerks in her hand. She smiles and her little tongue comes out to lick all around the head, then swirl over the top.

"Christ." I slide my fingers into her hair, gently, holding her head as she licks everywhere, getting me wet, then opens her mouth and takes me. A groan rumbles in my chest.

Her wet lips slide up and down my shaft, her fingers curled at the base, and when her other hand caresses my balls, the top of my head nearly blows off as my body surges with pleasure.

"Okay," I rasp. "Enough. I want to fuck you. Want to come inside you."

She eases back with a sultry smile, her lips swollen and shiny. I step out of the briefs tangled at my ankles and reach for her, flipping her onto her belly. The pink thong panties don't cover much. I palm her ass cheeks and squeeze them gently before dragging the thong down her legs and tossing it aside. Lifting her hips, I take in the view. Sweet Jesus, it's heaven, pink and perfect, plump and juicy. I caress her cheeks again, then drag my hand between her plump outer lips.

"Fuck, so wet," I marvel, sliding my fingers back and forth.

Face pressed to the bed, she mumbles something I don't understand.

"Need a condom, babe, be right back." I nearly fall off the bed, trying to get to my jeans. As soon as I'm suited up, I kneel behind her again. I glide the head of my cock around her wetness to make it easier to slide into her. Watching my cock enter her pussy is the hottest thing ever. So are her moans and soft wordless cries as I fill her, penetrating her slowly. Deeply. I pulse in her tight channel once I'm fully in, holding back the instinct to pound into her until she's screaming and I'm shouting. My skin buzzes, heat pumping through my veins.

Carefully, I slide in and out, then I pick up the pace. She pushes up onto her hands, arms straight, tossing a sexy glance at me over her shoulder. I fuck her harder, my hands gripping her waist. I slide a hand up her back to her shoulder and pull her up higher, then hold both her arms behind her as I drive into her. Her breath is coming in fast pants and soft cries. "Yes . . . yes . . ."

Her long hair flows down her back. I hook my arm through both of hers to clasp her shoulder again, sliding it around to her throat, so gently and carefully. She lets out a little sob that encourages me.

My cock tunnels in and out of her, her body jolting with each impact.

"So tight," I growl in her ear. "So wet for me."

"Yes. God yes. Fuck me . . ."

I release her arms and her throat, cup one breast and reach around to the front of her to find her clit. I nuzzle her ear, her hair, whispering, "I love . . ." I stop. "I love fucking you. Love that pussy squeezing me. Are you close? 'Cause I wanna make you come so hard." I circle wet fingers over her clit.

A stream of do-me-harder sounds falls from her lips as she covers my hand with hers, on her knees in front of me, my cock filling her again, and again. Sensation pours through me, racing up my spine, tightening my balls. I squeeze her tit, pinch her nipple, suck on the skin on the side of her neck, my fingers still working. She presses on them to adjust them just a bit, then tenses against me, her spine arching. "Oh God . . . ."

"There . . . that's it, gorgeous girl, come all over my fingers and my cock . . . oh yeah."

She's squeezing me and it's like lightning bolts to my balls.

"Oh Christ." Excitement pounds through me, robbing every thought, taking over everything. I need her. Christ, I need her.

She falls forward, on her elbows, head to the bed, and I pound into her as my release roars over me. Tingles grow at the base of my spine, pleasure corkscrews inside me. My balls tighten even more, white hot electricity burning from them up my cock and exploding. Sensation swamps me in huge, suffocating waves. I shout my release, then slump over her, my breathing harsh and ragged, my heart racing.

"I really don't know about this."

I smile at Arya when I'm back at her place the next day to pick her up. "It'll be fine. It's not that big of a deal."

Her face tells me she remains unconvinced.

"You know Everly and Bellsy. I mean, Wyatt."

"I never know who you're talking about." She grins. "You hockey players and your nicknames."

I shrug.

"Your mom's name is Chelsea, right?"

"Yes."

She nods. "I just don't want to forget. And your brothers are Noah and Asher."

"Yup."

"Do I look okay?"

She looks amazing. She's wearing a casual dress, flowered cotton, that leaves her shoulders and legs bare. Her hair is down in long, sexy waves that make me want to run my hands through it. "You look gorgeous. Perfect. Do you have your swimsuit?"

"Yes." She grimaces and holds up a tote bag.

"Great. Mom and Dad have a nice pool. We might want to jump in."

She swallows. "Okay."

I move closer and set my hands on her smooth shoulders. "Don't be nervous." I brush my lips over her cheek. "It's just a fun afternoon to celebrate Dad turning seventy-three."

I feel her relax under my hands and I find her mouth with mine. Kissing her will distract her from her nerves. Her lips soften and open for me and I pull her flush against me, enjoying the feel of her soft curves as I taste her.

"Okay," she says breathlessly, long moments later. "We should go."

I smile down into her eyes, giving her one last reassuring look.

Then I pat her ass when she moves to the door in front of me.

She flashes a mock reproving look over her shoulder. "Hey."

"Couldn't resist. You have such a sweet little ass."

She pauses to lock the door, looking up at me from beneath her eyelashes. "Well, okay, then."

I laugh and sling my arm around her shoulders to walk out to the street.

I'm trying to reassure her that this will all go well, but truthfully, I'm not a hundred percent sure of that. When my family gets together, things tend to go screwy. Today's party will be smaller, though, so I hope that means uneventful.

It's not far to Mom and Dad's place. Apparently, we're the last to arrive. I let us in the front door, but I hear voices out back, so we make our way through the great room and kitchen, and out onto the patio.

"This is the house you grew up in?" Arya asks with a whisper.

"Yeah."

"It's lovely."

"Yeah, it's pretty nice, I guess."

Mom must have heard us coming, as she's just about to enter the house as we step out. "You're here!" She hugs me, but her attention immediately goes to Arya. "Hi! You must be Arya."

"Yes." Arya smiles and extends a hand. "So nice to meet you."

"Yes, yes, likewise!" Mom studies her, smiling.

Arya hands over the bottle of wine she brought. "For you."

"Oh, thank you!" Mom beams at her.

I wave at Everly and Wyatt. "You two already know her. Arya, this is Noah, my youngest brother."

Noah politely stands from the lounger he's stretched out on to shake her hand. "Hi. I've been hearing so much about you."

Arya bites her lip. "Uh-oh."

He grins.

"And this is Asher, who's going to vouch for me for yesterday."

Asher stands too, grinning hugely. He holds out a hand to Arya. "I gather we almost met yesterday."

Arya's cheeks go cherry red. "Almost!"

"What's going on?" Mom asks.

"Tell you in a minute. Happy birthday, Dad." I clap my

hand on his shoulder and squeeze. "Arya, this is my dad, Bob Wynn. Dad, Arya."

Dad also stands, eyeing Arya. "Another blonde?"

I close my eyes, heat washing through me. "Yes, Dad, she's blond."

Arya shoots me a playful glance as she shakes Dad's hand. "Harrison likes blondes?"

"Seems like," Dad mutters.

"Arya's a yoga instructor," I say.

"That's right." Arya smiles. "I've been doing yoga classes with your hockey team."

Dad nods. "I've never tried yoga. But when I bend down in the morning to put my pants on, it hurts, so I don't think I'd like it."

I choke and Arya grins. "If you did yoga, it wouldn't hurt to put on your pants."

Dad snorts, but he's still smiling.

Everyone else chuckles too, exchanging glances. Dad seems to be having a good day.

"Happy birthday, Mr. Wynn," Arya says. "Thanks for having me here today."

"What can I get you to drink?" Mom asks us. "We have beer and wine, and pitchers of margaritas. Or iced tea or juice if you prefer."

"A margarita sounds great," Arya says.

"I'll have a beer," I say. "But I'll get it."

There's a fridge outside on the patio as part of the outdoor kitchen, and I grab a beer from it while mom pours Arya a margarita.

"So, what happened yesterday?" Everly asks. "Come sit here, Arya." She pats the arm of the chair next to her.

Arya bites her lip as she sits. "Let me first say that Harrison failed to tell me that Asher is his twin. You two do look exactly alike."

"Nah." I shake my head. "I'm way better looking than he is."

Asher flicks me a middle finger. "Our hair is different," he says.

Arya looks between us and nods. "Yes, now I can see that."

"I can't believe he didn't tell you that!" Everly says. "Oh, wait, I guess I could have mentioned it too." She shrugs. "I didn't even think of it."

Arya continues. "Anyway, I saw Asher at the pier yesterday, um, with a girl."

The family starts laughing.

"Oooh, who is she, Ash?" Everly asks.

He shrugs. "Her name's Camilla. First time we went out."

"I gather they were looking quite friendly." Everly catches Arya's eye with a sympathetic smile.

"Oh yeah." Arya grimaces. "Well, Harrison figured out what happened after he kept telling me he hadn't been at the pier over and over and I kept saying 'but I saw you!' "

Mom hands Arya her drink. "You're not the first girl that's happened to, if it makes you feel any better."

"So I heard." Arya shakes her head, her cheeks red again, but her eyes are dancing.

Whew.

"How about the time Asher broke up with a girl for you?" Everly smirks at me. "What was her name?"

"Never mind."

Arya snort-laughs. "Oh my God. Really?"

"Harrison didn't want to do it," Everly says. "He didn't want to hurt her feelings."

Arya shoots me a warm glance.

"I let her down gently," Ash adds with a grin.

"I hope you're using condoms."

We all fall silent and turn to stare at Dad.

"What?" He glares back at us. "You all better use condoms."

"I thought you wanted grandchildren," Everly says, lips twitching.

"Just from you." He points at her. "But Wyatt better marry you first."

We're all biting our lips now, trying not to laugh.

"You're so old-fashioned, Dad," Everly says, pushing his buttons. "You don't need to be married to have a baby."

He grunts. "I'm not old-fashioned. I'm practical. You better get a pre-nup signed too."

"Oh my God." Everly closes her eyes. "You did not just say that."

"Imagine if Dad *didn't* like you, Bellsy," I joke to him.

Bellsy shakes his head good-naturedly. He's known Dad for a while, playing for the team, but getting to know him better now he's dating Everly. It's a little awkward, dating the daughter of the team owner, but like I said, Dad actually likes him, so it's been going okay.

Dad never did have much of a filter, but now he just blurts out whatever he's thinking.

"How about you open your presents, honey," Mom says to Dad.

"I like presents."

"Don't we all," I agree.

Buying Dad a gift is a challenge. He has everything he wants. "My present is still in the car," I say. "I'll get it last."

We watch Dad happily open gifts from Ash, Noah, Everly, and Wyatt. Then we go look at what Mom bought him—a new potting bench, which has already been built and installed at the side of the house.

While they're admiring that, I hike out front and get my gift from the vehicle.

"I couldn't really wrap it," I explain to the others, as I set it on the potting bench. It's a clay pot with a plant in it.

"Wow," Dad says, fingering the unusual flower. "What is this?"

"It's a bat flower." The black blossom does look oddly like a bat. "It's a tropical flower. It'll get quite tall, which is why it's in that big pot." It's French pottery I thought would look nice with the patio stones. "There are care instructions on the tag."

"It's the ugliest flower I've ever seen." Dad grins at me. "Thank you."

I laugh. I can tell he likes it.

"Where do you want to put it? It needs filtered shade." I heft the big pot again.

Mom leads the way back to the patio. "Over here would be perfect. The trees give some shade on this side."

I set it down where she indicates.

Mom refills drinks and sets out bowls of snacks. "If anyone wants to swim, go ahead. The water's nice and warm."

"Want to hit the pool?" I ask Arya.

"I don't know." She flicks her gaze around. "I don't want to be the only one."

I dig into a bowl of Chex Mix, carefully avoiding the pretzels. "Okay, we'll wait a bit."

Arya picks up the pretzels I just rejected, then the cheese crackers, and munches them.

I stare at her.

"What?" she asks, about to pop another pretzel in her mouth.

"Don't you like the Chex?"

She blinks. "Um, no. They're cereal. Not snack food."

I break out into a huge grin. "You are fucking perfect."

"What?" Her eyebrows pull together.

"I *love* the Chex. And the little breadsticks. Hate pretzels, and the cheese crackers are meh. Therefore, we are the perfect Chex Mix combination."

She looks down at the bowl, then back up at me.

Oh shit. Did I screw up again?

Then she laughs. "I guess you're right. But how can you possibly hate pretzels?"

I shrug. "They're dry." I point at Ash. "When we buy Chex Mix, there's always pretzels and cheese crackers left that nobody wants. We like the same things."

"Well, save them for me."

I smile at her, warmth flooding my chest.

"Are you talking about me?" Ash says.

"Yeah." I gesture at the snack bowl. "Arya likes the pretzels and cheese crackers."

Ash laughs. "How does she feel about hard-boiled eggs?"

Arya wrinkles her nose. "I like them . . . ?"

"Do you like the white better, or the yolk?" I ask.

"I like the whole thing."

"Ugh. Damn."

She laughs. "Why?"

"Ash and I love the egg white, not so much the yolk. When we were kids, we'd give all the yolks to Noah. He loved them."

"Still do," he says. "You guys are weird."

Arya is looking more and more relaxed, laughing at our stories and jokes. "Okay,"

She says to me, "Here's one for you: do you like to eat the half-popped kernels left in the bottom of a bowl of popcorn?"

"What?" I gape at her. "Who would do that?"

She points at herself. "This girl."

I start laughing. "Well, okay, then! More support for my position."

"Uh . . . what position is that?"

I lean in closer to her ear and whisper, "Any position you want, baby."

She gives a strangled little laugh and pushes at my shoulder.

My siblings are watching with amusement. Luckily, my parents are standing over at the counter where the grill is, getting food ready for dinner.

"I'm ready for a swim," Noah announces. He pulls off his T-shirt, runs over to the deep end of the pool, and does a somersault into the water. In his shorts.

What a guy.

19

ARYA

M Y MOUTH FALLS OPEN AS NOAH LEAPS INTO THE POOL.

The others shake their heads and laugh.

"Good idea." Everly stands and sets down her margarita glass. "I'll go change. Did you bring a bathing suit, Arya?"

"Yes."

"Come on. I'll show you where you can change too."

I follow her, grabbing my bag where I left it near the door.

"There's a bathroom right here." She opens the door and flicks on the light. "I'll go to my old bedroom to change."

"Thanks."

The bathroom is small but lovely, with black and white patterned ceramic tile on the floors, white subway tiles on the walls, and black cabinets. There's a full-length mirror on the back of the door that I use to inspect myself once I have my bikini on. I turn to check out the cellulite on my ass and tug the suit down. It's my favorite, multi-colored stripes with a halter top.

I slip on a sheer tank dress cover-up, and slide a hair tie onto my wrist so I can pull my hair up when I get into the water. Then I grab the doorknob to leave.

The knob comes off in my hand.

I stare at it. What the . . .

I drop my bag again and study the door and the broken knob. I try to pull on the door, but it won't open. Shit.

Maybe I can fix it.

I try wiggling the knob back into the opening. I have no idea what I'm doing, but maybe if I can get it back into the right place, it'll work.

No luck.

I'm not sure how long I spend doing that, but I'm getting hot and sweaty and frustrated. I lean my head against the door. I'm going to have to call for help.

Great.

"Hello!" I call. "Anyone out there?"

Silence.

I don't know if Everly's still in her room or if she's gone back out.

I call again, louder. "Hello! Help! I'm stuck in here." Then I bang on the door.

Still nothing.

My head drops forward. Fuckety fuck.

I sit on the closed toilet seat and slump over. How long am I going to be stuck here? Harrison will come looking for me eventually, won't he? But how long will it take?

I sigh.

I eye the window at the end of the room. I'm pretty sure it's next to the patio where everyone is. I jump up and rush over to hammer on the frosted glass.

Nothing.

I let out another expulsion of air. Shit.

I eye the window again. It's pretty high up. Does it open? I sink my teeth into my bottom lip as I try to see. I climb onto the toilet, which isn't that close to it, bracing a hand on the wall as I lean over.

It does open.

Okay. I'm pretty strong. If I can get it open, maybe I can pull myself up and get out that way.

Oh my God. Do I really have to do this? Why hasn't Harrison come looking for me? I plop back down onto the toilet lid again, shaking my head. After a few more minutes, though, I have to try.

I can just barely reach the lever that unlocks the window, then I slide it open. Yay!

I pause, still hoping someone will rescue me. With a sigh, I turn to the wall. I grip the windowsill and hoist myself up, using my feet on the wall. Jeezus. My arm muscles strain. I'm determined to do this, so I grit my teeth and keep working until I'm high enough to rest my boobs on the sill. I pause, panting.

Okay. I got this far. I can do it.

I wriggle myself through the window. Now I'm half hanging out, but I'm headfirst and I don't want to take a dive into the shrubs beneath me. I peer through bushes and palm trees to see the patio. I can vaguely hear them talking over there.

I really don't want to make a scene, but . . . "Help!" I wait, then call again. "Help! Over here!"

A moment later, Harrison's face appears through the shrubbery. "Arya? What the hell are you doing?"

"I'm locked in the bathroom! Help!"

He starts to thrash through the shrubs toward me. Oh thank God! I'm going to live.

Just as he nears me, I hear the bathroom door open.

"Oh," I hear Noah say.

I am now painfully aware that my cover-up is scrunched around my waist and my bikini bottom is firmly wedged between my ass cheeks.

Heat flames in my face and I kick my feet in frustration and embarrassment.

"Okay, I got you," Harrison says calmly, reaching up for me. "Come on."

"I've got her!" Noah calls from behind me.

I close my eyes, mortification scalding my insides. Should I go out or back in? I'd rather face Harrison, I guess, so I push myself through the window and into his arms. I scrape a shin on the windowsill, and the shrubs scratch at my arms, but I'm free. Harrison catches me and holds me, and I bury my face into his neck.

"What the hell happened?" he murmurs.

"The doorknob came off." I can't look at him. "I guess I broke it. I couldn't get it back on and I couldn't get out. I called for help." I almost sob. "Nobody heard me."

"I'm sorry." I can hear the amusement in his voice, though.

I lift my head. He's already been in the water—he's wearing a pair of wet, black board shorts low on his hips, and rivulets run down his bare chest. His gorgeous, bare chest.

"Sorry, beautiful." He smiles at me. "I didn't know you were stuck in here."

"Didn't you wonder what was taking me so long?"

"Um . . . I would have."

Noah's face appears in the window. "You okay, Arya?"

I squeeze my eyes shut, imagining what he just saw. "Yes." I whisper to Harrison, "I think he got a good view of my cooch."

"*What*?"

"Shit." I press my forehead to his chest. "Now I'm embarrassed."

"Uh . . ." He feels around my butt and finds my bathing suit bottom. "You're not naked."

"Not totally." My face burns. "I can never face him again. Take me home."

He laughs softly. "Well, I can't say I'm happy that my brother may have gotten a look at your pretty pussy, but I don't think he saw everything. It's fine, sweetheart."

"I'm sorry I broke the door."

He presses a hand to my hair. "It wasn't your fault. Obviously, the knob was already broken."

Carrying me, he steps through the bushes and onto the patio.

Mrs. Wynn appears. "What's going on? Are you okay, Arya?"

"Yes." I wriggle out of Harrison's arms to stand and tug my cover-up down. "I'm fine. I'm so sorry, I broke the bathroom door."

She covers her smile. "I'm sure you didn't. We don't use

this bathroom very often anymore. I didn't realize there was a problem."

She's so nice.

Noah appears through the sliding doors, wearing a bemused expression. "You okay, Arya?"

Everyone's concerned about me. Too bad I'll never be able to look him in the eyes again.

"Yes, I just need to drown myself in the pool."

"I was about to come looking for you," Everly says. "I'm so sorry.'

"It's okay." I pull off my cover-up, drop it onto a chair, and walk straight into the deep end, letting myself sink to the bottom in the nice, cool water, where I wish I could stay.

However, I pop back up to the surface.

Harrison's treading water right in front of me. He eyes me with warm amusement. "Okay?"

"I'm fine." I roll my eyes. "Just when you want to make a good impression . . ."

"Don't worry about it." His big hands circle my waist and pull me closer. Our slick, wet skin glides together. I hold onto his shoulders, resisting the urge to wrap my legs around his waist, which I would totally do if we weren't surrounded by his family.

"Too many people here," he murmurs, his hands going to my ass. "If we were alone, I'd lift you onto the side, pull off this little bottom"—he plucks at my bathing suit—"spread your legs, and feast."

Oh dear God. I hope no one heard that but me. Inside, I'm melting. He's doing a very good job of distracting me from my embarrassment.

Harrison laughs softly.

The water is lovely and silky, swirling around us, sparkling in the sun. Our wet skin glides together in sensuous slides that are turning me on. And Harrison too, from the bulge I feel in his shorts. Daringly, I brush my hand over it as we play in the water.

Noah gets a ball and we do a little impromptu volleyball. I've always loved swimming, and having a pool is such a luxury. This is heaven, and so much fun with Harrison's siblings all cracking jokes.

Later, changed into dry clothes, we fill plates from the platters set out on the outdoor bar and take seats to eat grilled chicken and veggies, salads, and bruschetta on crusty, chewy bread. The conversation turns to hockey (surprise).

"What were you and JP nearly fighting about in that last game?" Everly asks Harrison.

He grins as he cuts his chicken. "I played a little prank on him."

"What did you do?" I ask, wide-eyed.

"I stuffed his gloves full of bubble gum."

"Eeeew!" My jaw drops. "Chewed-up gum?"

"No, no! It was wrapped. I laugh every time I think of him trying to shove his paws into his glove and trying to figure out why he can't get them on. And then when he sees the gum. Ha!"

"And then when he realizes who did it," Ash adds.

"You guys and your pranks." Mrs. Wynn shakes her head.

"It's tradition," Harrison says. "Especially when it's another Wynn."

The talk turns to playoff predictions, and I'm fascinated

by their analysis of how other teams will do, their strengths and weaknesses.

My gaze is caught by movement at the side of the house. I blink as two men walk around the corner, following the brick path to the patio. I gesture to Harrison beside me, who looks up.

"Jesus." His head jerks back.

Everyone else looks too.

"Mark! Matthew!" Mrs. Wynn exclaims, standing. "Hi!"

"What are you guys doing here?" Mr. Wynn growls, also standing.

"It's your birthday, Dad," one of the men says. I'm not sure who is who. "We thought we'd come by."

"You weren't invited," Mr. Wynn says bluntly.

The men and Mrs. Wynn exchange glances and I have a suspicion that she may have invited them.

"Well, have some food, since you're here." She gestures to the bar. "I'll get a couple more plates." She sets her dinner down on a table and hustles into the kitchen.

Harrison rises slowly and follows Mark and Matthew to the bar. "Can I get you a drink?" he offers.

They each take a beer and help themselves to food. Conversation has dried up, the atmosphere suddenly dense and heavy. I look around at the others.

"You haven't met Arya," Harrison says to his half brothers. "Arya, this is Matthew, and this is Mark."

I smile and shake hands. Matthew is clearly older and looks very much like his dad, his hair graying and receding a bit. Mark has merely a touch of gray, and his wide shoulders and lean build indicate a very fit and muscular man. "Nice to meet you."

Noah has pulled two more chairs closer to us and they sit with their plates.

"Happy birthday, Dad," Mark says, echoed by Matt.

"Well." Mrs. Wynn sits and looks around the group. She doesn't look fazed by the unexpected appearance of her stepsons.

Which is a little weird to think about, because her stepsons are about the same age as her.

She smiles serenely. "This is a good chance for us to all talk."

Mr. Wynn frowns. "About what?"

There's another tense exchange of glances.

"I feel like I shouldn't be here," I whisper to Harrison, leaning over.

He sets a hand on my back and rubs a small circle. "You're probably going to wish you weren't." He sighs.

My stomach tightens. This seems like it's going to be a very personal family discussion.

"Let me start," Everly says. "Mark, Matthew, I'm sorry that I blurted out all that stuff that night at the game. Actually, I'm not sorry I said it; I'm sorry I said it *there*. That wasn't the appropriate place for that discussion."

"I missed it," Mark murmurs. "But Matt filled me in."

"We're worried," Everly continues, shooting her dad a glance. "This family needs to come together. Now more than ever."

"You need to know," Mrs. Wynn adds. "The doctors have confirmed that your dad has Alzheimer's."

I watch Matthew and Mark. Mark's throat works; Matthew's jaw tightens.

"Are you absolutely sure about that?" Matthew asks. "What about a second opinion?"

"We've seen a several doctors," Mrs. Wynn replies. "They're all in agreement. And they're excellent doctors."

There's music playing from an outdoor speaker, but it seems to fade in the midst of the opaque silence that descends over us. I poke at a piece of grilled zucchini, wishing I could go get locked in the bathroom again.

"I'm not questioning the doctors," Matthew says, his voice rough. "Just . . ."

"You're in denial, like the rest of us," Everly says quietly. She swipes a finger under one eye but lifts her chin.

"What are you talking about?" Mr. Wynn asks irritably. "The doctors said I'm fine."

Everly's lip trembles. Harrison closes his eyes briefly.

Mark and Matthew look to Mrs. Wynn. She shakes her head, her expression pinched.

"This lawsuit has to be settled," Everly speaks up. "Now you know why."

Mark and Matthew exchange glances and slowly nod.

"I have some information put together," Mrs. Wynn says to them. "This isn't the time, but if we could sit down and go through it, I have a . . ." She stops. "A proposal, I suppose. After the playoffs, maybe?"

"You didn't steal that girl from your brother, did you?" Mr. Wynn suddenly demands.

He's looking at Harrison. And me.

My mouth falls open. I turn to Harrison, confused.

"No, Dad," he says.

"Good. Because that's a dick move."

"I know." Harrison leans closer to me. "He's thinking of JP." He pauses. "I don't think it's worth getting into it."

"JP stole his brother's girlfriend?"

"Yeah. Long story. Evidently, Dad's still pissed about it."

Then Mr. Wynn starts into a story about one of the years he won the Stanley Cup. It's a little rambling and doesn't entirely make sense, but I can tell that it's based on something that really happened. Everyone listens and reacts appropriately, smiling and commenting, but I can tell their hearts are breaking.

And I kind of feel like that too, because I hate seeing Harrison hurting. I finish my meal, set my plate on a small table, and reach for Harrison's hand. I curl my fingers around it and he reciprocates, twining our fingers together, and we sit like that. I want to think, from the way he's clasping my hand, that I'm helping in some tiny way.

Mrs. Wynn serves birthday cake that I can see nobody wants to eat, but everyone's acting cheerful. Matthew and Mark are quieter than the others, moving to sit beside their dad to talk to him in low voices while they pretend to eat cake.

"You okay?" I ask Harrison without looking up from my chocolate cake.

"No." He slants me a crooked smile. "I'm fucked up."

"I know." I reach for his forearm and squeeze it. "It's okay."

"You ready to go soon?"

"Sure. Any time."

He takes my empty plate a few minutes later and carries it into the kitchen.

Following him, I say, "We should stay to help clean up."

"Yeah." He surveys the mess of dishes on the counter. "Let's get these into the dishwasher."

We set about rinsing and filling the dishwasher. I toss crumpled aluminum foil and plastic wrap into the trash while Harrison finds storage containers, and we move leftover chicken and veggies into them and store them in the fridge.

Mrs. Wynn comes in as I'm wiping the counter. "Oh my God!" She stops and looks around. "Did you two do this?"

"Yeah." Harrison smiles at her, drying his hands. "It was Arya's idea."

She moves toward me with arms outstretched and my heart swells as she hugs me. She draws back and smiles. "Thank you. I'm glad you came and I got to meet you."

"I'm happy to meet you too. I do feel like I probably shouldn't have been here for some of that family business."

"It's fine." She glances at Harrison. "We need to think about how we're going to deal with this publicly. I think we should consult with Murray."

I have no idea who Murray is, but . . . wow. Bad enough they have to go through this, they have to go through it in front of the whole world.

"Yeah." He nods. "I don't think we need to do anything yet."

Everly enters the kitchen too, followed by Wyatt. "Oh! I just came in to help clean up." She surveys the room. "It's done."

"Perfect timing," Harrison says dryly.

She rolls her eyes.

"We're out," he says. "Thanks Mom, that was a great dinner."

He hugs his Mom while I hug Everly.

"Let's do drinks and appies again one day," she says to me.

"Absolutely!"

"The playoff schedule comes out tomorrow, and then we'll know what our life looks like for the next couple of weeks anyway." She slides an affectionate look at her boyfriend. "I'll text you."

"Sounds good."

We say more goodbyes, then climb into Harrison's SUV to head home.

"I'M NOT GOING TO BE VERY AVAILABLE FOR A WHILE," Harrison says the next day in his SUV. "We need to focus on the playoffs. We'll be traveling to Vancouver. Sometimes the team even makes us stay in a hotel here in town instead of our own homes so we're not distracted by family shit."

"And you have a lot of family shit going on."

"True that." His smile is rueful. "Anyway, I want to spend time with you as much as I can the next few days, if you're okay with that."

I smile. "I'd love that. I don't want to be a distraction for you. I know how important this is."

"Yeah." He reaches over and squeeze my hand. "I just don't want you to think I'm ignoring you when things get going."

"I'm okay with it. Seriously. I have my friends, I have my work . . . in fact, I just got offered a great opportunity."

"Oh yeah? What's that?"

"I'm going to do a rooftop sunset yoga class downtown once a week."

He shouts a laugh. "No shit? That's awesome!"

"I know, right? I just heard about it this morning. I'm excited. It's a cool thing. So, um, where are we going?" He's taking me out somewhere, but he's been mysterious about where.

"You're gonna love this." He grins and twists his hands on the steering wheel in excitement. "Puppies and Pints."

"Uh . . . what?"

"Puppies and Pints. We're going to Last Glass Brewers. Once a month they have these Puppies and Pints evenings where they bring in rescue dogs and you can go and have a drink and play with the dogs."

"Oh my God!" I press a hand between my breasts. "Seriously?"

"Yeah." He slants me a smile. "I thought you'd like it."

"Dogs! I miss my Roxy so much."

"I know you do. And I know you want a dog of your own, someday. Maybe won't be one of these ones, but you can enjoy them anyway and get some dog time." He frowns. "That sounds weird."

"No, it doesn't. I need dog time. I need puppy hugs. I'm so excited!" I clap my hands.

The event is being held on the patio at Last Glass Brewers. The hostess shows us out there and seats us at a table. Before we even order drinks I'm eyeing the dogs.

My heart!

I can't resist. I have to go see them. "I'll have whatever you're having," I tell Harrison, leaving him to order.

I cross the patio and crouch down beside a beagle. "Hello, my sweetie."

"This is Buster," the girl holding his leash says. "He's two years old. He's very affectionate and friendly."

I hold out my hand palm down which he sniffs, then I rub his chin. "Hi, Buster. You're a handsome boy, aren't you?"

He looks up at me with big brown eyes and I'm melting into a puddle of puppy longing.

Another dog comes over, tail wagging, eager for attention. He?—She?—is smaller, so I scoop him up. He lays puppy kisses all over my chin. I'm laughing as the girl from the shelter tells me this is Vita, an indeterminate mix of breeds who's only eight months old.

"You are so sweet." I cuddle him against me.

Harrison comes over with a plastic cup with beer in it for me. I set down Vita and take the beer. "Thank you." I beam up at him.

He crouches beside me and holds out a hand for Vita to sniff. "Hey, little dude."

I introduce them, earning an amused glance from Harrison. He rubs a hand down Vita's back. Vita moves closer, eyes closing, nuzzling into Harrison. My heart trips again, watching him rub the dog and smile at him.

This is heaven. Harrison and I play with the dogs and drink beer and laugh a lot. I squeeze puppy bodies and boop noses and rub bellies. Harrison seems to enjoy it too, even though he's apparently never had a dog. At one point I catch him watching me as I plant a kiss right between the eyes of Buster the beagle. My skin tingles everywhere at the heat I see in his eyes, and for a few seconds I actually forget the puppers.

"Thank you," I say softly.

He quirks an eyebrow.

"For bringing me here. I love it."

He smiles slowly. "I can see that. I'm glad."

My heart is already full of puppy love, and it swells even bigger. I want to throw myself at him and kiss him all over and . . .

I'm getting feelings for this man. Big, soft, tender feelings. Huge, scary feelings.

20

HARRISON

The coaching staff has told everyone to take care of whatever family shit we need to deal with before the playoffs start so we aren't distracted by it.

I can't really take care of my family shit; nothing's going to change Dad's situation. That weighs heavy inside me, but I'm going to have to accept it and put it aside for now.

I'm also aware this isn't a good time to be starting a relationship. It's the playoffs. We need to win. I'm trying to earn a permanent place on the Condors' roster. I'm trying to show my dad I can do this and make him proud of me . . . and he's dying.

But I can't stay away from Arya. From the moment I laid eyes on her, something drew me to her. And my family can eat rocks about the fact that she's blond—it's not that at all. It's the softness that glows in her eyes, the joy that shines in her smile, the affection she showered on those puppies, the way she held my hand when things got tough at my parents' place. The way she's got big jock hockey players doing yoga. Maybe I'm crazy, but being with her makes me feel . . . stronger. Better. And I need to be my best right now.

Outside of practices, workouts, and team meetings, and her class schedule, we spend almost every moment together for the next few days.

We go for a bike ride and end up lying in the sand dunes near Venice Pier, staring at the ocean, letting the sun warm us, and talking about everything. She takes me to Leo's Creamery for ice cream and I find my new favorite—dark-roast coffee and white chocolate. We lie in bed reading, and she's amused that I'm reading a Kresley Cole book, one of her favorite authors. We discover other authors we both like. We go shopping and buy a deep fryer, then to Whole Foods for ingredients, and spend an evening trying to create deep-fried pizza. We have a few failures.

"It's basically a Pizza Pop," I say as we remove one golden-brown treat from the oil.

"A what?"

"A Pizza Pop. Oh right. That's a Canadian thing."

"Oh yeah! We had them in Winnipeg when we went there! I love Pizza Pops." Then her face falls. "Damn. I thought we were creating something original."

"We totally are. No Pizza Pop will rival our unique creation. Let's see how it tastes."

We dig in.

"This is the best one yet," I proclaim.

"I agree. Great Pizza Pop." She grins.

We do couples' yoga. I have no idea what this even is, but Arya convinces me to try it.

We're on my living room floor and she's telling me we're going to do Plank on Plank.

"You can do a plank, right?" she asks me.

I scoff. "Of course I can do a plank." I get down on the floor into a straight-arm plank. Then she gets on top of me the other way, gripping my ankles, her ankles on my shoulders. I tighten my core even more to support her weight on top of me.

"See?" she says triumphantly. "Not even hard. Let's try something else. Front Bird."

"Whut?" When she's off me, I lower myself to the floor and roll over to stare up at her.

"Yes, like that." She nods. "Bend your legs."

I do so, and she stands in front of me, positioning my bare feet against her pelvis. She reaches over to grip my hands.

"Okay." She grins at me. "Ready?"

"Sure . . ."

"Lift me up with your feet."

My eyes widen. "Okay." I push at her hips and she stretches out above me, her body flat, straightening her arms. Following her lead, I straighten mine too, propping her up over me like she's flying. "Holy shit."

She laughs. "See? Front Bird."

"This is awesome." It strikes me that she has to trust me to let me do this, because I could easily drop her. "What happens if I grab your boobs?"

She starts laughing, and so do I, and that's the end of that pose as we both collapse onto the floor, me making sure to cushion her fall.

"Let's try that again and see if we can let go of our

hands."

I'm skeptical, but we do it, and goddamn if it doesn't work. Slowly, she releases my hands and extends her arms to the side, then stretches them back, balancing on my feet. I keep my arms up in case I have to catch her, but wow, she's got this. She's so strong. Our eyes meet and we smile and focus on each other and on the pose, a connection drawing out between us. Fuck, she's amazing.

We do a few other poses, which require that we hold onto each other and not let go or we'll fall, and it's pretty cool, the engagement and trust we have to have with each other. This feels . . . intimate. Being totally present in the moment. Trusting each other.

Her trusting me makes emotion blaze through my chest. I can't even speak for a moment. This is what I've wanted.

"You okay?" She blinks at me, forehead furrowed.

"Yeah. Can you do a headstand?"

"Yes."

"Show me."

With a smile, she gets down on her knees and elbows. She interlaces her fingers, dips the top of her head to the mat, her hands cupping her head. She pushes her ass up into the air, which is spectacular, adjusts her position a little, then pulls her knees slowly to her chest.

"Holy crap," I breathe, watching her balance on her head and elbows.

Her movements unhurried and sure, she straightens her legs, toes pointed toward the ceiling.

"Wow. You're amazing." I move to stand behind her.

When she parts her legs, I can't resist. I slide my arms around her waist and pick her up, upside down. She lets out a little screech and smacks at my thighs. "What are you doing?"

I bury my face in her pussy, then slowly lower her to the floor, her head between my legs. She grabs the backs of my knees, laughing. I join her on the floor and we roll around together, kissing and laughing.

Then Ash walks in on us.

"Uh . . . sorry." He stops in the opening to the living room.

"We're just doing yoga," I explain.

His eyebrows rise. "Suuuuure." He waves a hand and heads to his office.

Arya's flat on her back on the floor, still laughing. "Oh my God."

I lean over her and smooch her lips again. "I'd rather be doing you."

She laughs harder.

"Maybe we should do our couples' yoga in the bedroom."

"You like the couples' yoga?"

"Are you kidding? I get to put my hands on you and put my face between your legs. What's not to love?"

Late Monday night I leave her at her place, alone, and go home to my solitary bed so I can get a good night's sleep. Tomorrow night the playoffs start.

We ended up two points ahead of Vancouver, so we have home-ice advantage, and start the series at home Tuesday night. This is the first time I've ever played an NHL playoff game, although I've played in plenty of playoff games in the AHL. I've gotten advice from some of the veterans, and the team has a sports psychology consultant from UCLA working with us. He tells us that mental and emotional skills are just as important for the playoffs as physical skills.

There are vets like Jimmy, Olle, and Richie who have a lot of playoff experience, albeit years ago. There are brand-new guys like Eddie and Meals. And then there are guys like me, who have some experience with it, either in the NHL or AHL.

Brian knows we don't want to sit through hour-long meetings talking about this stuff, so he gets us watching short video clips of experienced professional athletes talking about focus, dealing with pressure, and visualization. Even a pro golfer talks about each shot he takes being the most important thing in the world at that moment. We listen to guys talk about blocking out everything else and dealing with pressure by keeping things simple and remembering to breathe.

Breathing makes me think about Arya, and what I've learned from her, which increases my confidence that I can do this.

"Embrace the pressure," Brian tells us. "Let your talent and your training come out. And don't focus on the outcome of the game. Sounds like it doesn't make sense, because you have to win. But you need to remember the process of the game, focusing on doing what it *takes* to win, not on the need to win."

The team even has a playoff theme: "Now's our time." It's on everything—banners in the dressing room, on the walls in the corridors, and in the motivational video the team put together for us.

I text Arya from my bedroom Thursday afternoon

just before I leave for the arena. I've had my nap, I'm dressed in my suit, including my lucky Wolverine socks, sitting on my bed. Once I get to the arena, I'll put my phone in my locker and won't look at it again until after the game.

She texts me back.

Are you nervous?

Yeah. No. Excited. Okay yeah nervous.

I laugh out loud and rub my mouth. I feel like I'm electrified, buzzing with energy. I have to control that energy.

I'll be there cheering you on.

Good.

You'll be great. Remember—breathe.

Yep!

I want to say more. I wish she was here so I could feel her, wrap her in my arms and kiss her. I'd like to end the text convo with a *love you,* but it's too soon for that. I just have to be patient. One thing at a time.

Okay I'm off. Have fun at the game.

Ash is in the living room. He too is heading to the game, also dressed in a suit and trying unsuccessfully to tie his tie. He makes a frustrated noise.

I smile and walk up to him. "Here." I start the knot

from fresh, twirling the silk fabric expertly and then snugging the knot up. "There you go." I slap his shoulder.

He grins. "Thanks, man."

"I'm out." I start to move away.

"Hey."

I stop and look at him.

"How're you doing? Okay?"

"Yeah. Good." I suck in a breath and nod.

He steps forward and gives me a bro hug. "Good luck."

I hug him back. "I thought you were neutral."

"I am." He smirks. "Don't tell anyone I'm cheering for my brother."

The laughter eases some of my tension and I jog out to my SUV.

AFTER THE GAME, I'M SITTING IN THE LOCKER ROOM, HEAD down, sweaty, and exhausted, still wearing my pants and half my gear.

We lost.

The mood in the room has dimmed considerably from before the game, when the energy was high, spirits buoyant. And yet, I don't feel as shitty as I would have expected.

"It's game one," Jimmy says. "We'll figure out what went wrong and we'll fix it for the next game."

We all make noises of agreement.

"We got this," Bellsy adds.

I already know my own mistakes. Fuck. I didn't play my worst game ever, but it sure wasn't my best either. A stupid turnover led to a goal that I'll be kicking myself over for a long time. Except I'm not supposed to do that. Put it behind me. Learn from it. Look forward.

Yeah, all the clichéd advice and platitudes don't actually help that much. It's easy to say forget about it and move on; it's not so easy to do.

There are no post-game drinks or parties tonight. We've done the media stuff, including answering tough questions from my own goddamn brother. At least his questions aren't stupid, unlike that idiot from WXN who asked me why I turned over the puck to Vancouver's leading scorer. What. The. Fuck. I had to bite my tongue to keep from saying that out loud.

At home, I stretch out on my bed wearing my boxers and call Arya. Much as I want to see her, I know I need to stay away, stay focused. But we can talk.

Arya immediately says, "That was so good in the first period when you skated through all those guys! I thought for sure you were going to score."

"Yeah." I didn't score, but it had been a good play.

"And then you and Edvin and Pavel . . . that face-off when Edvin scored . . . that was amazing!"

"We lost, you know," I say dryly.

"I know. I'm sorry. But I thought it was a good game. Of course, what do I know?" She laughs softly. "But really, it could have gone either way."

"True."

Surprisingly, not rehashing everything that went wrong is making me feel better.

I talk about the pressure and how I thought I was doing okay with it, but it must have gotten to me. With Arya, I'm not afraid to tell her shit like this. I know she won't laugh at me or think I'm weak. And she doesn't try to give me advice, like everybody else in my family I talk to. She just listens and lets me know she gets how I'm feeling.

After we're done talking, I set my phone on the bed and close my eyes. I focus on my breathing, just as Arya taught us, trying to empty my mind.

It's hard. I want to relive the game. I want to relive sex with Arya. I want to think about the next game. But I try to push those thoughts aside.

WE LOSE THE NEXT GAME TOO. THIS ONE REALLY SUCKS. We played hard. We did all the right things. We scored four fucking goals. We can't blame it one player, but we all know Bergie let in a couple of soft ones in the third period, and that did us in.

"We should have been better in front of him," I tell the media when I'm asked about that. "That's our job. We can't play like that. We can control the mistakes we made and support him better."

This one hurts more than the first game, because if we're playing our best and we can't win . . . never mind. Don't finish that sentence. We can do this. Coach tells us and I know it's true—we just have to keep playing our game. He reminds us of all the things we can't control, that we have to focus on the things we can that will give us our best chance of success.

Now we've lost our home-ice advantage. We go to

Vancouver for the next two games. We're determined and trying to stay positive. It's hard to ignore, though, that almost everyone is hurting in some way, and we're all exhausted. But we know we can beat this team.

I'm sitting at home after the game. Ash is still out. I could call Arya, but I miss her and I want to see her. I know she's home.

I sit and debate whether it's a good idea for about ten seconds, reminding myself that we're leaving in the morning for Vancouver. But I don't want to wait until we get back to see her. I need to see her *now*.

Flushing my good judgment down the toilet, I grab my wallet and keys and jump into my vehicle. Arya's place is only a few minutes away.

I pull up in front of the house. The light over the front door glows, and lights are on inside. Smiling, I jump out and stride up the sidewalk to the small yellow house.

I lean against the wall after I ring the doorbell, waiting. I get a little lost in thought, thinking about Arya, and then realize a minute has passed and she hasn't answered the door. I ring the bell, again, frowning. I can hear it, so I know it's working.

When there's still no answer, I pull out my phone and text her.

> Hey, answer your door.

After a few seconds, the little dots start jumping around and then her reply arrives.

> What? Is that you?

Yeah.

A few seconds later, I see her peer through the small window and then slowly open the door.

"Hi!"

She stares at me.

My smile fades.

Her eyes and mouth are drawn tightly, eyelashes fluttering.

"What's wrong?" I ask.

"What are you doing here?"

"I missed you. I wanted to see you. I just thought I'd drop by . . ." She's decent, dressed in leggings and a sweatshirt, so it's not that I've caught her naked, having a bath or something.

She presses a hand to her heart. "You scared the crap out of me."

I gnaw on my bottom lip briefly. "I did?"

She closes her eyes, looking like she's going to cry. "Yes."

"I'm sorry."

Her jaw tightens and she opens her eyes to glare at me. My insides squeeze up.

"Why the hell did you come over here without telling me?" she demands.

I blink. I don't move. "What?"

"You can't do that!" she cries, shaking her head and frowning.

"Calm down." I hold up my hands, palms out.

Her eyes widen.

Right, right. Telling women to calm down is the wrong

thing to say. "I mean . . ." Frantically, I try to think of what to say. "Can we sit down and talk."

"No!" She's trembling now. "No, we can't."

"Arya, come on, I just stopped by to see you, it's no big deal. If it's not a good time—"

"No, it's *not* a good time."

I gape at her. What the fuck? I didn't do anything wrong! I dropped by to see her without calling ahead of time. That's not crazy, when we've been seeing each other and sleeping together and . . . what the *fuck*?

My belly churns with a toxic mess that burns its way up to my chest. "Okay," I bite out. "*Fine.*" I spin and walk back to my vehicle.

21

ARYA

I feel so stupid.

I know I totally overreacted to Harrison showing up at home the other night. First, someone showing up at the door, at night, when I was home alone, scared the shit out of me. I thought I was doing better, being home alone at night, but someone at the door I wasn't expecting had visions of Lucas flashing in front of my eyes, his erratic behavior and his threats coming back to haunt me.

Then, as I was cowering in my bedroom with my phone in hand, I discovered it was Harrison and I was so relieved I almost started crying, and then I was mad at him for scaring me like that and mad at myself for being so scared. I didn't handle it very well.

And I made him angry, with my irrational response.

I sink down onto a chair in the living room, staring into space.

If I'd told him what happened to me with Lucas, maybe he wouldn't have been so pissed. I didn't want him to know about it, but it dawns on me that I probably should have told him. I remember why I told Everly and the others . . . because making friends and building connections with people requires honesty. Vulnerability. I didn't do that with Harrison, and he's the one I most want a true connection with.

He's in Vancouver now with a game tonight, so I can't even see him to apologize. I don't know when is a good time to call him. I don't want to distract him. So I don't do anything while I figure that out.

I keep myself busy all day with classes, but when I get home that night, Taj is out and the house is quiet and empty.

I am so messed up.

There's no way I deserve a boyfriend like Harrison.

I don't know what to do about this.

I check the time, but I don't know why, because I don't know his schedule. I have no idea what he's doing on the road.

I have to do something. I have to at least apologize to him. So I opt for a text.

> I overreacted last night and I'm sorry.

I don't get a response, but I didn't think I would.

I'M OBSESSIVELY CHECKING MY PHONE LIKE A TEENAGE GIRL waiting for her crush to call. Luckily, I can't bring it into classes with me on Saturday, so that distracts me for a while.

I go for a bike ride between afternoon and evening classes, finding the spot where Harrison and I made out in the sand near the Venice Pier. I sit with my arms wrapped around my knees and stare at the ocean, the wind blowing my hair around. I really screwed up and the timing was the worst. Normally I could have tracked Harrison down and apologized and explained to him. He's off playing for the biggest championship in his sport and I'm a jerk.

I can only hope he's more focused and together than I am. Because I won't be able to bear the guilt if I've messed up his head before an important game. But he's a professional. I'm sure he's fine.

I get home a few minutes before Taj and we make a late dinner together. We haven't done this for a while, I've been spending so much time with Harrison.

"You're really quiet," he comments as he cuts tofu into cubes. "You okay?"

"Yeah." I pause, then sigh gustily. "No." I tell him what happened the other night.

He pauses in his slicing, tilts his head, and gives me a long look.

"I know, I know. I freaked out." I press my fingers to my mouth for a few seconds. "I was scared someone was at the door, but even when I saw it was him, I was so pissed at him for doing that! It just . . ."

"Brought back memories?"

"Yes." I drop my head forward. "Oh my God, yes. I was terrified. All I wanted was to get away from him, to make sure the door was locked and I was safe. I ended up in bed with the covers wrapped around me, shaking like we were having an eight-point-oh earthquake."

"Ari." His tone is gentle. "It's okay."

"It's not okay!" I pause. "I should have told him about Lucas."

He frowns. "You haven't?"

"No." I hang my head. "Another screwup. If he knew, he probably wouldn't have dropped by like that. Or at least he would have understood why I freaked out."

Taj gives a terse nod.

"I know, I know, I fucked up. Wait. I know I'm not supposed to be hard on myself when that stuff happens. I just feel like I should have handled it better. I pissed him off, and . . ." I stop because of the pinch at the back of my throat.

"You really like him."

"Yeah. I think he's a good guy. Now that I've had time to calm down and think about it, I actually like it that he just dropped by like that. He said he missed me." I blow out a sharp breath. "I missed him too." Which is crazy, but that's where we are.

"So, you made him feel like shit because he wanted to see you and did something spontaneous."

I drop my head forward. "I'm an asshole."

"I didn't say that." His voice gentles. "But I know why you reacted that way. *He* doesn't."

"True." Sighing, I meet Taj's eyes.

"What are you going to do about it?"

"I texted him an apology. But I haven't heard back." My voice quivers.

"Ah."

"You need to tell him what happened."

"Oh yeah, *that'll* make him feel better."

"If he can't deal with it, then it's for the best. But you can't have any kind of relationship without honesty."

"That's true." I purse my lips. "But I can't tell him now. He's out of town, and when he gets back . . ." I pause. "Unless they lose these two games in Vancouver. Then they'll be out of the playoffs. Shit." I slump against the counter. "But if they're still *in* the playoffs, I don't want to distract him. He hasn't even read my text."

Taj grimaces. "I'm sure he's just trying to focus."

"Yeah." I nod. "I thought of that."

We make dinner then watch the game together. I've been so distracted by what happened that I forgot to be nervous about the game.

"They need to win this game," I tell Taj, who already knows this. I wriggle around on the couch waiting for the opening puck drop.

"You need a glass of wine."

"Okay." Not going to argue with that.

Taj fetches us each a glass of Merlot from the kitchen. I settle in cross-legged with a cushion on my lap.

Taj used to go to hockey games with me in college but hasn't watched much since then, like me. But we basically know what's going on, groaning when the Condors take a penalty, sitting on the edge of the couch when there's a scrap behind the Condors' net, throwing our hands in the air when they score.

"Yes!"

Harrison assisted on that goal by Eddie Rintala. Whoop!

It's not a pretty game, with lots of skirmishes and quite a few penalties. My insides are knotted. The Condors are coming out hard, but I hope they aren't going *too* hard and risking the game with their physical play. They have to feel the pressure of this third game.

They come through with a win, though, the score four–three.

I throw myself back into the couch cushions and blow out a long breath. "Whew!"

"Pulled that one out of their asses," Taj says colorfully. "Wasn't sure they were gonna do it."

"I know! Now we have hope again."

"They play again in Vancouver, right?"

"Yeah." I catch my bottom lip between my teeth. I wish Harrison wasn't so far away after I screwed up.

We watch some of the post-game coverage, interviews with players I know, like Jimmy and Bergie and Eddie. I'm proud when they replay the first goal, and one of the TV guys talks about how well Harrison has been playing for the Condors since being called up.

Then Taj changes to the "Disasters at Sea" episode he's recorded.

I give my phone a long look. I refill my wine glass. I try to watch "Disasters at Sea."

I don't hear from Harrison that night. I don't hear from him Sunday, or Monday, the day of their next game.

I do hear from Everly.

She texts me an invitation to come to her place to watch the game with her friend Lacey, who I've learned is Théo Wynn's girlfriend.

I don't know if I want to go. I know Harrison's angry

and/or hurt. I talked to Taj about it, but I don't think I want to tell Harrison's sister how I screwed up. Except, she knows why I freaked out.

The fact that I haven't heard from Harrison (although the text message now shows that he's seen it . . .) makes me feel sick.

Of course, he *is* busy. And that's an understatement. I have no idea what it's like to be in his shoes, with that much pressure. I should just go to Everly's and cheer him on, and we'll figure things out later.

Taj is out with Ziggy so I can use his car. I drive to the address Everly gave me. It's a beautiful complex of townhomes.

She gives me a big smile and a hug when she opens the door. "Hi! Come in."

"Hi. I brought wine." I hold up the bottle for her.

"Perfect! Come and sit. You know Lacey."

I smile. "Hi! Nice to see you again."

"You too!" She pats the cushion next to her on the sectional.

"Would you like red or white?" Everly asks, heading toward her kitchen.

"White, please."

The TV is on, although the game hasn't started.

"Do you get nervous watching?" I ask Lacey, sitting.

"Oh my God, yes!" She bounces a bit. "I'm a wreck! I'm scared as a rabbit in a fox hole."

I hear Everly snort from the kitchen and I smile, relaxing a little for the first time since Harrison left my place.

Everly hands me a glass of wine in a big, beautiful glass with a delicate stem. I swallow a giant gulp.

"I haven't met Théo," I say. "You have to point him out to me."

"I guess he doesn't come to your yoga classes." Lacey wrinkles her nose. "He should do that. I'll point him out if they put him on camera, but he watches the game from the visitor's GM box."

"It's a playoff game. I'm sure they'll go to him a few times," Everly says, making herself comfy in a big armchair with her own glass of wine. "Dad's there too."

"How's he doing?" I ask.

She sighs. "Well, okay, I guess. But he's definitely changing." She presses her fingers to her mouth for a moment.

"Sorry, I didn't mean to make you sad."

Everly grimaces. "Don't apologize, it's not your fault. It's just hard."

"I'm sure it is. I could tell that day at his birthday party. I'm so sorry."

Everly flashes a grateful glance. "Thanks. It would be nice for him to see the Condors do well. Who knows if he'll even realize what's going on this time next year."

That's so depressing. My chest aches with sympathy for her and her family. Including Harrison. In fact, I ache for him the most. "I hope they win, then."

It's not that I'm that much of a Condors fan. And I do care about Bob Wynn, although I hardly know him. What I really care about is . . . Harrison.

I want him to win. I want him to be happy. I want him to succeed and for all his dreams to come true.

Wow, we haven't even known each other that long and I'm all invested in his life. What does this mean? Have I fallen for this guy?

That's a really stupid question. Of *course* I've fallen for this guy.

Hard. I finally got brave and took a risk with a man, a man I'm now sure is a *good* man, and then because of my stupid hang-ups, I freaked out and pushed him away.

A bunch of TV guys are talking about the game, including an exchange about the incredible chemistry between Harrison, Pavel, and Edvin, which makes me sit up straight and pay attention, my smile as big as a blimp.

"How important is chemistry for a line, Don?" one dude asks the other.

"Well, Tim, chemistry is hard to define. Often it's because the players are familiar with each other. But these three have only been playing together a short time, so that's not it. I tend to think it's the type of players that are put together that makes the difference. They all have a great work ethic and good defensive responsibility, but when you combine Wynn's ability to set up scoring chances with Rintala's incredible shot and how Volkov gets in on the puck and sets the forecheck, they're a wicked combination."

I meet Everly's eyes and she's beaming as much as I am. We both laugh.

I love it that she's proud of her brother.

Oh God.

It's fun watching the game with these two. Lacey's extremely vocal and animated, with a lot of cheering and swearing. A *lot* of swearing. It makes me laugh. Everly is more controlled, but she knows more about hockey, seeing things that Lacey and I don't. She seems to know when a player is going to score before the puck even goes in the net. I'm jealous. I need to learn more.

"Oh my God, cross-checking," she says in despair, falling back into her chair. "Archie, you idiot."

I didn't even see that, but we have a penalty.

"It's okay," she mutters. "Our PK is really good."

"Uh . . . what?"

"Penalty kill."

I nod. That, I get.

To our delight, the Condors score a goal! Shorthanded! We're up by one now.

Sadly, before the penalty is killed, the Canucks tie it up.

We all curse. Even Everly.

It's a back-and-forth game, but in the end, the Condors lose. By only one goal, but that doesn't matter.

Lacey, Everly, and I all look at each other glumly.

"Damn." Everly holds up her empty wine glass. "Who else wants a refill?"

"I better not. I have to drive home." I make a face.

"I'll have one," Lacey says. She looks at me. "I'm staying here tonight, since Théo's away. You should have too."

"Yeah, we should have planned a sleepover." Everly unfolds her legs and stands. "Be right back. Arya, you want some pop or water?"

"That's okay. I should go."

It's bizarre how sad I am about this loss. I know I'm feeling it for Harrison.

When Everly returns, we all exchange hugs. "Thank

you so much for inviting me. It was way more fun watching with you than alone."

"Of course it is." Lacey grins. "But you can watch with us any time. If they win their next game here, there'll be another in Vancouver. Are you coming to the home game on Wednesday?"

"I . . . I'm not sure." I nibble my lip. I don't know what's going on with me and Harrison.

We're not doing team yoga right now, because their schedule is so intense with all the travel. So I don't know what will happen when he comes back tomorrow.

I know Everly and Lacey watch the game from the owner's box, so even if I went, I wouldn't see them.

"Well, we'll text," Everly says.

I drive home. I need to think.

I'm falling in love with Harrison, and right now, this is not a good thing. I am such an idiot.

Stop.

I know better than to call myself names like "idiot." I'd never say that to someone else, so I shouldn't say it to myself. I *do* have hang-ups, but they're real and they're justified. I've been so much better lately, although I know I may never totally get over what happened to me. But I'm living and I'm doing my best, every day.

At home, I walk into my bedroom and sink down to the floor in lotus position, hands on my knees. I inhale a long breath.

I breathe in courage and breathe out doubt.

I've got this.

I just need to figure out what to do about it.

Harrison comes home tomorrow. Well, late tonight;

Lacey said they'd be flying home right after the game. But he'll go home and go to bed.

I need to apologize to him. I need to explain to him. Not excuse my behavior, but I want him to understand why I reacted the way I did. He may be angry at me and I wouldn't blame him if he is. And if he can't get past that or accept my, um, shortcomings, I'll deal with it. Somehow.

I try to breathe out my doubts, but it's hard because I really don't know if trying to contact Harrison tomorrow is the right thing or the wrong thing to do. I don't want to disturb him during such an important time, which would make it easy for me to put it off. But he deserves to know how sorry I am. It's probably best to get it out there and then move on.

I text him in the morning.

> Do you think we could talk? I'd really like to explain what happened. But if it's not a good time I understand.

Taj drops me off at Prana today for my eleven o'clock class.

When that's done, I check my phone in the teacher's lounge, and I have a voice mail. Shit! I missed Harrison's call. He sounds quiet and serious in the brief message. I hit his number to call him back, but dammit, I get *his* voice mail. I too leave a message. "We're playing phone tag, sorry." I briefly outline my schedule for the day then glumly end the call.

I eat a salad in the teachers' lounge, scrolling through social media. My attention span is short, so I'm barely paying attention to what I'm reading, skimming through new posts and pictures of cute dogs.

Then my phone rings. Harrison's name appears on the screen.

My heart leaps and I stab at the phone to answer. "Hi."

"Hi." He pauses.

"Sorry I missed your call," I say, even though I said that in my voice mail. "Um, do you have a few minutes to talk? Or maybe we could meet up. I know you're probably busy."

"Yeah, we can meet up. You're done at six?"

"Yes."

"I'll pick you up there."

I can hardly breathe. "Okay." I swallow. "See you then."

Whoa. Okay. I did it. He's going to see me. I have no idea what's going to happen, since he said next to nothing. My belly's all fluttery and it takes all my focus to get through my afternoon classes.

He's waiting in the loading zone when I walk out of Prana a few minutes after six, carrying my yoga bag, still dressed in leggings, tank top, and a long, loose sweater. My feet pause when I see him sitting in his SUV. My heart kicks against my ribs, then I start forward again, crossing the sidewalk. As I reach for the door, he looks up.

His expression doesn't change. His usual smile is absent, but his eyes flicker. A big purplish bruise marks one cheekbone. Sympathy pain twinges in my belly, seeing that.

I slide in and close the door. "Hi."

"Hey."

As I buckle up, he puts the vehicle in gear and pulls out onto the street.

"Where to?" he asks.

"Um, we could just go to my place."

He nods.

"Thanks for making time for me," I say, my voice tentative.

He makes a harsh noise, his jaw tight, staring straight ahead.

"Sorry about the loss last night," I add. "I watched the game over at Everly's place."

He goes very still. "Oh yeah?"

"Yeah. We were all cheering for you. Lacey was there too."

"Thanks. It sucks."

I suck on my bottom lip and nod. Words bounce around in my head, but I say nothing until we get to my place. I unlock the door and lead him into the living room. I've gone over what I need to say a million times, but still, my palms are sweaty and my mouth dry.

I gesture to the couch and he sits. I sit too, tucking a leg up under me so I can face him. "Um, you got my text the other day?" I ask.

"Yeah."

"I really am sorry I overreacted."

"I guess it was a bad idea to arrive unannounced. I apologize too." His words sound stiff.

"It wasn't that bad." I pick up a cushion and pluck at it. "And I wanted to explain to you why I freaked out over nothing."

He nods. Our eyes meet and heat flames over my skin, my insides quivering.

"For one thing, I get a little nervous when I'm home

alone at night. I didn't expect someone to come to the door."

"Understandable."

"But when I saw it was you . . . I shouldn't have freaked out more. But I did." I sigh. "I have to tell you a story."

"Uh . . . okay." His lips firm and his eyes narrow as if he anticipates this isn't going to be good.

"A few years ago, I went on a date with a guy I met on a dating app."

His body immediately tenses. For a moment, neither of speaks, then he grits out, "Go on."

"His name was Lucas. He seemed nice—very charming. Handsome. In hindsight, I had little . . . hints that I should have paid more attention to. He came on really strong, telling me how beautiful and perfect I was, but I thought he just really liked me. I agreed to see him again, because why not? He was fun."

Harrison grunts.

"Before we even went out again, he dropped by my apartment. Just to say hi. I thought it was weird, and my roommate Leah just laughed it off and said, 'Wow, he's really into you.' I had this uneasy feeling about it, because that seemed odd, but it was sort of flattering that he liked me that much."

"Christ." He scrubs both hands over his face.

I take a deep breath and continue. "After our second date, I knew I didn't want to see him again. He came on too strong, and just . . . made me feel uncomfortable. So I told him that. He . . . didn't take it well."

Harrison closes his eyes, his mouth a thin, tight line.

"He knew my name and phone number and address.

He kept phoning me and texting me. Showing up at my apartment unannounced. The first time I wasn't there. He scared the hell out of Leah, and she understood why I was creeped out. Next time he came back, I was there—luckily, so was Leah. We got him to leave. But he kept doing it."

My voice has started shaking with the memories of that time.

"He got weirder and more aggressive, and the things he said started scaring me. He thought we were . . ." I pause. "Meant to be together."

After several beats of thick silence, Harrison says, *"Fuck."*

I bite my lip.

"I am so sorry," he growls. "Jesus, Arya."

"It's okay. You had no idea."

"I'm an idiot." He swallows. "Go on."

"He was following me places . . . he'd show up at West Acres—the shopping mall—if I was there, or if I was having dinner with friends at TGI Friday's he'd walk in. It was freaking me out. I kept telling him to go away. At first I tried to be nice—stupid me! Then I got blunter. And he got creepier." My voice hitches. "He started getting threatening. He texted me asking what I'd do if I was attacked. Would I scream? Fight back?"

"Fuck me." Harrison reaches out for me, drags me against him, and presses my face to his chest. "Fuck. Me."

I nod against him, still shaking both with memories and with the relief of being in Harrison's arms again, feeling safe enough to tell him the rest. "I reported it to the police. They didn't seem all that worried. Then he slashed the tires on my car." Harrison makes a harsh noise in his throat and his arms tighten. "I reported that too. They didn't do anything. He kept threatening me. I was so scared . . . all the time. Scared to go to work, scared to go home, scared to be home alone. I didn't know how this was ever going to end. Then one night I was going to the gym after work, and he followed me . . . grabbed me and dragged me into a park. He had a knife."

Harrison's body is shaking against mine now, his skin clammy.

"I was so lucky someone else saw it . . . and screamed for help and called the police. But he st-stabbed me a bunch of times . . . mostly my hands and arms. I was trying to defend myself."

"Fuck! *He stabbed you?*" He jerks back to stare into my eyes. His are dark and anguished.

I nod.

"The scar on your shoulder . . . ?"

"Yes. I have a scar on my right arm too." I hold up my arm and touch it. "The ones on my hands have healed up and you can't see them so much."

"Jesus. Jesus fucking Christ." He takes one of my hands in his, turns it over and inspects my palm.

"He's in prison now," I assure him. "But it was an awful time. And . . . it was hard to get over."

"You're not over it."

"No," I agree softly. "I probably never will be, entirely. After the trial, which was short, mercifully, since he pled guilty, I thought I'd feel closure. Feel safe. But I didn't. That's when I decided to move here. I wanted to get away from where it all happened and start over."

He nods.

"I'm working on it," I tell him. "I went for counselling. Practicing yoga has helped."

"I can't . . ." He stops, sounding strangled. "I can't believe the things I said to you. And did. Showing up at your class. Christ." He shakes his head and lifts me away from him. Bowing his head, he leans forward, elbows on his knees. "I'm so fucking sorry."

"It's okay." I rub his shoulder, his back. "*I'm* okay. I'm working on being stronger. I have to live. Take chances. Learn to trust people again."

He stands abruptly. Shakes his head. "Jesus. I must have scared the shit out of you. Over and over. Fuck."

He faces me, standing there, fingers curled into his palms, tension making the veins of his arms stand out. My mouth falls open as we stare at each other.

"I'm sorry, Arya. So, so sorry. I'm so fucking pissed at myself. I can't . . ." He shakes his head again. "I better go."

22

HARRISON

I'M THE STUPIDEST FUCK IN THE WORLD.

I can't even deal with the rage that's boiling up inside me. I need to punch something, preferably my own face.

I drive home. The house is dark. Looks like Ash is out somewhere.

In my own room, I kick off my shoes violently and fall onto the bed. Hands curled into fists, I stare at the ceiling.

I relive every stupid moment where I screwed up, things that seemed harmless and innocent. Well, they *were* innocent. I may be an asshole, but I'm not as much of a psycho as that Lucas fuckhead. The idea of her being threatened . . . afraid . . . attacked and hurt . . . *Jesus*. My chest feels like a blade is twisting inside it. I almost can't breathe with the pain.

I can't fucking *bear* the fact that I scared her like that too. Even though I meant her no harm, it still scared her. I also can't stomach the fact that, all along, I was so oblivious to her distress. I just ignored it, telling myself I just had to try harder.

You don't get what you wish for, you get what you work for.

I thought I was being determined. Working for what I wanted. In reality, I was being a fucking stalker.

Who the fuck gave me that advice? Oh yeah, Coach. Thanks a lot, man.

Unable to lie still, I roll off the bed and march into the kitchen. I open the booze cupboard and pull out a bottle of scotch. Leaning against the counter, I pour a generous amount into a glass and down half of it.

I know this is a bad idea, but I have a feeling alcohol will ease the twisted knot in my gut. I swallow another mouthful.

I pestered her, stalked her, told her we were meant to be. I remember her rushing out of that restaurant and then telling me she was triggered. I *knew* that meant something bad, but I just kept going, insisting on taking her back in there and seeing her again. I want to beat myself with a hockey stick for being such a nutwaffle.

I pace the house, walking from room to room, staring out the front window, then through the back-door window into the small yard. I remember sitting out there with Arya, drinking mojitos and making out. Taking her into my room.

I drop my forehead against the cool glass.

I really did believe we were meant to be together. Everything just fit. Except I'm an asshole and she deserves better.

I fill my glass again and wander into my bedroom. I sit on the bed. I've tried to keep the room neater since Arya first came here. I close my eyes and my shoulders slump. Nothing fucking matters.

I fall asleep with my clothes on. When I wake up at about five in the morning, my mouth feels like someone stuffed it with a dirty sock and my brain is pulsing in my skull.

I roll over and bury my face in the pillow. My neck is stiff.

Shit. This isn't good.

I drag myself into my bathroom where I down a couple of Advil with a big glass of water. I brush my teeth and wash my face, and then I go back to bed for a couple more hours.

Things are tense. We have to win the game tonight or we're out of the playoffs. People are saying we should be happy we made the playoffs after a drought so long, but there's no way that we're happy. We made the playoffs and we want to go all the way. We're competitive, professional athletes. We're not giving up.

Except I'm not feeling it. I'm dragging my ass on the ice, shooting half-heartedly and missing the net.

"What crawled up your ass?" Bellsy says tightly, skating up close enough so that only I can hear. "Get your shit together, man."

"What?" I glare at him. "I'm good."

"You're not good, you're skating like you've got a piano tied to your ass. Are you hurt?"

I snort. Hurt? All I can think of is some psycho attacking Arya with a knife, cutting her. I want to puke over the side of the boards.

Bellsy stares. "What?"

I roll my eyes. "Later. Come on, let's go."

We join the drill.

Yeah, this isn't a good time to be having a breakdown. Bellsy's right. I need to get my shit together.

I try to focus when we're talking about our penalty kill. And what we need to do to beat Vancouver.

"Okay," Coach says, pointing at the whiteboard. "The attacking defenseman on this side is gonna try to pinch in, but if the puck gets chipped out, the defending forward in the hash marks is now up higher, and suddenly he's racing the defenseman who has to retreat, which could lead to a shorthanded breakaway."

I usually have a lot to say in meetings. Today, not so much. I don't care.

Then I see Dad sitting in the stands, watching.

I *have* to care. I can't be like this. What happened to my determination to achieve my goal, never mind the team's goals? I don't have time to waste—we might have one game left. Dad is dying and losing his memory. I need to make him proud of me *right now.*

I'm terrified that I can't do that. I screwed up everything with Arya and I'm going to screw up this too. I've never measured up to my father and I never will. The thought that I'm letting him down when he's at his most vulnerable makes me burn with frustration. My chest tightens and my throat closes up. Pressure squeezes me from all sides, and I almost can't breathe. I don't even want to play tonight.

"It looked like you didn't even want to be there."

I feel like shit. I'm sitting in Dad's office, and Mom is here too, like she is so often now.

We won the game last night, but it sure as hell wasn't because of me.

I don't reply to Mom's comment. It's true, but I don't want to admit that.

She knows, though. She's been a hockey mom long enough that she knows when her kids aren't playing well and don't even want to be on the ice.

I hitch one shoulder and attempt a smile. "I made some mistakes. I'll work on them."

"What's wrong?" she asks, her voice gentle but strong.

I lift my head and meet her eyes, my jaw slackening. "*What's wrong?*"

Her shoulders slump and she tips her head back briefly. "Okay, yes, I know things aren't great, but you can't let this impact your play." She lowers her chin and again holds my stare. "Is there something else going on?"

Again, I don't answer. I rub the back of my neck and shift my focus to Dad who's listening, frowning.

"What's her name?" he barks, out of the blue.

"Who?"

"The young woman you're seeing." He pauses. "I can't remember her name."

A burn hits my chest. It takes a few seconds to squeeze the word out. "Arya."

"Yes. Her. What did you do?"

I narrow my eyes at him. "What did *I* do?"

I catch Mom trying not to smile. "Did something happen, Harrison?" she asks more tactfully.

It's my turn to slump. I slide down in the office chair, legs stretched out in front of me. "Sort of."

"Do you want to talk about it?"

"Not really."

"It might help. Obviously, something's getting to you. And yes, I know you're concerned about Dad—I understand that."

"Do you?" My chin rests on my chest. "Do you really know what it's like trying to live up to the King of Hockey?"

For a moment the room is dead silent. Then she makes a soft noise. "Oh, Harrison. Is that what this is?"

I blow out a breath. "Partly." I stare at my track shoes.

"Tell me."

My dad was always the one I went to for advice. Hockey advice. Woman advice. Money advice. Not that Mom and I aren't close; it's just different. But Dad's . . . different now. And Mom's looking at me with a soft expression of love and concern and compassion.

I remember Arya saying parents love being asked for advice. I don't know how much Dad understands but I'm going to ask anyway.

I tell them about what Coach said to me last month when I got called up, about how I've coasted through my career. How much I want to be a regular in the NHL, to live up to the Wynn reputation. To make Dad proud of me.

My mom listens, nodding. At one point she shifts her chair closer to me so she can set her hand on my shoulder and squeeze gently.

Dad's still sitting behind his desk, but he stands and comes around it. "Look, son. There's a lot of pressure in this league."

"Yeah."

"And . . . I guess even more so if you're a Wynn."

I meet his eyes. I nod slowly.

"Pressure is hard to handle," he continues. "Nobody can teach you how to deal with it. You have to learn yourself."

That's probably the most real advice I've gotten. I thought I'd done pretty good with the pressure, but yeah, it got to me. "Sorry, Dad."

He frowns. "Sorry? For what?"

"I don't want to let you down. I don't want to let the team down."

"You only let us down if you aren't trying."

"Harrison." Mom speaks up. "What Dave said about coasting . . ."

I frown at her. "Yeah?"

"He may have a point."

I scowl. "I work hard!"

"I know you do," she says quickly. "But . . . there have been times where I think you haven't really given your all."

Shit. That's just what Coach said. I stare at her. "People expect me to be like Dad. But I'm not."

She smiles. "That's exactly my point, you're not. You're your own person, with different strengths and different flaws. I think . . . if you feel you can't be like your dad, sometimes you don't try to be your best. *Your* best."

Our gazes hold for a moment, then I look down at my feet again, processing. "I don't know who I even am," I say quietly. "I just know what I'm supposed to be."

"You're supposed to be *you*. Nobody else. We've never expected that of you." She grips my hand. "Believe in yourself. Take the risk of giving it your all. Win or lose, then you know you've done that."

"It's not winning or losing, it's how you play the game." I shoot her a wry smile. "You know who says that? Losers. Losers and their coaches."

She chuckles. "I know winning is important. Especially if you're a Wynn." She glances at Dad with amused affection. "Do you remember what I told you about losing, when you were younger?"

I screw up my face. "Uh . . ."

"It was a quote from Nelson Mandela. He said, 'I never lose. I either win or learn.'"

I nod. "Yeah, I remember that."

"I tried to teach you that so you would learn from your losses. And grow and be better and stronger. But if you don't learn anything . . . then you *have* lost."

Oh man. Mom knows how to get a knife straight to the heart of the matter.

"And I'm not just talking about hockey games," she adds. "I'm talking about life."

I blink at her.

"Here's another saying. If you try, you risk failure. If you don't, you ensure it. Take a risk. Give it your all."

I slowly sit up straighter. That rips a hole in my gut. "You really think I've done that? That I'm lazy?"

"No! Not lazy. That's not what I'm saying at all. I'm saying maybe it's fear that's holding you back."

I gape at her.

"And I'm sure you've never even realized it."

I stand abruptly. I've had enough of this conversation. I

feel shitty enough without Mom pointing out my failings. Fear? Jesus!

"I have to go. Good talk, Mom." I start toward the door.

"Harrison." Dad speaks up.

I turn and look at him.

"I *am* proud of you. Don't ever doubt it. I love you. You're a good man. *That's* what matters. *That's* success."

Pressure builds behind my cheekbones and my eyes burn. Jesus.

I walk back to Dad. He wraps his arms around me and we hug it out. "I love you too, Dad," I choke out, squeezing my eyes shut at the stinging. I slap his back, then step away to leave before I burst into blubbering tears.

I nearly make it out of the building, but I run into Everly. She gives me a sharp look. "What's wrong?"

I sigh and rub my face. "Nothing."

"Riiiight. Come in here." She grabs my arm and drags me into her office. "You look terrible."

"Thanks." I pause. "Mom just told me I'm a coward."

I expect her to assure me I'm not a coward. Instead, she asks, "Why?"

I tell her about the conversation. "She thinks I'm afraid to try my best because I'm afraid I'll never be as good as Dad."

"Ah. Is she right?"

"Who can ever be as good as Dad?"

"So true." She sighs.

I drop into a chair. "Also, I screwed things up with Arya." My voice chokes up.

"Oh no." She takes the chair next to me, studying me. "You really like her, don't you?"

"I love her." I squeeze my eyes shut. "I know it's fast, but I felt it the first time I met her."

When I crack an eye open to look at her, she's smiling gently, not looking judgmental or incredulous. "What happened?"

"I've been a total idiot. I chased after her and wouldn't take no for an answer. I didn't know . . ." I trail off. I can't tell Everly about Arya's history; that's hers to share.

"You didn't know what happened to her?"

I meet her eyes. "You know?"

"Yes."

I blow out a breath. "I kept going after her. I kept thinking what Coach told me—I had to work harder for my dreams. And that's what I was trying to do."

She shakes her head. "You can't treat a woman the same as you treat hockey. You can't make someone care about you. She does or she doesn't."

I nod glumly. "Yeah. That's what I was doing. I was treating her like I've been treating my hockey career—something I could just power through, work hard, never give up. Like Coach told me to do. But I had no idea what she'd been through. I was like a fucking stalker," I choke out. "I went to her class so I could see her. Pushed her to go out for a drink with me. I didn't take no for an answer. Then she told me what happened . . . how she was attacked, and I hate myself. I feel like shit."

Everly frowns and tilts her head. "*You* feel like shit."

"Yeah."

"Uh . . . Harrison." She pauses.

I wait.

"How *you* feel right now doesn't really matter."

My head jerks back. "What?"

"Jesus! She spilled her guts and told you the most horrendous thing that ever happened to her and how it affected her and *you* feel like shit?" She smacks my shoulder.

My mouth drops open and I flinch at the blow, although it's not hard.

"This isn't about you! Come on! You're making this about you when *she's* the one who's been through hell."

I gape at her.

She's right. I left Arya because I couldn't deal with how I felt, how I'd treated her.

"I fucked up even worse than I knew," I whisper, closing my eyes and slumping back into the chair.

"Yeah, you did. Oh my God. You need to do something."

"I need to see her. But we're leaving for Vancouver in . . ." I check my phone. "Half an hour. Shit."

"Call her. Text her. Do something. You need to at least apologize." She shakes her head, and I can feel her disgust with me.

I deserve it.

"Yeah. Yeah. I'll call her." I stand, gripping my phone.

"Stay here. I'm late for a meeting." She hustles out of her office, closing the door behind her so I'm alone.

I try calling, but Arya doesn't pick up. I leave a pathetic voice mail, but somehow I know she's not going to call me back.

I try again on the plane, and again get voice mail. This time I leave a longer message. "I need to see you," I say in a strangled voice. "I need to apologize. I'm an asshole and I don't blame you if you never want to see me again, but please just let me tell you how sorry I am."

It's not good enough. I know it isn't.

While the guys chirp and joke around the entire flight to Vancouver, I'm collapsed in a window seat, head against the wall of the plane, staring at nothing, thinking about everything that happened today. Mom's honesty. Dad telling me he's proud of me for being a good man, when I'm not a good man, I'm so far from that. Then Everly giving me shit for being a selfish jerk. Shame burns a hole in my gut.

23

ARYA

"You were right." I sniffle a little, staring down into my cocktail. It's lime and pineapple juices with a hint of ginger. And vodka. A lot of vodka.

Taj rubs my shoulder. "I'm sorry."

"I told him what happened. And he couldn't handle it. You were right. How could we have a relationship if he couldn't deal with it?"

He sighs. "I actually didn't think that's how it would turn out. He seems like a decent guy."

"Other than the stalking."

"Come on," he gently chides me. "You know he wasn't stalking you the same way Lucas was."

"I know. I was nervous at first, but . . . I wanted to be brave and it didn't take me long to realize he's a good guy." I sigh. "And I'm working on not beating myself up over taking the chance. I thought I was ready for it. Turns out I was . . . but he wasn't." I sip my drink. This is going down like water on a hot summer day after a 10K run. "They won last night, though. Yay."

"You don't sound very happy." He picks up his beer.

"I am happy. For him. They needed to win to stay in the playoffs, so that's good. He didn't play very well, though. Not that I know much about hockey, but he seemed . . . invisible. He didn't seem to be on the ice much, and when he was, he didn't do anything."

"Shit."

"I know. I was worried about talking to him during the playoffs in case it distracted him. I don't want to be the reason they lose."

"Uh . . . they won."

"Right."

"Also, that's giving yourself a lot of credit—the whole team losing because of you?" He lifts an eyebrow.

I snort-laugh. "Oh my God. You're totally right. I'm being a drama queen. Thanks for keeping me real." Then I sigh again. "I just want him to do well and be happy."

"He was probably happy they won."

"Yeah." I nod, yet somehow I know he wouldn't be satisfied with his performance last night.

"You haven't heard from him since?"

"He called me earlier. Twice. I was in class, but he left voice mails. He says he wants to apologize."

"For . . . ?"

"I don't know."

"Call him."

"I just said I don't want to be a distraction. He's in Vancouver. At least it's not a do-or-die situation for them, but it is for Vancouver, so I'm sure they'll be fighting hard."

"Don't leave him hanging."

Slowly, I move my head up and down. "You're right. I'll text him. I need to think about what to say."

We hang out at the Golden Fish for a while, and I drink way too many Mexican Mules and try to smile when Indigo and Arlo and Ziggy join us. Inside I'm cold and weary, with an uncomfortable heaviness in my chest.

When we get home, I make myself some tranquility tea, and holding my mug, I sit cross-legged on my bed, my phone in front of me.

I still don't know exactly what to say. As usual, though, just being honest is the best thing, painful as it is.

I finish my tea, then tap in my message and read it about ten times. Then I send it.

24

HARRISON

Landon looks after our travel arrangements, hotels, and meals all year long, but during the playoffs it's even more important that everything is taken care of for us. We're super spoiled arriving in Vancouver, being whisked to our hotel and checked in and not having to worry about bags or gear or lost reservations.

It's also great that we're in the same time zone. It can really mess you up, flying across the country and having to deal with a two- or three-hour time difference.

Our bus takes us to the Rogers Arena for a practice, then back to the hotel. A bunch of us go out for a walk before the team dinner. From our hotel, we can walk to Gastown. The weather is cool and damp, the area is bustling with people. We pass bars and restaurants and funky shops, meander the brick pavement of Maple Tree Square past the statue of the man this neighborhood is named for, "Gassy Jack" Deighton, and move on to the famous clock.

I don't really hear what the guys are yammering about as we walk to the restaurant we're meeting at for dinner, Boucher. The restaurant is kind of industrial-chic, with low lights, lots of brick, and exposed ducts. It seems appropriate to order the salmon, even though I'm not hungry at all, a cold lump amassing in my stomach.

I force myself to eat some of the salmon. I'm only drinking water tonight, and the waiter keeps refilling my glass as I guzzle it down.

Everyone's finished dinner and chilling when my phone vibrates. I pull it out to check it. I have a text. From Arya.

Finally.

My heart bumps in my chest. I stare at my phone, then tap the icon for the message.

It's long. My eyes skim over it and I force myself to slow down and read it all from the beginning.

Hi Harrison. I got your voice mails. I don't want to bother you when you're away and I know it's a big game tomorrow but I wanted to let you know I got your voice mails and you don't have to apologize. I'm okay and don't let what happened with us interfere with the playoffs. I watched the win last night, congrats. I'll be cheering for you tomorrow. I know things worked out for the best with us. What happened to me was terrible and I'm working on getting past it but I know it's a lot for other people to deal with. I understand. Going out with you was scary for me, because you're the first guy I've wanted to go out with since Lucas, but I wanted to be brave and take the risk. I've learned that fear means I'm doing something that matters, and even though things didn't work out, I know I'm stronger because of it. So thank you and good luck.

I read it again. And again.

"Harry's picking up the tab for all of us tonight."

My head snaps up to stare at Bergie. "What?"

He grins. "What the hell, man? Pay attention."

"Sorry. Just got a text."

"Ah. The future wife."

I haven't said anything about what happened, because it's embarrassing that I'm such an idiot, plus I know Arya wouldn't want me telling the guys about her stalker.

Going out with me was scary for her, but she wanted to take the risk.

My throat clogs up. And I hear my mom telling me, "Take a risk. Give it your all."

Maybe I *have* been holding back. Maybe I *have* been afraid. If I never measure up, I don't want it to be because I didn't try.

I want to be as strong and brave as Arya.

She left her family and her hometown and a job she enjoyed, to move across the country so she could feel safe. She started a new career, made new friends. That's gutsy.

I remember how nervous she was when I invited her for a drink . . . how upset she was when I made that stupid comment about us being meant to be together, how apprehensive she was when she wanted to take an Uber home instead of telling me her address. Like she thought I'd be pissed off.

Jesus Christ.

Yet she kept seeing me, even though I was being an idiot. Now, knowing what happened to her, I admire that so goddamn much. It swells up inside me, a hot and powerful force that makes my heart expand in my chest. I love her even more.

"Must have been a good text," Jabber says.

"Was it a sext?" Scotty asks. "Did she send a dirty picture?"

I roll my eyes. "Jesus. No."

This text message was clearly meant to end things between us, and to end things between us on a friendly note. No hard feelings. Ha. She has no idea. I'm wrecked over this.

I don't want things to end between us. But clearly, pushing her harder isn't going to be the right thing to do. So . . . I'll give her up, if that's what best for her. If she needs time, I'll back off. If she needs to be left alone, I'll do it. I just want her to have what she needs and to be happy and safe.

But . . . there are a couple of lines in her text that bug me . . . *I know it's a lot for other people to deal with. I understand.*

She should be pissed at me for bailing because I couldn't deal with it. Because I couldn't deal with my own guilt, which doesn't even matter in the face of what she's been through. I should have been there for her when she spilled her guts to me, and I ran away like a stupid kid. And now I'm a thousand miles away, and I can't get to her. I've got a game to play tomorrow and I need to be here for it. Not just *here*, present. All in.

Right now, I feel like the only thing that matters is setting things straight between Arya and me. But it also matters that I prove I'm not afraid. And now it's not about showing my dad I can do it, or my mom, or even Arya—although I want her to be proud of me.

It's about proving it to myself.

THE SCORE IS TIED, TWO–ALL. ONE OF THOSE GOALS IS mine, and I assisted on Eddie's. I fucking love playing on this line with him and Pavel. We've really clicked and our styles complement each other. Adrenaline courses through my veins where I sit on the bench watching the play as the third period comes to a close. Christ, looks like we're going into OT.

We all jump to our feet as Jimmy and Archie go in on the Canucks' net. There's a bunch of whacking and smacking, but the whistle blows as their goalie covers the puck. I hop over the boards for a line change along with Eddie and Pavel.

Eddie takes the face-off but loses the puck to their center, who flicks it over to his winger, and they're off up the ice. We race after them, Bellsy and Jabber defending. Bergie's alert, standing tall in goal as a Canuck player skates toward him. The Canuck player tries to shoot the puck, but Bellsy tips it away from him, except another Canuck is there and pokes at it. I see it squeak through Bergie's legs and behind him.

Shit!

I don't know if the puck has enough momentum to cross the line, but I'm not taking that chance, so I dive for it, my stick outstretched, and sweep it away only an inch from the goal line as I slide on my belly. My shoulder and hip smash into the post, but I don't even care. I've gotta get back up and make sure the Canucks don't have the puck again.

Just as I'm on my feet, my body throbbing, the horn sounds to end the third period. The guys are mobbing me, slapping my back and my helmet in thanks for saving that goal.

"That woulda been the game!" Bellsy cries. "Holy fuck!"

I make it off the ice and into the dressing room. Teddy checks out my shoulder and hip. I think I'm okay, just bruised. He gets me ice packs and, with my jersey off, I stretch my legs out in front of me, grinning like a fool even though we haven't won. Yet.

WE PLAY A WHOLE PERIOD OF OVERTIME WITH NO SCORING. We're dying. The winner will be the team that doesn't literally die on the ice. Both teams are playing great, both goalies are like goddamn brick walls.

Now we're into the second OT period. We have to finish this. My legs are seizing up, my shoulder is stiffening, but I keep going. We have to fucking do this.

Bellsy has the puck at the blue line and takes a shot at the net. There's a crowd in front, and somehow the puck is deflected to the corner. Pavel goes in and scoops it out as Eddie and I both go to the net. I look up at Pavel. He's looking at Eddie, and so is the Canucks' goalie, but I know . . . somehow I fucking *know* . . . that puck is coming to me. In perfect timing and reading, Pavel slides the puck over to me and I tip it in as the Vancouver goalie watches Eddie.

I'm fucking jumping up and down, stick in the air, laughing. "Holy fuck! Holy fuck!" I'm immediately mobbed, the entire team coming off the bench. We just won the series.

"Fuck, yeah!" Eddie yells near my ear.

Guys are jumping on each other, hugging, smacking each other. It's nuts, but holy fucking shit it feels good.

The Canucks are sitting on their bench dejectedly, others leaning on the boards, heads down, shoulders slumped. Dave and Stan and Teddy are shaking hands and hugging behind our bench. Eventually we slow our celebration—you'd think we just won the cup!—and start back toward our bench. We have to do the handshake line, and I gotta say, it feels a lot better doing it when you've just won the series. But we've all been trained from the moment we put on skates that good sportsmanship is paramount, and we shake hands and hug and thank our opponents for a hard-fought series.

I see Théo come onto the ice. He was watching the game from the visiting manager's box high above . . . with Dad.

And there's Dad behind him.

I don't think he should come on the ice in street shoes. He seems frailer these days. So I skate straight to him before he's taken three steps. I open my arms. A smile breaks across his lined face and we hug. "You did it, son." He slaps my back. "You goddamn did it."

"I did." I grin too. I might never stop grinning.

Okay, I do have other problems lurking at the back of my brain. But right now, I'm smiling.

"You worked your ass off out there." Dad grips my shoulder. "That's determination."

I nod, choking up. I'm not the only one who's emotional. Dad's eyes are watery and so are most of the players', to be honest.

I stay beside Dad as he joins in the handshake line, making sure he stays upright, though I'm trying to be discreet about it so as not to embarrass him. My chest is bursting with pride that I had a role in getting this team to the next round of the playoffs. I'm also feeling relief and satisfaction.

I fucking did it.

25

ARYA

I'M CONSIDERING STARTING RAGE YOGA CLASSES.

We could drink beer and swear and yell. Let go of all our anger and frustrations. The idea is really appealing to me right now. We could be Zen as fuck.

But the reality is, I'm ready to do a Saturday SUP class at the marina. Everyone would probably be taken aback if I yelled at them to release all the fucking tension in their neck and shoulders. An alternate way to higher peace and motherfucking acceptance. Ha.

There's an ache in my chest because I miss Harrison and I'm so, so sad that things are over between us, but after watching the game last night and what he did, I feel happy and proud and . . . satisfied.

I still don't know if I did the right thing sending him that text. He didn't respond, which I didn't expect. But it didn't negatively impact how he played, so that's good. They won their game and they're going on to the next round of the playoffs. It might even be against the Golden Eagles, if they too win their next game.

So I feel at peace with how things are. I'll just try not to think about Harrison and how much fun we had together and what an honest and honorable, determined and talented man he is, and even though it didn't work out with us, I had that time with him. I'm really using those affirmations, repeating them over and over. I can't compare how I feel now to how I felt after Lucas assaulted me; it's totally different, but damn, it hurts. It hurts a lot.

I am capable of anything.

I lead the class outside. The clear, blue sky and sparkling water help ease the heaviness inside me. Not completely, but a little. I turn my face up to the sun and let its warmth seep into me as we paddle away from shore. Despite the beauty all around me, an aching longing fills my chest, a wish that things could be different.

We find our places and drop our anchors, and I begin the class. "Stand-up paddleboard yoga is a great way to develop mindfulness, focus, balance, and breath skills. These are all important for being present during this practice. Let's start in Mountain Pose, holding your paddle like so." I demonstrate. "Feet together, big toes touching. Inhale and lift your paddle above your head, using it to keep your arms level. Exhale as you bend your knees, bringing your thighs as low and as parallel to the board as you can."

As I bend my knees, I look straight ahead and see someone paddling toward us, apparently a latecomer to the class. Except the class is full and . . . my eyes widen as I take in the size and shape of the man on the board.

Harrison.

He's wearing shorts and a T-shirt, his biceps bulging as he digs his paddle into the water and rows in strong, even strokes, the board skimming across the ocean toward me. Sunglasses hide his eyes, but I recognize him.

He finds a spot not far from me, drops his anchor, and slides his sunglasses up onto his head, revealing dark circles beneath his eyes.

His eyes meet mine.

Sunshine bursts in my chest. My breath stalls and my heart crashes against my breastbone as we stare at each other. My lips tremble into a smile that he returns, his eyes warm and crinkling up at the corners.

Why is he here?

I need to gather my wits. Blinking rapidly, I continue. "Shift your weight into your heels, enough that you could raise your toes off the board if you wanted. Breathing smooth . . . even . . . deep."

Harrison moves into the pose smoothly, his powerful thighs flexing as he bends his knees. My jaw loosens, even though I've seen those thighs many times.

I manage to maintain my composure and lead the class despite the thoughts ping-ponging around in my head. I'm on autopilot, which isn't fair to the others here, but at least I keep going. It's a challenge to not look at Harrison, and every time I do, he's watching me, and our glances collide with a visceral impact that nearly knocks me off my board.

Don't want that to happen again, nope.

"Bring your hips down even lower and lift through your heart, spreading your shoulder blades apart . . ." I look around at the group. These are all people who've been here before. "Go deeper . . . deeper . . ." My eyes flick toward Harrison.

He smirks at me and arches an eyebrow.

Damn him and his dirty mind! Now I want to laugh!

We move onto other poses, inhaling fresh air as the ocean breeze wafts around us. I fill my lungs and control my breathing, hoping to steady my galloping pulse. "Now . . . inhale . . . exhale and fold forward. Place your paddle on the board, and your hands on either side of the board . . . roll your shoulders away from your ears, inhale . . . extend the spine forward."

I lead them through the Cobra Pose. "Tuck the toes and press back to all fours . . ." I lift myself onto hands and knees, then lift my butt in the air. "And into Downward-Facing Dog."

"I feel really connected to my dog spirit," Harrison says.

This is the first comment he's made since he joined us. My head is down and I can't see him, but I swallow a giggle.

We flow through Warrior 1 and Warrior 2. Some are wobbling a bit on their boards, but as I glance over at Harrison, he's steady as a rock.

Steady. As a rock.

I love that.

"Find your Plank Pose . . . either on your knees, or legs straight." I work on maintaining my focus, moving through poses. "Enjoy the movement of your body on the water. Connect with your breath." We're all still and quiet for a moment. I don't look at Harrison. "One more breath."

We move into Child's Pose to finish, relaxing into the silence and gentle movement of the water beneath us. But my body is vibrating with nerves and excitement because as class ends . . . I'll talk to Harrison.

At one time I would have been anxious about him showing up like this. But I'm not. And I know I haven't totally conquered my fears and the trauma, but I do know that I trust Harrison.

We paddle back to shore. There's a little chatter, and laughter from the rest of the group, but I stay behind them. Harrison paddles near me.

"Okay," he says. "Push me in the water."

My head whips around to stare at him.

He holds his arms out wide. "Push me in. I deserve it."

My lips twitch. "I'm not pushing you in."

He grins, and it's the most gorgeous, uplifting smile I've ever seen. I can't help but smile back at him, my heart jumping in my chest. "You should."

"You're crazy."

"Yeah."

I tip my head, eyeing him. I dip my paddle and push, and I'm nowhere even close to touching his board, but he wobbles as if he's losing his balance, windmilling his arms dramatically, and then he falls backward into the water with a shout and a splash.

My mouth drops open and my eyes pop wide. "Oh my God!"

He comes up spluttering. "I'm okay."

I cover my smile with my fingers. "What are you doing?"

The other people in the class are at the shore and have turned to watch.

"I deserved that," he says loudly. "Don't apologize."

Now I'm really laughing and in danger of falling in myself. "Harrison, you nut. Get back on your board."

The water is shallow enough for him to walk, and he tugs his board along, grinning.

Inside Stand-Up Guy Paddleboards and Makara Yoga, everyone returns their boards and disperses. Harrison's gone too. My shoulders slump and I look around in confusion. Then he appears from the men's change room, dressed in dry clothes—a pair of jeans and a T-shirt—his hair still damp.

He approaches, his gaze fixed on me with solemn focus, and stops in front of me. "Can we talk?"

I nod, my heart hammering.

"I'm not stalking you," he assures me.

"I know."

"And I didn't come here to pressure you. Just to talk. If that's okay."

I nod slowly.

"Maybe we can go over to Bandits for a drink."

"Sure. Let me grab my things." I head into the changing room for my bag. I slide my feet into flip-flops and check my appearance in the mirror. Not that I can do much about it. My cheeks and nose are a bit pink from the sun, my hair's in a ponytail that's coming loose. Whatever.

I rejoin Harrison and we walk outside to cross the parking lot to the restaurant.

"Are you limping?" I ask, stopping short.

"Maybe a bit." He rubs his left hip. "Had a run-in with a goalpost last night."

"I saw it." I catch my lip between my teeth. "Are you okay?"

"Oh yeah. Stiff and bruised, that's all." He rolls his left shoulder too.

My stomach clutches at the thought of him in pain.

We resume walking. "Congratulations on the win last night."

"Thanks." He beams a big, wide grin.

"You played fantastic."

"I did." Then he laughs. "It was a team effort."

"When does the next series start?"

"We don't know yet. Eagles and Blues play tonight. Then we'll know who we play against and when."

"It would be . . . funny if you played against the Eagles."

"It would be a great matchup," he says. "Might cause some family strife, though." He rolls his eyes. "As if we don't have enough of that."

"Anything new happening with that?"

"Not really. Everyone agreed we'll deal with things after the playoffs."

"Right."

We sit outside on the patio since it's a nice afternoon. A potted palm flutters near my head as I settle into my chair, taller palms outside the patio swaying in the ocean breeze.

"Are y'all eating today or just having drinks?" the server asks us.

"Just drinks," Harrison says, then looks at me. "Unless you want food?"

"No, I'm good. I'll have a margarita, please, on the rocks."

"You bet." She looks to Harrison, who orders a beer.

"This beer is gonna taste great. Haven't had one in nearly two weeks. Although I did overdo it on scotch the other night." He grimaces, then meets my eyes.

I tip my head. "The night we talked."

"Yeah. Wasn't doing so hot the next day. I needed to get my shit together. Had a painful convo with my parents. And then with Everly. She gave me hell and told me what a selfish prick I am."

My eyes widen.

"I am so, so sorry, Arya." His voice is full of sorrow, his eyes shadowed with regret. "For so many things."

My lips quiver. I keep my gaze fastened on him.

"I did awful things to you," he goes on, his voice deep and thick. "I thought I was being determined, going after what I wanted. I wanted you." He meets my eyes, his dark and sorrowful.

I blink rapidly. "I-I know."

The server brings our drinks, pausing our conversation for a moment.

"But that wasn't the right way to do it," he continues. "I had no idea what you'd been through and I was an idiot, showing up at your classes, pushing you to go out with me. I want you to know that I didn't leave because I can't handle what happen to you. I left because I realized what an asshole I'd been to you. And then . . . the worst thing, which I didn't even realize until Everly kicked my ass, was freaking out when you told me what happened to you. I was so guilty and ashamed about how I'd behaved, and it shouldn't have been about me, it should have been about you and what you went through, and I wasn't there for you."

"Oh, Harrison." My throat aches and I swallow painfully.

"You said I scared you . . . and I'll never forgive myself for that." His voice catches on the last word.

"No!" I sit up straight and reach out a hand to cover his. "You didn't scare me."

"You said that . . . you were scared."

"I didn't say that." I grip his hand tightly. "I was scared because I didn't trust myself. I didn't trust my judgement. I *wanted* to go out with you. I really liked you. I mean, I was nervous about it, but it wasn't you who made me nervous. It was myself." I pause. "I don't know if I'm making any sense. Please, please don't think that you scared me."

Our eyes meet and hold as I beg him not to think that.

The air thickens and pulses around us.

"One of the things I've had to work on is trusting myself," I continue in a low voice. "I blamed myself for misjudging Lucas when I first went out with him. I was afraid I'd never be able to have a relationship with someone because I was too stupid to know when someone wasn't a good person."

"Christ, Arya, you're not stupid."

I roll my eyes. "I felt stupid. And since then, I've been afraid to trust my own instincts. I was so horribly wrong that time. My instincts were telling me you were a good guy, but I was afraid to believe that."

He lifts his chin. "That night I showed up at your place . . . I did scare you."

I close my eyes. "Okay, yes. I know your intentions were

good, though. You didn't mean to scare me. That's the difference between you and . . ." I don't even want to say something that compares him to Lucas, because there's no comparison. "It was *my* hang-up. And I know I overreacted. I told you that."

He nods slowly, then lifts his chin. "Okay. I get it."

"I should have told you." My throat squeezes. "I should have told you what happened, and then you'd understand why I was so cautious and nervous. I'm sorry."

"Aw fuck, Arya, this isn't your fault."

"I guess we were both messed up."

"Yeah." He picks up his beer and takes a few big gulps. "I understand, though. I understand if you're not ready for a relationship. You've been through a lot. I'm not here to pressure you, I sure as hell don't want to do that. I just wanted to apologize. If you need to be left alone, I accept that."

I stare at him. "Oh."

There's another stretched-out silence weighted with uncertainty and unspoken questions.

"Is that what you want, Arya?" he asks quietly.

My mouth goes soft and my chest aches. I press a hand there. Is there still a chance for us? Once again, I need to be brave. I need to be honest.

"No," I whisper. "That's not what I want." I blink at the prickle in my eyes. "I want you."

His eyes widen and his jaw loosens. For a moment he says nothing.

I'm aware of my chest rising and falling with shallow, rapid breaths, but everything else has faded away, the people around us, the seagulls crying, the boats moving in the marina.

"Really?" he finally says. He sets down his beer and reaches across the table for my hands.

I give them to him, our fingers curling together tightly. "Really."

He closes his eyes. I study his face. He's so handsome, his wide mouth now pressed firm, his square jaw dusted with stubble, his thick eyebrows pulled together above his imperfect nose. Love for him expands rapidly in my chest, pinching off my airway so I can't breathe.

When he lifts his eyelids, his blue eyes blaze at me, melting me. "I really want you too."

I smile tremulously.

"That sounds all wrong," he says hoarsely. "It's a lot more than just wanting you. I want to be with you. Always. I'm falling in love with you, Arya."

Now my lips really quiver, my heart knocking around in my chest. "I'm falling in love with you too."

"Ah." His fingers squeeze mine so tightly it almost hurts.

"Easy, big guy." I wiggle my fingers, and he eases the pressure.

"Sorry, sorry."

I smile.

"I'm so sorry for everything I did," he goes on. "I can't believe I was so insensitive. I could tell you were nervous sometimes, and I just steamrolled ahead."

"You really didn't," I say softly. "You have no idea what steamrolling really is." I roll my eyes.

"Christ. You're right."

"I needed to know that you were really interested in

me," I add. "I was afraid I was scaring you away with my insecurity. I'm glad that you didn't give up on us."

"Fuck." He drops his head forward. "You're amazing. You're way too good for me."

"No, I'm not. We're good for each other, I think."

He picks up his head. A slow smile pulls at his mouth. "Yeah. I agree." He gives his head a shake. "We need to get out of here. I need to kiss the bejesus out of you."

I laugh. "I'm good with that."

2 6

HARRISON

"YOUR PLACE OR MINE?"

Arya laughs at the cliché. "Mine is closer."

"Perfect." I pause. "Do you have your bike here?"

"No. I came with Taj."

"Ah. He's still working?"

She smirks. "Yes."

"Also perfect. Although I have to be honest, I don't care if he's at your place or not, even if we break your bed banging our brains out."

Her smile beams and we can't keep our hands off each other as I drive like a Formula 1 racer to her place. She's incredibly tempting, in a pair of tight little shorts and a sports bra, although she put on a sweater before we went to Bandits. I stroke a hand down her smooth thigh, over her knee, and back up.

Watching her lead that class was seductive as hell. Yoga's not supposed to be sexy, but when Arya does it, it sure is. The graceful way she moves her strong, flexible body turns me on. She has an actual six pack that's particularly visible when she arches her back and, Jesus, that's hot. Even her face when she closes her eyes and breathes, the look of serene focus, is sexy.

I park on the street and we enter the little cottage she shares with Taj. I spin her around, set my hands on her hips and direct her toward her bedroom.

"I don't want you to think I'm only interested in sex," I tell her. "But right now, I'm only interested in sex."

She laughs softly, not resisting my efforts. "Good. Me too."

"It's been eighty-four years . . ." I lament.

She laughs louder. "Slight exaggeration."

"Feels like it." In her room, I slide the sweater down her arms, my hands lingering on her skin. "You made me so hot during that class."

"Um." Her chest rises and falls rapidly. "That's not supposed to happen."

I bend my head and kiss the corner of her mouth. "Can't help it." I tilt my head and kiss her fully, at first soft presses of my mouth, then my tongue sliding out to lick over her bottom lip and inside. With a moan, she opens to me and wraps her arms around me, pressing that tight little body against me. "Fuck, yeah," I groan into her mouth. I tug the hair tie off her ponytail, then gather up fistfuls of her hair in my hands.

My blood rushes scalding hot through my veins, lust pulsing in my balls.

I release her hair and slide my hands down to her butt. I love squeezing those firm cheeks. I pull her tighter against me, my aching dick pressing against her belly. "God, I missed you."

"I missed you too. So much." Her head falls back to allow me to glide my tongue over her throat, suck her skin so gently, then kiss my way back up to her mouth.

I want her out of these little clothes. The shorts come off easily, but the bra gives me trouble. It's so frickin' tight I don't know how she can breathe.

With a soft laugh she wrestles it off over her head.

"There." I feast my eyes on her tits, Christ, I love them. I cup them gently, reverently. Then my gaze lands on her scar. I go still, and so does she. I trace my fingertips over it, then raise my eyes to her. "I will never, *ever* hurt you. I swear to you."

Her eyes shine and her plump bottom lip quivers. "I know. I trust you, Harrison."

Emotion pushes at the walls of my chest. Those words mean so much.

I capture her mouth in another long, soulful, achingly sweet kiss.

Her hands slide up under my T-shirt, up my sides, over my pecs, which makes my dick twitch. I release her long enough to pull my shirt off, then she pushes my athletic shorts down. She pauses, gentle fingertips lingering on the bruises coming to color on my hip.

I back up toward the bed, bringing her with me, still kissing her. I kneel on the bed and pull her onto her knees too, and I bend to take a nipple in my mouth. She moans, sliding her hand around my neck, over my head, holding me to her breast. Her long hair falls all around us.

As I suck and tongue her nipple, I slide a hand down

between her legs. "So wet," I whisper against her skin. "I love that." I slip my fingers back and forth between her pouting lips, grazing her clit. Her hands are all over me, up and down my back, my shoulders, scratching my scalp, lighting me on fire. We're both making needy, gasping, filthy sounds as our mouths and tongues slide together, desperate for each other, wanting more, more.

Her body undulates, rising and falling on her knees to the rhythm of my strokes, then she sets a hand on my chest, pushing me to my back. I smile as she climbs on top, straddling me.

Gorgeous. So fucking gorgeous.

She smiles too, then bends to kiss my chest, flicking her tongue over my nipples. Electric need burns through me, my engorged cock throbbing.

I hope she still has condoms in her nightstand. I stretch my arm out to yank open the drawer. I overdo it a bit, and it crashes to the floor. "Oops."

She meets my eyes, her lips curved. "Easy there." She rolls off me and hangs off the side of the bed while she searches for a condom. This gives me an excellent view of her ass, and I palm one cheek.

She pops back up, pink cheeked, hair tangled around her face, holding a small package. I start to take it from her, but she moves away, straddles my thighs and opens it. My dick is straining against my belly. Carefully, she lifts it, bends to kiss the tip, then rolls on the latex.

Her hands on my cock ignite every nerve ending. I watch, enthralled, my skin prickling all over, desperate for more of her touch.

Her eyes on my face, she shifts herself over me and lowers that sweet pussy onto my cock.

"Aaaaaah." I clasp her waist, her wet heat enveloping me, taking me in. "So good."

"Mmm."

I'm filling her, fighting not to lift my hips and thrust up into her. She begins to move on me, up and down. Her hands press on my chest and she slides them up over my neck. I turn my head and suck her thumb into my mouth, holding her gaze as she moves on me. As I suck, her pussy clenches tighter around me.

Her eyes heavy lidded, she tosses her hair over one shoulder and leans forward to kiss me. My hands roam over her waist, her back, her ass, while our mouths meet in a molten, explosive kiss.

As she shifts back, I push up to suck her nipples again, wrapping an arm around her. My cock slips out of her pussy and we both make a dismayed noise. Reaching behind her, she finds my shaft and slips it back inside her. Pleasure engulfs me again.

I suck and nibble for long moments, absorbing her soft noises of delight. Then I fall back to the bed. With one hand on my chest, the other pressed into the mattress, she raises and lowers herself, liquid heat sliding along my cock . . . faster . . . faster. I grip her butt cheeks, squeezing, helping her move on me. "Christ," I groan. "I can't stand it . . . you feel so good."

"I love it too." She rides me harder, panting. Pushing against my chest, she straightens. She sweeps her hair back with both hands, lifting her breasts, her nipples hard and crimson from my mouth. I watch her moving, and it's fucking glorious.

"I fucking love being under you like this, watching those pretty tits bounce." My head falls back into the pillow, my mouth open, heat and pressure building. We stare at each other, a connection between us I've never felt, a hot sweetness, a bond of lust and passion, affection and admiration. "I love you."

"I love you too."

I worship her. I want to spend my life protecting her, cherishing her, being the best man I can for her.

Then her movements change, her pussy rocking against me, grinding, the noises she's making increasing their tempo. I grip her hips and she releases a low wail as her head drops forward and she presses through her orgasm. Her pussy squeezes me, squeezes . . . sensation twists inside me, fiery and torturous, but it's also exquisite. Hot pressure builds, fast, violent, consuming, rocketing to a peak. It's joy and rapture and relief and thankfulness. It's bright and dark, thunder and lightning, frightening and yet safe. It's beauty and love and everything I've ever wanted.

"I'm glad you played so well last night. I was worried you'd be distracted."

"I definitely had a lot to think about. I knew I had to be brave."

She rolls her head on the pillow. "What do you have to be brave about? You mean your dad?"

"That too. But right now, it was about hockey."

I tell her what Mom said to me, about being afraid I couldn't live up to my dad, about how at first I was pissed off, but then realized maybe she was right. And about how Dad told me the hockey didn't matter, it mattered that I was a good person. "But I didn't feel like a very good person. I felt like a selfish coward. But you . . . you made me feel . . . I don't know. Inspired, I guess?"

"Really?"

"Yeah. You went through something . . ." I stop. Swallow. "Something horrifying." I squeeze her tighter in my arms. "I hate it that that happened to you. Fucking *hate* it. But you're living your life. You came here, started a business . . . you're brave. And strong. And I couldn't help but think that I need to be brave too."

She burrows in closer to me, hiding her face.

I stroke her hair tenderly. "Do you believe in love at first sight?"

She shifts and leans her head back, a small crease between her eyebrows.

I touch my fingertips to the crease, smoothing it. "Hey. It's okay if you don't."

Her bottom lip wobbles. "Do you?"

"Yeah." I hold her gaze steadily. "Is this too soon?"

"It should be too soon. This all happened so fast."

My heart knocks, but it's okay. I'm prepared to wait and be patient.

"But no." Her eyes go liquid. "It's not too soon."

I close my eyes on a wave of relief and elation. *Thank you, thank you, Jesus.* "I love you, Arya. I think I did the first time I saw you."

"You were such an ass." A tear slides from the corner of her eye and I catch that with my fingers and brush it away. "Knocking me into the water really created a good impression."

I choke out a laugh. "I know. I'm still an ass. I'll probably do things that piss you off or make you wonder what the hell you're doing with me."

"It's possible." She's trying not to smile, I can tell. "But I'll probably do things like that too. I think that's all part of it. I love you too."

I gather her up against me and press her face to my chest. "Please tell me when I'm being an idiot. The last thing I ever want to do is hurt you or scare you."

She nods. "I know. But we'll both screw up. Remember?"

I caress her hair. "Remember what, sweetheart?"

"Unalome. The journey isn't a straight line. We make mistakes and go sideways and sometimes backward."

"Right." I press her closer still. "Now, we'll do it together."

HARRISON

I walk into the house. Ash is on the couch with his laptop on his knees, the TV on to the Montreal–Ottawa game he must have recorded. He glances up at me. "Hey. Where've you been?"

"At Arya's."

"Ah."

He doesn't even know what happened, and I don't feel like telling the whole ugly story since things are fucking fantastic now.

"Good game in Vancouver."

"Thanks." I grin. "I had my ass kicked by a few women."

He arches an eyebrow. "And yet you're smiling about it."

"I know, weird, right? First Mom told me I was a coward. Then Everly laid into me about Arya. And Arya gave me a sweet little hoof in the hiney too."

"Uh, wow."

I sit in an armchair and meet Ash's eyes. "Why didn't you ever try to go pro?"

Ash's eyes widen, then narrow. "You know why. I wanted to be a journalist. I wanted to write about hockey."

"Yeah? Is that the truth?"

He shakes his head slowly. "Of course."

"Because Mom suggested that maybe the reason I've never tried my hardest is because I'm afraid I can never be as good as Dad." I purse my lips. "I think she might be right."

Ash is silent.

After a moment, I look at him. Our eyes meet.

"Shit," Ash says. "Mom's pretty smart."

I often know what Ash is thinking without him saying it. He's thinking that maybe he was afraid, too. So he didn't even try. "Yeah," I finally say. "She is." I pause again. "Dad was pretty awesome about it. Even though I wasn't sure he even understood what was going on."

"He has his moments."

"Yeah." I exhale harshly. "It really sucks."

"I know."

"It's so hard seeing him not able to drive anymore. Not being able to hold a conversation, sometimes. Being confused."

"Fuck." Ash leans his head back. "I know. I hate it. I feel like . . . he's already died."

"Sometimes it's not him. It's like . . . his body is aging, but his mind is getting younger . . . like a child." My eyes burn and I scrub a hand across them. "What the hell are we going to do without him?"

"We'll do what we have to do. We don't have a choice." Ash's quiet wisdom calms me.

"Yeah. I guess that's true. We can't be him." I pause. "But we can our best selves."

Thank you so much for reading! I hope you enjoyed Harrison and Arya's story. It was so much fun to write. If you'd like to read more about them, click here and add your name to my mailing list to get their epilogue!

https://kellyjamieson.myflodesk.com/feojffst5v

ACKNOWLEDGMENTS

Thank you, readers. I love to share my stories with you. I also love to share my passion for hockey along with the passion of two people falling in love. Thank you so much for buying and reading my books—I am forever grateful!

ABOUT THE AUTHOR

Kelly Jamieson is a best-selling author of over sixty romance novels and novellas. Her writing has been described as "emotionally complex," "sweet and satisfying," and "blisteringly sexy." She likes coffee (black), wine (mostly white), shoes (especially high heels) and hockey!

Kelly appreciates your help in spreading the word about her books, including sharing with friends! Please leave a review on your favorite book site! You can also join her Facebook group, Kelly Jamieson's Sweet Heat Reader Lounge, to hang out with her, and for exclusive giveaways and sneak peeks of future books.

Visit her website at www.kellyjamieson.com or contact her at info@kellyjamieson.com

WINDY CITY KINK

SWEET OBSESSION

ALL MESSED UP

PLAYING DIRTY

BREW CREW

LIMITED TIME OFFER

NO OBLIGATION REQUIRED

ACES HOCKEY

MAJOR MISCONDUCT

OFF LIMITS

ICING

TOP SHELF

BACK CHECK

SLAP SHOT

PLAYING HURT

BIG STICK

GAME ON

LAST SHOT

BODY SHOT

HOT SHOT

LONG SHOT

BAYARD HOCKEY

SHUT OUT

CROSS CHECK

WYNN HOCKEY

PLAY TO WIN

IN IT TO WIN IT

WIN BIG

FOR THE WIN

GAME CHANGER

BEARS HOCKEY

MUST LOVE DOGS…AND HOCKEY

YOU HAD ME AT HOCKEY

TALK HOCKEY TO ME

THE O ZONE

GOOD HANDS

SCORING BIG

MERRY PUCKING CHRISTMAS

LIGHT 'EM UP

STORM HOCKEY

CROSSING THE LINE

STANDALONES

THREE OF HEARTS

LOVING MADDIE FROM A TO Z

DANCING IN THE RAIN

LOVE ME

LOVE ME MORE

2 HOT 2 HANDLE

FRIENDS WITH BENEFITS

LOST AND FOUND

ONE WICKED NIGHT

SWEET DEAL

HOW SWEET IT IS

HOT RIDE

CRAZY EVER AFTER

ALL I WANT FOR CHRISTMAS

SEXPRESSO NIGHT

IRISH SEX FAIRY

CONFERENCE CALL

RIGGER

YOU REALLY GOT ME

SCREWED

FIRECRACKER

BIG WITCH ENERGY

HATE ME UNDER THE MISTLETOE

* 9 7 8 1 0 6 9 0 7 0 6 6 1 *